That Which Destroys Me
by Kimber S. Dawn

Dedicated To Trina Taylor...
You're the greatest friend I
could ever hope for, the single
person in my life that loves me
for both all my faults and
weaknesses, as well as my
strength and stubbornness.
You make me a better me, sissy.
And I ♥ you hard for
everything you do for me, and
see in me, even when I see
nothing at all.

TABLE OF CONTENTS

Chapter 1

The Fucking Good Life

WESLEY

Jesus Christ, her voice may have raked down my spine like fingernails on a chalkboard, but her mouth felt like a goddamn hoover on my cock. No, better yet, like a Dyson. Their slogan is 'It never loses suction', right? I'll be damned if I haven't been fucking Cindy? Candy? Whoever's throat for a solid twenty minutes... and I must say, she hasn't lost suction.

I drive my hands in her hair yanking, thrusting my hips harder, forcing her to take it all. In between her gagging, the head of my cock slips through the ring of muscles, bringing me further down her throat. I'm ready for this shit to be over. I'm ready to get this bitch out of my penthouse in all honesty. "Yeah, bitch. Fucking swallow that cock like a good girl. Mmm hmm." I smack the side of her face and clamp my fingers around her chin bringing her eyes to mine, "Be a good little cum slut. Don't you dare spill a drop, you hear me?"

Dumb bitch nods before I grasp my fists back into her hair and yank her face back where it belongs. I feel her gagging again around my cock and her tears trickle onto my thighs right before I shoot my cum down her throat. "Fuuuck!"

Well...now shit's just awkward. I want to tell her to go, but I don't want to be a total dick, especially with mine still out and within her reach. You know what I mean?

"Oh my gawd, Wes... Please, please baby tell me I can suck you until you're hard again, let me ride you. I need it. SO bad."

Chalkboard, nails... yep, fuck politeness.

"Nope, sorry sweet tits, but it's about your bed time and my

1

bed don't have time for you." I stand and tuck myself away, securing my johnson behind the metal gates of my khaki pants zipper. I grab the C named woman up from the floor and ignore her childish pout while leading her toward and out the door of my penthouse. "But Wesley..."

"Goodnight Cindy, and seriously, I meant it when I said don't call me babe, I'll call you." I wink before shutting and locking the door.

I hear her muffled voice through the door, "It's fucking Christy you asshole!"

Oops, hey at least I remembered it started with a C.

After I shower and grab a beer from the fridge, I sit on my bed with my laptop going through this evening's emails. I'm usually at the office Monday through Friday, however I never really have a day off. Don't get me wrong, I don't have to work my ass off by any means, I just always have to be available and prompt with responses to emails and texts and shit.

My cell rings after I've responded to the necessary emails and logged off my laptop. "This is Wesley."

"Hello, Mr. Jacobs. This is Rachel. How is your evening?" I grab another beer from the sub zero fridge chuckling at Rachel's polite and demure behavior.

"My evening has been shit, Rach. You know there's this thing called caller ID on all cell phones, so there isn't any need for you to introduce yourself when the person answers."

"Yes, sir. I am aware. And I apologize for your having a non-satisfying evening. That is a terrible shame."

"Oh, no. Don't misunderstand me, it was satisfying. Just sucks when they won't disappear immediately afterward."

Her audible gasp is something I find hilarious. However I keep my laughter suppressed.

"Come on, Rach. I just had you on your back, as well as bent over my kitchen table last night, love. There's no need for you to act as though I'm the scandalous one, now is there?"

I almost spew the mouthful of beer across the black, veined marble counter top when she clears her voice and returns with, "Mr. Jacobs, please. We are both professionals, surely we can act as such and keep our personal affairs out of our professional business."

"If that's how you want it sweet tits. So, whatcha got for me Rach?" I fall back into my oxford leather couch and relax, sinking into its comfortable texture with a sigh.

"Well I have over ten messages from your father that have gone without a reply. He is threatening my employment if you don't reply to his eleventh. Can't you just grab any damn intern and shove them into the mailroom or copy room, Wesley? Don't make me lose my job over this, please."

"Victor can't do a damn thing to you or your employment, Rach. Don't let him get your panties in a knot, babe. It's a waste of very fine silk, I promise. Just make sure there's a list of respectable interns on my desk on Monday morning, okay?"

"Yes, sir. And thank you for being in my corner, too. I appreciate it very much, Wesley."

"Anytime, Rach." I tap end and toss the phone on the coffee table before running my hands through my hair and sighing.

I really have no time to have a sniveling little intern on my heels. And if I had *ANYONE* to hand this shit off to, I would. I would love to put them in the mailroom, but honestly, when it comes to anything that is a product of Jacobs Publishing, if it isn't five stars … well, it's always five fucking stars, so never mind.

This is just the perfect shit icing on my even more shitty cake.

"Thanks, Pops. Can't take that I'm running this motherfucker better than you ever did because I have the balls that you didn't."

Why the hell am I talking shit to my old man out loud?

I make my way into the master bath and turn the shower full blast on hot before heading into my bedroom and pouring a tumbler full of scotch and downing it.

I really had well laid out intentions to stick to just beer tonight, but... I don't know how much, if any, more I can take off my old man trying to still dictate my life from afar. I just don't.

After I pour myself another crystal tumbler of scotch, I head back into the bathroom setting it down on the vanity counter top a little harder than necessary. I strip and walk into the reason I bought this penthouse.

Double-sided shower stall the size of the average American's bedroom. Over 75 showerheads... Um yes, I'll take it, and the penthouse too. Just saying.

As soon as those beautiful showerheads begin pummeling my skin and easing my muscle tension, the migraine that Cindy's or Candy's, or whoever she was, voice created begins to ebb.

My muscles are so loose that I barely manage a quick scrub and wash my hair before getting out of the shower.

I hook the towel around my waist, grab my scotch, and flop into bed without spilling a drop.

No, this isn't a superb practiced maneuver, I'm just that fucking good. Well that and it's damn near a nightly routine.

I hate to sound like a spoiled little pussy, but I have found myself asking this question more and more lately, when in the fuck did my life become so goddamn sad?

I don't understand this conundrum. I have every rare car available. I own a penthouse in every major city, plus homes on four different beaches, one in the Colorado mountains, and the ranch in Wyoming that I've only been to the one time I signed the papers on it. I have women falling over themselves to get the chance to choke on my cock and I have more success than I know what to do with on every level.

So I ask: When and how did my life become so goddamn sad?

The only time excitement even strikes is when I'm at Chained, the BDSM club that is the only reason I made NYC my home.

That's what I need.

I need to get my ass back to Chained. Find a suitable sub.

4

'Cause these bitches like Candy or Cindy... They closely resemble eating baked lays, when what you really want is a damn fat ass bacon cheeseburger.

Yeah, I'm putting a call into Chained tomorrow.

That'll shake me out of this shitty funk I'm in.

Chapter 2

The Fucking Shitty Life

"Seriously? Trina there isn't one fucking internship! Not one! Gahhhhh! Why? Dammit, I just won't do the internship leg of this program. I refuse."

I can't take it anymore. My head hits my keyboard, as my perfect, angelic, sister from another mister sets a glass of chilled Moscato next to my laptop. "Babe, listen to me. *You* need to pipe the fuck down. This is it. Right here, Stell. Everything you want is at your fingertips. Now jump on that motherfucking bull and ride that bitch for 8." She leans over and pulls my pony tail until my neck is arched at an odd angle and locks eyes with mine, "And then, You. Are. Done." Her smile is one she stole from Satan himself. I know it.

"Let go of my hair, bitch." Trina kisses the air then heads towards the couch in the living room. I grab that perfect, beautiful, delicious glass of wine and chug that bitch. After a pleasure-filled moan and a exaggerated sigh I set the glass down and ask her over my shoulder, "You get enough bottles to get us both drunk, sis?"

"Nope, just one bottle. Not even enough to get one of us drunk."

"The hell? You fucking tease. That's a waste!" I stand up and hurry into the kitchen and fill my glass to the rim with the chilled wine. I look up smirking like the Cheshire cat at my best friend from across the butcher block island that separates our loft's living room from the kitchen. She is glaring knives at me. "What?"

"You know what," she sets her kindle down on the end table. "I'll let it slide tonight. Go on, get it all out. You're pissed, you're upset. Now come on, lets get this pity party done and over with so you can accept what you can't change and move on with it."

I damn near swallow half the contents of my glass. "Trina, *I will not* work for that asshole. He is a player. He is a pompous dick head that thinks he's God's gift to women. No." Shaking my head to emphasize my adamancy, "Will. Not."

"Why? I don't understand that part, Stella. You of all people can handle anyone, and I mean *anyone*. That's just his reputation, hell you'll probably never even see the bastard!"

"Pasta's ready, you want one or two pieces of garlic bread, babe?" I say while rationing out a cup on each of our plates."

"Ahh, just half of one." Trina fills both our glasses with the remaining wine before she and I head to the living room and sit at the coffee table to eat our supper.

This is the norm for us. Neither one of us has ever understood how people can sit in hard chairs to eat at an actual dinner table. To us, it's at least in the lower twenties of our 'Why the fuck do people?' list.

I've known Trina for more than five years, we instantly became friends in junior college. She's my kinda bitch and I'm her kinda bitch. Neither of us take shit from one another; but at the same time, we never hold back.

Trina's a real ass bitch and I honestly love the hell out of her for it. One thing about me you'll probably learn pretty quickly is I can't stand being around fake ass bitches.

Another reason that I have always considered Trina my sister is because anytime I try to twist some shit up in my head, either to point the blame on me or on someone else and it's bullshit, Trina calls my ass out. Calls it like she sees it and I'll be damned if she isn't *always* spot on.

I'd like to say I help her mentally overcome her own demons and shit too. But I get the feeling that if this were a friend competition, yeah... she'd kick my fucking ass.

"Stell, answer the question. What is it about Jacobs Publishing House? You lived in complete and utter hell for the first sixteen years of your life, why can't you live with working in a prestigious firm as an intern for one year?"

After I swallow the food in my mouth, I take a sip of wine. Setting it on the table, I look up at my friend. "You're right, T. I can do it. I'll be fine."

She picks up a noodle and tosses it at my face, "Answer the question!"

"Shit! Just... look, okay I don't want to fucking talk about it. Period. Just leave it alone."

I scrape the remaining pasta into the trash, rinse it off in the sink and set it in the dishwasher. "You're night to do dishes. I gotta go hop in the shower. I have five more firms to meet with tomorrow morning, starting at eight." I sigh padding across the hardwood floors towards my bathroom.

Once I've showered and done my nightly routine—brushed my teeth, flossed, applied night moisturizer—I hop in bed and curl up with my Kindle and this hot as hell yet perfectly twisted motherfucker named Twitch.

Fuck yes, Twitch. Slap a belt around my neck and fuck me like you're mad at me, baby.

I know, it is extremely odd that given the abuse I suffered by foster fathers, brothers and even weird 'uncles', you'd think I'd be more apt to find a nice boy. One that opens doors and holds me before and after making love. But, in all honesty, I can't even make it through one date with a pussy-ass little boy.

Not that I date. Hell, if my hymen hadn't been obliterated by my bastard father, then the bastard men I lived with in foster care... I'd probably still be a virgin... No, who am I kidding? I would still be a virgin.

I do just fine with my Twitch's, Caleb's, and Jesse Ward's... Thank you.

My eyes begin getting heavy somewhere during a non-sex scene and I finally end up passing out. My dreams are fun at first, Twitch laden, if you will. But they take a dark turn right before I slip into a REM cycle.

Blood. Blood is everywhere. Soaking my hands, knees. It's everywhere. I'm scared. I'm cold. There are no lights on. It's dark, but I can still see his form silhouetted by the sliver of moon just outside the dirty trailer's window. It's cold. The blood is seeping into my sweatpants. It's everywhere. So are the screams. They are everywhere too. I cover my ears to stop them, but the blood on my hands smears on the sides of my head. When I feel the blood drip down from the sides of my face and onto my neck, my vision blurs from my tears. Why am I crying? I don't like this man. I hate him. I can't remember a time where I didn't hate him. All he does is hurt me. It's all he has ever done, for as long as I can remember. He's never been kind like my friend, Jill's, daddy. I don't know why my tears are falling. I don't know who keeps screaming. But I need them to stop.

When I go to open my mouth and scream at them to stop, I realize I'm already screaming...

Those are my screams...

I'm jerked awake, drenched in a cold sweat with screams tearing through the membranes that cover my throat and esophagus.

The entire frame of my body trembles as I pull myself from bed to start a warm bath. I peel the soaked clothing from myself. Instantly it causes flashbacks to bombard my consciousness.

As I sit in the tub huddled around myself with my chin resting on my knees, my eyes are fixed, staring at an old rust stain under the faucet.

My father's breath in my ear, his weight on my back, the sounds of him grunting. Pain. Fierce, agonizing pain shredding the lower half of my body. Until his weight finally cuts off the circulation to my lower torso and extremities making everything numb. I can't evade them. The memories, they continue battering my mind. Piercing through my consciousness and all I'm able to manage is to sit there

9

and stare, watching the water drip over that fucking rust stain.

I lose concept of time.

I want to fucking cut so goddamn bad. It makes shit more clear. Makes it easy to focus. Focus on the shit I need to do, the next step. Like I don't know… Say, get out of the fucking bathtub. Change my sweaty sheets. I haven't cut in almost ten years though.

I haven't felt the urge, or need to - at least not this strong - in almost five years.

It has to be all this pressure I'm under. Fuck, I don't want to go back to therapy. I really don't want to talk about my repressed memories. All the therapist ever wanted to talk about is me killing my father at the young age of seven to stop him from hurting me again.

"Babe? You okay? I thought I heard you crying." I feel Trina's dark brown eyes scan, searching my turned face while I continue staring at the damn rust stain. "You're still in your sports bra and panties, Stella." She pulls my hand that was resting on the edge of the tub into hers. "Your hands are cold," I see her fingertips brush the water from the corner of my eye, "The water's ice cold, Stella, come on…" she pulls me from the water, my eyes still haven't left the stain, I feel a warm towel swathe around me. "Come on, sis, let's get some clothes on you… You sleep with me, 'kay?"

She turns the lights off in the bathroom and I blindly follow with that stain fixated now in my mind. I somewhat recall her drying me off, dressing me in a big warm hoodie and yoga pants, then tucking me into her warm bed.

I fall asleep, still staring at that fucking rust stain seared behind the lids of my eyes.

Chapter 3

Families are A Bitch- Even The Rich Ones

WESLEY

As I step out of my Audi R8, grab my brief case and Starbucks espresso, a nine walks by fucking the shit out of me with her eyes.

Are you kidding me, bitch? It's too goddamn early for this shit.

No — I am not a morning person, nor am I a Monday person. Yes — I'm over these bitches constantly looking at me as if they hold sexual promises as well as all the answers to my deeply rooted, confounding disorientation where life is concerned.

The fuck did I say? Don't look at me like that, dammit. It's fucking Monday morning.

When I slam into my office, Rach almost drops the bottle of water she has halfway to her mouth. "Rachel." I nod as I make my way towards the solid mahogany double doors that lead to my inner-sanctuary, the head office, the throne that the king of Jacobs Publishing House sits upon, mothafuckas.

Rach is hot on my heels, "Mr. Jacobs..."

I spin around and advance until I'm leaning over her like the prey she is, our faces a breath away when I whisper, "Rach, It's Wesley or Wes." I grab her chin in between my thumb and forefinger. Grasping it hard, I growl, "My cock's been in that pussy, Rach. From that point on, you lost the right to be polite. Stop acting so goddamn virtuous, do you understand me?"

My eyes slide down her face and I watch as her neck bobbles, trying to swallow... She does swallow too—Just in case you were wondering.

In a breathless fluster of mumbled words she finally replies, "Wes," She clears her throat, "Wesley, your father, Mr. Jacobs is in your office, sir."

Oh, huh. I should probably be embarrassed, especially after the way I've just, well whatever. I'm not. I'm pissed! Not at Rachel, at my fucking father. Mr. Jacobs.

The scowl on my face is not something I could mask, even if I wanted to. I stalk into *my* office and there they are - Victor and Josephine Jacobs - somehow looking down on me standing over them at my full six-foot-four stature.

They're the embodiment of rich pompous pricks. So am I, but at least I don't look down my nose like an asshole at people.

I'm a product of my father's infidelity. Josephine, my step mother, was almost eighteen when she married my father at forty-five. On the day after my father's forty-sixth birthday, yep, you guessed it—I was born to a stripper-slash-escort girl my father had been having an eight year affair with during his frequent business trips to New Orleans.

Now, anyone that knows me knows I love my ma. She's a great fucking woman. I don't blame her for what she had to do in order to feed her younger brothers and sisters while cancer ate her own mother alive.

My plans of becoming a football star with a law degree and being able to care for my mother financially, allowing her to live in the lap of luxury, were thwarted by a football injury they'd originally said would prevent me from ever walking - much less running - again.

For as long as I can remember, I allow the simple fact that I run five miles a day help calm my demons, help soothe the hate that I've always had to keep reined in and in all honesty it isn't working anymore.

After my scholarship was pulled because of the injury, my father brought me to the Dallas area and tried to get me enrolled in several bitch ass schools. But when you come from playing quarterback for LSU, your square shape doesn't fit in everyone

12

else's peg holes—well not those holes anyway.

We agreed on Texas A&M where I threw myself into every damn socialite and sorority girl's pussy within a seventy-five mile radius. That and my studies, acing shit left and right until I'd graduated first in my class with a bachelors in Science of English, then my masters in communication.

With my father nearing his seventies, he eagerly handed over the power of our prestigious, and highly recognized family publishing business—to me, his single living heir.

In less than a year, I'd handed almost every one of the authors my dad represented over to the very capable hands of a very different publishing firm than the one I had Jacobs headed towards becoming.

I kept two authors that pops had kept hidden in the basement. One, a very cutting edge and no-holds barred writer that, quite frankly, didn't give a flying fuck if you liked his work or not. Scott's books were out of this fucking world. His shit was raw. It was pure. It was fucking real. I kept him.

The other was an erotica author, but Melanie's shit was much darker than the Fifty Shades books. Again, raw, gritty, erotic talent.

Melanie, Scott, and I packed up the whole fucking Dallas building and moved to NYC. The three of us slapped Jacobs on Madison Ave. Between the three of us, we brought in fifteen new upcoming erotica or cutting edge authors—no cookie cutter bullshit, no happily ever afters. Fuck that. Those were a dime a dozen. And I wanted Jacobs Publishing to be one of a kind!

That was almost ten years ago. Now I have more than two hundred authors, every fucking one of them think outside the box and more than bend the rules in the writing world. Seventy-eight percent of them have been at one time or another on bestseller lists.

Victor was once a millionaire. Now he was a fucking billionaire, many times over. Did he and Josephine spend that money like it there was no goddamn tomorrow? Fuck. Yes.

Did they approve of the direction I took their prominent publishing business that had been in the family for over a hundred years?

Fuck. No.

"Pops," I nod, "Josephine..." I kiss her weathered cheek, "You've aged like shit, my love. Glad to see it."

"Wesley." My father chastises. "Do not speak to her that way. We're here to discuss business, not squabble like children. Keep your petty childish behavior to ..."

"Get. The. Fuck. Out." I glare into his eyes. "There is no goddamn business for us to discuss, old man. You're over eighty years old." I glance at his crotch, then look over at Josephine, "Speaking of shit - Josephine, is he in adult pampers, yet?"

In a flurry of mink, diamonds and curses, she stands quickly moving to exit my office. Before slamming the doors, she calls over her shoulder, "Victor I'll be in the car, dear. I refuse to be treated this way by the son of one of your whores."

The doors slam behind her as I move around to sit behind my massive mahogany desk, steeple my fingers and commence glaring at my father.

After I'm finished with our glaring contest, I jerk my head towards the double wood doors, "Leave. Now."

"Son, acquiring an intern is the last business request I will make. JPH has always participated in, and been recognized in the Publishing Intern Accreditation Society. My grandfather, your grandfather and I helped not only make PIAS the respectable organization it is; Wesley, we built it. It's important to at least continue, even if you do have them proofreading smut."

The sinister laughter that rumbles from me has my old man's spine straightening. In the most condescending tone I have, I reply, "Smut, huh? I must say, it is utterly bemusing to me how you can allow words like accredit and respect to roll so gallantly from your old shriveled tongue, then - THEN - have the audacity to spat the word smut, at me?!"

14

I abruptly stand, causing my chair to crash into the floor-to-ceiling glass wall behind me before stalking around my desk and grabbing this motherfucker by his tie. I jerk him up until our faces are an inch away from one another. "Get the fuck out of this building you old motherfucker. You needed an heir to head this business. Well, here I am. I needed you to at least attempt to take care of my mother, Kathy! My *MOTHER*. And you never lifted a finger to help us when I was a kid. Well guess what, the roles have reversed. I will take care of my mother. But I would do almost anything to ruin you financially. However, if I do, I can't take care of the woman that raised me."

I smooth his tie out before grasping the lapels of his suit jacket. "You alright, pops?" I smile glacially at him.

"F-fine. I'm fine." He stutters.

"Good," I say patting his shoulder. "There's the door. Please do us both a favor and excuse yourself."

After he's been gone for five or ten minutes, Rachel comes in with today's schedule, rattling on.

I, however, am still seething pissed. I watch her mouth as it moves and the urge to fuck those red puffy lips isn't what skates across my mind. My eyes slide to her throat. That, that little fucking neck, is what I want. My hands wrapped around it, choking her until her eyes bulge and she claws the skin from my wrists.

Chained. DAMMIT. I never called! I need to put a call into Paul, let him know I'm coming. Line up some subs for me. He knows my flavor.

And it ain't fucking vanilla.

I chuckle at my thoughts, but they're interrupted by Rachel, "Sir? The intern list? I was explaining that I've researched the top twenty. Honestly, I can only see one, maybe two, candidates." She nods to the list on my desk that's gone unnoticed until this moment.

I snatch it up with a sigh and look over the names, their degrees, and the colleges they attended. "Which two, Rach?"

"Well, Christopher Wells; he comes from a long line of highly respectable names. He's the 'maybe'. And Jackson Brands; his family also includes an incredible amount of well-known names. And his Master's degree is from Oxford, so..."

I look up from the list of names, blinking dumbly at her.

"I mean I went through... I researched every name on the list, Wes. What? Stop looking at me like that!" Her giggle instantly reminds me of C-names voice, causing my head to collapse back, hanging over the back of my chair. I shove my thumb and forefinger into my eyes.

Am I attempting to gouge my eyeballs out? Fuck no!

My goddamn brains? FUCK. YES.

Groaning in exhaustion, I remove my hand from its attempts at a digital lobotomy and raise it to shut her the hell up.

"Jesus Christ, Rach. Stop. Shut your mouth. You realize that this..." I point to the list, "...I am aptly capable of handling? These little pussies..." I glance down to the highlighted names, "...Christopher and Jackson, are not the caliber of interns I'm looking for."

"Well, like I said, I went through every name. And those two gentleman," She starts ticking her fingers off with her reasons— which leads my mind back to wrapping my hands around her throat, "Are extremely educated, come from a long line of some of the *best* publishers and editors. They each have exceptional references and are without *rap sheets*."

I smirk at this cocky bitch, steeple my fingers and lean forward, "Rachel... I want the ones with the seediest pasts, longest goddamn rap sheets, from families that have no idea how to even spell publishing... That are from the top colleges. *That* is what I want." I point to the list, "And if there isn't one here, I'll need you to call my pops, and tell him to go fuck himself. Then, send him and Josephine a fucking Edible Arrangement, with nothing but chocolate covered bananas. Understood?"

As she rushes out of my office spitting, quite honestly the

saddest attempts of curses and threats I've ever fucking heard, my eyes fall to the list of names.

I'm going to find a damn intern. And when I'm done, they'll be nothing less than five goddamn stars.

Chapter 4

Families are Bitchin'-Especially The Poor Ones

"Shit!" I scream as the heel of my shoe gets snagged in a manhole cover. The next thing I know, I'm on my fucking ass in front of God and everyone; bloody knees, broken high heel, and papers stating all five firms are no longer accepting applications.

If I was a bitch, I'd fucking cry. I swear to Christ I would.

But I'm not.

After gathering all my shit, I half walk half hobble the last four blocks to my and Trina's apartment. I struggle up the stairs with one six-inch heel and one no inch heel, but don't worry. I make it! I unlock our door, shove it open with my hip and look up to find Trina cleaning the shit out of the kitchen. Tossing my keys and purse on the foyer table, I ask "The hell are you doing, babe? Smells like a bleach bomb blew up in this place."

"Oh my God! What happened to *you*!?!" She scurries from the kitchen towards me and I look down at my bloody legs and kick off my heels, well… whatever, you know what I mean.

"What's it look like? I busted my ass. That's what happened." exhaustion evident in my voice.

"Looks like you tried to bathe a cat!" Her laughter sounds more like a cackle, "With your fucking feet!" Aaaaand the cackling continues.

"Yeah, I guess it kinda does. I'm gonna hop in the shower. Today sucked gorilla balls - fuck that - it sucked King Kong gorilla balls. I've been defeated. And I fucking despise defeat. You get any wine?" I ask stripping off my clothes and heading to the shower.

"I got four bottles of Riesling, to celebrate... But fuck it, we'll have a defeat party instead. And I'm only attending because I know you haven't cried a day in your life."

"Fuck yeah! The first three bottles are mine though! No negotiations!" I call out on my way to the bathroom.

Before I can close the door I hear her non-negotiations, "Okay, that's cool. Because Bo and Eve are coming over! They're bringing wine to celebrate too. Err... Dance in defeat, I mean."

"Shit!" I slam the door closed and turn the shower to scalding hot.

Bo and Eve are two of my best friends. Trina met Bo when he first moved to New York. They tried dating, but it never really went far. I absolutely adore him. He is the funniest, kindest man I know.

And Eve? Eve's the oddest fucking NYC model you'll ever meet. First of all, Eve is a complete and utter softy! No balls. At all. She is the most unsure, uncertain goddamn beauty queen I've ever met. However, she's real as fuck and I dig that. Eve and Bo went on one date, that's all it took. And they've never looked back.

Fucking beautiful thing, isn't it? *Gags*

Trina, Bo, and Eve have been my family for the last four years. Quite honestly, I don't know if I would have made it with my sanity intact without them.

However, even with them being my fam, I still just wanted to shower, drink three bottles of wine, and pass the fuck out.

Like I said; I'm tired. I'm defeated.

After I shower, I walk into the living room and I'm immediately bombarded by my 'family'. Eve walks up to me with a goblet of Riesling in her outstretched hand and a smile that quickly turns into a frown. "Sorry, Stell." She whispers.

"I'm okay." I grab the wine glass and set it on the nearest

surface before hugging her neck. When I lean back and see her sad teary eyes, it almost kills me. "Don't look at me like that Eve. I said I'm good. 'Kay, babe?" She nods, causing her tears to spill over onto her cheeks.

Shit, I need to get drunk—Fast.

"*HOLY FUCK!!!*" I pull my pillow over my face. When I smell Trina's shampoo I realize I'm in her bed. I have not a clue how the fuck I made it to bed. I knew when I stood up to get another glass of wine last night and the room went sideways that I should've stopped.

I'm pretty sure I landed in Trina's room because I couldn't make it any further down the hall. It happens. *Shrugs* Even to the best of us.

I just roll until I kinda fall out of bed then walk bumping into walls and shit on my way to the bathroom.

After I've showered and swallowed WAY more Motrin than the bottle suggests, I walk into the kitchen to start the coffee maker before making a beeline to the living room and flop down onto the couch. I spot Bo and Eve on a pallet on the floor and I can't help it, I laugh.

"What the hell's so funny, Stell?" Bo asks from the floor.

"We're too old for this shit. You know it?" I reply still giggling.

After the coffee maker stops brewing, I sigh before getting up and making my way back into the kitchen. "You and Eve want a cup o' joe?"

"Nah, I want my damn bed. Any bed will do. This floor fucking sucks."

"Go get in my bed, you dork. I didn't even make it that far last night. Hey, where's T at by the way?"

"Work." He tries to wake Eve, but ends up having to carry her. "We're going to lay down and try to sleep this hangover shit off.

Oh, and before T left, she said you got a call." He nods towards the sofa table. "Message is right over there."

He and Eve disappear down the hallway.

I make my coffee – black, one Splenda. After taking a sip, an extremely grateful sigh crosses my grinning lips. "See? Shower and coffee; that's all I needed to make this day go from shit to good." I tell the room.

I grab my laptop and snatch the message from the sofa table before curling up on the couch.

Taking another sip of coffee my eyes scan the message:

Stell—

Sorry bitch, I know you're in hangover hell. But your boy Wesley called. You have an appointment for an interview at 10. Wear the heather gray pencil skirt and the silk off-white capped sleeved blouse. Black fuck-me peep toe pumps too. You're good girl. The skirts long enough to cover your injuries from bathing that cat with your feet. I love ya, sissy.

T.

P.S. His number is 555-2398. His receptionist said it was the direct line to his office. ;)

"You have got to be kidding me! How? *FUCK*!" I crumble the message before tossing it in the trash and slamming my way into Trina's bedroom headed straight for her closet. I dig out the oldest, ugly mu-mu dress and lay it on her bed. After grabbing my makeup and sitting in front of the mirror on the floor, I carefully apply my make-up. I pin my dark brown hair up into a sloppy, sexy bun and pluck the hair to create little wisps of hair around my face and at the nape of my neck.

Only after I've finished, I realize how much attention I spent to detail. *SHIT.* I will look utterly ridiculous if I try to rock this face and hair in a goddamn mu-mu.

"Fuck it. This is it, Stella. This is your last damn chance at an internship. Wear the damn fuck-me pumps and the skirt."

Have I mentioned that I despise defeat?

When I walk into Jacobs Publishing building on Madison Ave., my head is high, my shoulders are back, and my heels click with purpose.

I smile at the man behind the security desk. Speaking quietly, I ask, "Hi. I'm Stella Reese. I have an appointment with Mr. Wesley Jacobs. Which floor is his office on?"

"Top floor, ma'am— the 70th." He smiles.

My hand pats the desk before I nod and head towards the elevators.

I'm lost in the thoughts waging a war inside my mind when the elevator doors open, physically shoving me from my thoughts. I jerk, straightening my spine before walking from the elevator.

"Well... Here goes nothing. Please GOD. Wesley Jacobs, don't remember me."

I enter the main headquarters of Jacobs Publishing House.

Hell no, I'm not nervous.

I'm scared out of my fucking mind!

Chapter 5

Who The Hell is She?

WESLEY

I ended up taking over the fucking list of Rachel's as soon as I realized she was blatantly ignoring the four females on the list.

Yeah, bitch. I clocked your bullshit five minutes into our second convo over this intern bullshit.

I spent over an hour on the list. Which was about fifty-seven minutes longer than I'd needed to. Because I'd known in the first three minutes that Stella Jolie Reese—the girl with a Master's in English from Columbia University that had been earned from a full scholarship and who'd also spent most of her life being bounced from foster home to foster home in every shit town scattered throughout Louisiana—That girl...was mine.

There was no two goddamn ways around it. Stella Reese. Would. Be. Mine. My fucking intern. Mine. I plan on taking this little thing and turning her into everything.

IF she's as badass in person as she is on paper.

And don't worry... I'm fully prepared to be sorely let down.

"Mr. Wesley, your ten o'clock is here."

I roll my eyes at Rachel's snooty ass voice before telling her, "Send Ms. Stella Reese in, Rach." I slam the phone down in its cradle before glancing at the clock to note her timeliness; then I shrug into my suit jacket and sit back down behind my desk.

I pick up my fountain pen and continue going over this quarter's numbers. And yes, I'm only trying to appear busy, goddammit.

Her soft knock fucking pisses me off, causing me to shout, "Come in!"

Keeping my eyes down but training my mind on watching her in my peripheral, I witness as she opens not one but both double doors with both hands and walks in this mothafucking office like she owns the bitch.

Without invitation, she curtly waltzes to the chair in front of my desk before slowly sitting. Her legs cross and she leans over before placing a file on my desk and clearing her throat, "Mr. Jacobs, Hi. I'm Stella Reese. Thank you so much for this opportunity. It is... Well, it's, ahh... I appreciate it." She smiles brightly at me over my desk.

Now, at some point, I've set my pen down, steepled my fingers and began taking in little Ms. Reese from the top of her head to her waist—it's all that's visible from where I sit.

Narrowing my eyes on her hazel ones, I smirk above my linked fingers. Never unlocking her gaze, I explain, "Stella, you're quite welcome for this *appreciated* opportunity. Now, I want you to realize that there were more than fifty people on Jacobs Publishing intern list. After my secretary had completed her research, you were not one of the final names—It's in your good fortune that I don't trust her, and even more that I've always followed my gut."

I lean back into my chair and allow my eyes to run over her petite frame. She is a delicious 10+ at least! My fingertips slide her file towards me. When they're close enough, I glance down before looking back up and locking eyes with her again.

"Quite frankly, you're the only intern I plan on interviewing, Stella, with that being said, your being here for the interview tells me you want the internship that Jacobs is offering. Am I correct?"

Why are her eyes growing wider?

"No... I mean," She shakes her head before clearing her throat, "Yes, sir. Jacobs has become my last resort. Without this internship I will be forced to forgo the intern division of the program."

Soooo... After sir, all I heard was the 'wa wa wa' sound Charlie

Brown's parents make. Gibberish. Just a bunch of fucking gibberish coming from the softest, most fuckable lips I've ever laid my eyes on. I'm in the middle of making a solemn vow to myself, my thoughts and internal promises of fucking the goddamn hell out her mouth, when she interrupts. She fucking whistles.

Whistles! I snap my attention from her mouth to pierce the hazel eyes that are constantly flashing from topaz to peridot. "Eyes up here chief. Got it?" She motions to them with her hand.

I grab the file I had Rachel put together and slam it in front of her, causing her to flinch. I pluck the pen from my desk and set it beside the file. Not once do my eyes leave hers. "Initial on the short lines. Sign on the long one, last page." I smirk before nodding and settling back into my chair.

I know I can't fuck little miss Reese. Well, I mean I can, but I won't. I'm turning over a new leaf. I realize women like Stella and Rachel, and even that girl you met earlier... What the fuck was her name? Oh, Casey, right, anyway I've accepted that these women are comparable to putting a Band-Aid on a bullet wound. And I'm not sure why I've continued to attempt forcing myself into this mold that society has of how a relationship should be. Especially when you look at every other aspect of my life... I don't fucking conform to shit. They try to tell me to stop bending the rules, I snap the fuckers in half.

So, for that reason, I will not fuck Ms. Stella Reese.

But Jesus fucking Christ—Do I want to.

Thankfully, I got in touch with Paul and have plans to visit Chained this weekend.

I can wait until then to get my cock wet—Don't worry, I got this shit.

An exasperated sigh leaves Stella's beautiful fucking lips as her head comes up from signing the paperwork. She slides the folder across the expanse of my desk, "Okay. All initialed and signed. Do you have a curriculum or a schedule for me? I didn't see any mention of hours per week in the forms."

25

The devils grin snakes its way onto my face. Leaning forward in my chair, I lower my voice to the lowest, devious tone I possess. "You're fucking mine, Stella Reese. All. Mine. You will be at my heel Monday through Friday from seven am until six pm, you will be available and easily accessible to me twenty-four hours a day, seven days a week. You will work directly under me, and me alone, for the next three hundred and sixty-five days, and when I'm finished with you, you will be nothing less than a five fucking star publicist. Is that understood?"

Okay, so... As soon as the first sentence fell out off my mouth, any and all control over the remaining words that I originally maintained fucking vanished.

And from where I'm sitting, Stella seems to have gone as pale as a ghost, broke out into a sweat, and is chewing that goddamn bottom lip of hers to hell.

"I asked you a question. Answer it." I say sternly.

She stops chewing on her lip however the 'O' her mouth is currently forming is making my cock swell so hard, it's almost unbearable.

"Close that pretty fucking mouth of yours. You won't like what happens to it if you don't."

She snaps it shut and begins squirming in her seat. I sit behind my massive mahogany desk and watch in fascination as she pulls her confidence up around her and I find it somewhat amusing.

"Monday through Friday, seven to six. Got it. Able to be reached twenty-four/seven. Got it. Yours? Never." She leans over my desk with a detested looking smirk on her face, "Not in a million fucking years. Your employee? Yes, sir. Got it? And if you ever, *EVER*, talk about my mouth in the context you just did, I'll have your ass in court for sexual harassment quicker than you can steeple those fucking fingers of yours again. Understood?"

She stands from her chair before snatching her file from my desk and flipping it open. After setting a piece of paper on the top my desk, she spins on her heel before making her way to exit the double doors of my office.

But before she can close the door I get the last fucking word in, because I always get the last word in. It's what I fucking do. "Rachel has your new work cell phone. Make sure to get it from her before leaving. Goodbye, Ms. Reese."

Long after Stella's left my office, I remain sitting there, staring at the doors she walked through. Weird, and I mean weird as fuck shit begins shifting around in my chest. And my mind? Fuck don't even ask where that damn thing went. Because even I don't know.

I do, however, know three things. One, I like Stella Reese—a-fucking-lot. Two, I could not have chosen a better intern for Jacobs Publishing. And three, those goddamn subs Paul has lined up, every damn one of them better look exactly like Stella Jolie Reese.

I shove my fingers through my hair and fist them before settling my elbows on my desk and staring at her fucking initials on the forms.

"Shit! What in the hell was that? Who in the hell is she?" I ask the paperwork on my desk.

No, it doesn't answer.

"Shit!"

What the fuck is today? Thursday. Okay. Yeah—I totally have this shit. All I have to do is wait one day. Totally got this shit.

Chapter 6

Who The Hell Does He Think He Is?

I was *SO* ready for that interview. I walked in that bitch, head high, shoulders squared. Ready! Until I saw him again for the first time since I was thirteen years old. I'm almost certain I was able to pull off my nonchalant attitude. Well, until he told me to close my... What did he call it? Pretty fucking mouth?

Yeah, after that, I knew I had to get the fuck out of there. All that *'mine, you are mine'* bullshit didn't surprise me at all. It's classic Wesley Jacobs. C-l-a-s-s-i-c. Wesley. Jacobs. He hasn't changed at all in the last fourteen years.

So no. I was fully prepared for that little dirty, sexual innuendo-riddled speech.

Well... I guess it's time for me to explain why I was so adamantly set against doing my internship with Jacobs Publishing. I'm not sure if I'll ever tell Trina, but you... You probably should know this tidbit to fully grasp what the hell is going on, as well as fully understand my reaction to all this.

I was probably nearing the fourth foster home when I landed in a new home. They lived in a small town in northwest Louisiana. I was excited when I first met the family. They had the whole Brady Bunch thing going on with a daughter of their own as well as two other foster boys. The house was clean. It was a little small and old, but it seemed nice.

I settled in quickly, but never could really seem to fit in. I tried to adapt my personality as best as I could, but it was impossible. My shy and quiet cards didn't work. My abrasive stand-up-for-yourself cards also didn't work. When I combined the two decks, shuffled and tried playing those, shit just got even worse.

The friendship I initially hoped would form between Jessica, their daughter, and I never even had a chance. She told me within the first twelve hours not to speak to her. That we were not sisters and she planned for my ass to be gone before the week ended.

The boys were older than me, but Sam, the oldest, seemed to take me under his wing. If he and his friends were going to a baseball game, he always let me tag along. If they went out to the lake to fish or to just hang out around the bonfire at night, he'd also let me come.

I zeroed in on Sam's friend, Wesley Jacobs, the first time I laid eyes on him. He was beautiful. I didn't care that I was only twelve. In my mind, I was close enough to thirteen; so him being seventeen was easily brushed aside in my preteen fixated mind. I truly believed I was in love with him and that if I could change myself enough, in time, he would notice me and love me as much as I loved him.

As a product of the foster care system, you immediately conform—you become a chameleon. Your survival depends on your ability to become whatever or whoever others expect you to be, and by foster home number four, I'd honestly thought I'd mastered this skill.

I was sorely mistaken.

I turned thirteen in May. By the time mid-summer came, I was at the pool almost every day. The sun had tanned my skin to the perfect golden tone and puberty was making itself known by causing my boy straight hips to fill out and my breasts grow into a decent B cup. Before going swimming every day, I would French braid my hair and spray a mixture of peroxide and water to help the sun create natural looking highlights.

By the time the Fourth of July weekend rolled around, I had completely transformed myself from the pale skinned, dull, dark and stringy haired girl with nothing but a gaunt, boy figure into the beginnings of an attractive young woman.

Armed with a mini skirt I'd cut off to mid-thigh (it was originally long enough to reach my ankles) and a white eyelet strapless bustier top, I slipped my old ugly black rubber flip flops on and ran out the back door to avoid being seen when Sam honked his horn for me to hurry my ass up.

His reaction to my choice of clothing was exactly what I was hoping to achieve from Wesley.

Sadly, that night was not only the night I lost every ounce of hope to ever find or believe in love. It was also the night I lost the only friend I'd ever had, as well as the last remaining vital part of my soul.

As soon as we pulled up to the beach at the lake I kicked my ugly flip-flops off and jumped from Sam's truck. Excitement was zipping through me as soon as my toes sank into the sand.

Make a note of this moment, because this is the last time in my childhood that giddiness would ever consume my already grim life. Morosely, it would also be the turning page in my life, the domino that is tipped and leads to my being homeless and truly knowing what life is like with absolutely nothing.

I skipped over to where the keg was when I saw that Wesley was the one handing out the red solo cups of beer. I'd never drank before, but what the hell? I wanted to act as old as I looked.

After waiting for the five people in front of me to collect their cup I walked up smiling at Wes, waiting, hanging on his every word and body movement.

He never even spared a glance in my direction. His fist pumped the keg filling the cup. Then he handed it to me before grabbing some chick's ass as she walked by. Somehow, I managed to blink the tears away and swallow the lump in my throat, then I tucked my tail between my legs and quickly walked away.

Sad, huh? I know. There is honestly nothing that leaves a deeper wound than being so that when you do, in that fleeting moment, everything you've obsessed about and yearned for - for months - would all finally transpire. Only it doesn't.

I wholly believed that entire squabble of bullshit for merely five more hours of my life. Having drunk more than three cups of beer, I knew my ass needed to keep itself planted right where it was: On the log near the bonfire Wes had made. Yep. He walked right past me, dragging logs then dry grass before sitting on his haunches less than two feet away and kindled a fucking fire. He never looked my way, not one damn time.

Most of the party guests had either left or wandered into the surrounding woods to take their groping a few hundred steps further while I sat and stared into the fire until nothing but embers remained.

I wasn't naïve, being molested the first three or four years of my life, then raped repeatedly by my father as well as two different foster fathers... I knew what the hell was going on. I'd just never, well besides Wesley, actually wanted to participate in any petting or groping, much less taking it further.

I heard some yelling coming from the woods to my left, but shrugged it off and kept stabbing the embers with the stick I'd found and had been hanging out with for the last two hours.

I was a little shocked when Sam and Courtney came out of the woods. I covertly ducked my head and watched from beneath the veil of my hair only to witness her rearing back and slapping him across the face. Snickering too low for anyone to hear, I went back to poking the coals and charred wood.

A few minutes later Sam stumbled over to me, "Stell, come on. Time to go."

"Thank God! Sorry, but this party freaking blew." I stood up dusting the sand off my ass and started following Sam as we made our way to the parking area. Once we were close enough to Sam's truck, I realized Wes's truck was parked diagonally in front of Sam's. When I saw him stand on unsteady feet and begin unbuckling his belt and pull his thing out, I blushed in embarrassment and then mouthed "Thank you, Jesus."

A smirk crept its way onto my face, but quickly dissolved when I heard a female voice purring right before Wes told her,

"Goddamn right you little whore. Fucking suck that thick cock." His hands delved into her long blond tresses before he yanked her face into his crotch and his head fell back. "Suck until I cum or I'll spew my load into your fucking eye. You hear me, bitch?"

To say I was sickened was a horrid understatement.

I was so overwhelmed with disgust, my mind utterly consumed with hatred for this fucking asshole that I'd placed on a pedestal and worshipped for the last eight months that I didn't realize what was happening when Sam let down the tailgate of his truck.

Honestly I didn't know until he had me pinned, bent over with my skirt flipped up over my ass and felt the metal grating of his truck biting into the flesh covering my hipbones. He shoved his hand between my legs before he grabbed the panties covering me and yanked them down.

I screamed, as loud as I could. I let the cry for help, the shrieking words, "Wes, please! Help me Wes, please fucking HELP ME!" tear their way from my soul, claw up my throat and pierce the night with nothing but moans and grunts as an answer to my pleas.

When Sam shoved my panties so far into my mouth, I gagged struggling to breath around the suffocating material.

And vaguely, somewhere between my sobs and tears, I remember - I'll always remember - as my best friend, my only friend, my brother shoved himself from one hole into another, having to listen to Wesley Jacobs reach orgasm.

The sound was so disturbing, it caused me to heave every drop of beer I'd consumed that night. And after I lost the contents of my stomach, I then drowned in it.

That's why... You wanted to know why I was so goddamn fucking set against working for him? That's fucking why.

And never fucking ask again.

Sam tossed my lifeless ass out of the back of his truck, and hauled his ass from what I could gather.

I woke up in a hospital days later—utterly shocked. I honestly didn't understand why I was still alive. I'd been hanging outside the pearly gates with some woman claiming to be my mom and an older woman that kept apologizing for her 'shitty piece of shit' son. So yeah, I was confused when I woke up in a hospital bed. But not too confused to know I needed to run if I planned on staying alive.

Remember that deep wound and biting pain I mentioned earlier when Wes ignored my existence?

Yeah, turns out I had no real fucking grasp on what pain really was... Ten weeks later, after living on the streets and ducking from every cop car or authoritive looking adult, I fucking face-planted into the sidewalk, crippled by pain so fiercely, that even after *ALL* the shit I'd been through, lived through, remained conscious through, *THIS* pain...It took me past my goddamn knees.

The pain of an ectopic pregnancy twisting and rupturing your fallopian tube... It takes you past your knees.

It brings you to your fucking face.

easily brushed off by someone you've watched for months. Someone that has consumed both your every waking thought as well as your dreams. It's hard to describe the bite or pain you feel when you've done *EVERYTHING* just to capture his attention for a space in time; knowing.

Chapter 7

Convince a Woman to Submit

WESLEY

From the moment Stella left my office, my worthless mind has done absolutely nothing but think of her - imagine her in every fucking sexual position - on her knees, bent over my desk, sitting proudly on my cock and riding me to kingdom cum.

None of it is as fucked up as when I stood in the kitchen downing tumblers of scotch and looked up to see her sexy little ass in nothing but one of my button up shirts, unbuttoning it as she walked towards me with a smirk on her face, only to vanish into thin air when I reached my hand out to feel her skin when she got close enough to touch.

Shit's fucked up, right?

A shitty day, a shitty night, and another shitty day later I remove my jacket and tie, leaving them in the R8 before stepping through the double doors of Chained, unbuttoning the first few buttons of my shirt on my way into the club.

Fucking euphoria instantly thrums through my veins and I fucking love it. This is exactly what I needed. I feel alive for the first time in... Well shit, since the last time I was here.

See if I try to avoid the caged beast inside me again. You won't. Because I'm fucking done denying myself this. Finished.

I look around the club's main floor interior as I head toward the bar. The walls are covered in black satin with chains embedded every foot or so, each chain reaches the ceiling before it's strung to meet in the middle of the club where an enormous crystal

34

chandelier hangs.

Black and off-white leather chaise lounges with low tables holding several tea lights are scattered throughout this area of the club.

And because I was so fucking antsy to get here, to get Stella flushed out of my system I'm one of maybe twelve occupants on this early Friday night.

I order a scotch and unbutton the cuffs of my shirt before rolling them up my forearms. I nod when the bartender slides the crystal tumbler of scotch in front of me.

"Wes, what's up, man? Long time."

Shit! I don't know this guy's name. Joe? Jon! It's Jon, I think...

"Yep, been a while. Paul in yet?" I ask before sipping my drink.

"Let me check for you." He heads over to a phone at the far end of the bar and speaks to someone before heading back in my direction.

I raise my empty tumbler before he can speak, "Hey, bud. Mix me another, yeah?"

"Wes it's a two drink maximum," He looks at his watch, then back up at me and asks, "You sure you wanna blow through both before nine?"

My eyebrow shoots up, "The fuck'd I say?"

"All right, man. It's your call. Paul's headed down by the way."

Oh shit yeah.

I rub my hands together like a kid in a candy store before I turn to face the club.

"Here ya go, man."

"Yep." I say grabbing the tumbler and turning back around to face the club. Thankfully a few more patrons have recently shown up.

Women in their business suits with men kneeling at their feet.

35

Men in their business suits with women kneeling at their feet.

There are a couple of Doms taking it overboard wearing a cape and shit… Yeah, they don't have a sub kneeling at their feet.

I'm chuckling at my inner musings when Paul walks up to me.

"Wes. How are you friend?" We shake hands and I smile looking towards club.

"Doing good, Paul. You?" I jerk my head motioning at the club. "Business is doing great I see. Place looks great."

My eyes scan the area noting the recent renovations.

And come to a screeching halt as they land on Stella Jolie Reese.

"What the FUCK is she doing here?" I realize too late that I've asked the question out loud.

Paul's eyes follow my line of vision and land on the two women and guy that have walked in with Stella.

"Oh, that's Eve Arras, she's here for the Jacques' Boudoir magazine shoot." He sips from his tumbler of bourbon, "I believe Eve was the center fold of the lingerie add. Not sure though."

"Really, Paul? So, you just let vanillas float around your establishment amongst the people living the lifestyle, and for no other reason than because they hit the center fold of a lingerie add?" I sigh setting my drink down.

"Oh, no." Paul shakes his head before reiterating, "They go no further than the main bar area."

"What's allowed here? I mean—Shit." I curse. I want Stella out of here. She has no damn business being in a club like this.

This entire fucking shit is absolutely absurd!

And dammit if Jon was fucking right. I shouldn't have used up my two drinks so early. *FUCK!*

"You ready to meet the subs?" He extends his arm in a 'right this way' motion.

My eyes shoot back over to where Stella and her model friends are laughing, having just a fucking grand ol' time.

"Hey! The brunette goes nowhere. You fucking understand me, Paul?" I demand as I point in Stella's direction.

"She's not a member, Wes. It doesn't matter what the hell you say. They will not even know there are other areas in this building. Much less be allowed into those said areas. Do YOU understand?"

"Thank Christ, okay, lets go see what you have lined up for me." I stand from the bar and head in the direction he gestured to earlier.

We're in the elevator headed to the 13th floor when he speaks again. "I have two blondes and a brunette sub that are looking for Doms. All three of them are like you, somewhat new members of Chained and have the same tainted understanding of the lifestyle that you have."

"Damn. Just one brunette?" I ask as the elevator doors slide open.

Paul stops right outside the door. "Wesley, the color of their hair is not of any importance. You know that. So before you go after a sub just based on her hair color, you need to get your goddamn head on straight. Now."

An exhausted sigh slips out at the same time I roll my eyes. "Yes, Paul. I am fully aware of that. I just would have liked a few more brunette subs to choose from, that's all."

He narrows his eyes on mine before opening the door and motioning for me to enter. After I've stepped into the small meeting area Paul closes the door leaving me with the three subs.

All three are nude with their hair pulled back in a bun at the base of their necks. All three are kneeled perfectly, palms facing up resting on their parted thighs. All three faces pointed downward, backs bowed, reminding me of something Michelangelo would sculpt.

I stalk towards the brunette first.

What? Don't look at me like that. I want the damn brunette to fucking work out, okay?

My hand slips under her chin tilting her face up until her eyes meet mine.

Damn it. Dark brown.

Smiling at her I ask, "What's your name?"

Quietly she responds, "Heather."

I nod and flick my hand for her to stand before verbalizing the command as well. "Heather, stand. Let's sit over there," I point to the sofa and low table, "I want to know about you. And you're going to tell me. Understood?"

"Yes, sir." She quickly stands to follow me to the sofa. I motion for her to sit.

"You may sit. Relax. We're just going to talk, get to know one another."

After we're both settled on the couch, I begin. "I'm Wesley Jacobs. I'm dominant by nature and have been in and out of the lifestyle for over ten years. However, I plan on finding a sub that is looking for the same things I am from a relationship and sticking around. I've tried to pacify my pallet with vanilla and to be quite honest I'm fucking starved. That's all for now, so tell me a little about you."

Her eyes remain on her lap staring at her twisting hands. "Well, I'm twenty-three, I'm taking some courses at the junior college to get my license to be a dental hygienist."

My fingertips tilt her chin bringing her eyes up to mine. "When you speak to me, look at me. I can't see if you're telling the truth without reading your eyes while you speak. Continue." I nod urging her to finish.

Her fidgeting is already grating on my nerves.

She continues telling me her life story. But I don't hear a word.

All I can think about is Stella in that fucking red dress. It hugged her every curve like it was made, tailored just for her beautiful little body. All that long brown hair in big curls hanging down to her

38

waist.

Fuck. Heather isn't going to work.

I look at the other two subs, unmoved from their perfect submissive stance.

Nope.

Bloody. Fucking. Hell.

And then it hits me.

Paul could bring me a goddamn harem of subs, but if one of them isn't Stella Jolie Reese, then they won't do.

I've got to get inside of little Ms. Reese's head... Find out if this girl has even one submissive bone in her body.

And God fucking help me if she doesn't.

God fucking help her if she does.

Chapter 8

Defying a Dom

Can someone tell me why the *HELL* I'm in club known for BDSM? I'm so damn nervous I can hardly sit still. Plus, this damn dress keeps riding up and if I pull it down any further my tits are gonna fall out of the top.

I cannot believe I let Eve and Trina talk me into this shit.

Let's go to a BDSM bar and see how they party they said.

It will be fun they said.

Yeah, sorry, I'll stop.

Once I gain the bartender's attention, I smile, "Hey. Ahh… Can I have another glass of white Zin?" He nods at my hand. "Oh, you want to see my stamps?" I hold my hand and smile again. "I'm not sure why I got them, but this shit better wash off before Monday."

"Stamps, plural. Two-drink maximum, babe. Sorry. You've had your two." He turns to walk away and I try to stop him.

"Two fucking drink maximum? What the fuck kind of bar has a two drink maximum?" He just shakes his head and continues moving towards the other end of the bar.

"Seriously? Are you fucking kidding me you asshole?! It's a bar!"

"A bar where Doms come to find subs. A bar where Doms bring their subs. No one wants a drunk Dom that takes shit too far. And no one needs a drunk sub that forgets her safe word." Wesley's voice is like dark chocolate covered sin, his words are smooth as silk sliding from his tongue. Instantly, I am soaked between my thighs.

Hell no I don't have panties on either. Who the hell wears panties anymore? Oh, right... The smart bitches. *SHIT!*

I briefly wonder if I can play deaf - pretend I don't know he's talking to me. But when his large warm hand circles my arm above my elbow and gently squeezes - well, even I know the shudder that goes through every molecule of my body is one that's clearly visible.

Before I can turn around his lips brush my ear and he softly speaks, "I saw that, Ms. Reese."

I turn nudging my face into him before I can make sense of my body language. "Why does that not surprise me, Wesley Jacobs? Of course you notice the things I rather you wouldn't."

He runs his nose from behind my ear to the nape of my neck, planting his face into my hair before breathing in deeply and whispering, "I don't know what the fuck that means. Honestly, I don't care." His grip on my arms tighten and he pulls my back flush against his massive chest and torso. Immediately, I become aware of his massive erection. I cannot keep the smirk from my face if I wanted too. "Come with me, Stella. We have a lot to talk about, love."

If I were smart, if I had more wine in me, I'd do exactly what I should—I'd tell him to fuck off. But I've only had two glasses of wine and apparently, I'm not as fucking smart as I thought I was.

I nod, wave goodbye to my friends and follow Wesley fucking Jacobs out of the BDSM bar.

Yeah... How you like those cookies? They look sweet. Fuck it, I guess we'll see, won't we?

Once we're at his black looking sports car—I have no idea if it's a Hyundai or a Jag—he opens the passenger door for me and moves the stuff from the seat to the back of the car before stepping aside. "My place?" he asks as I slide into the softest fucking leather seat my ass has ever graced.

I nod before he shuts the door and quickly makes his way

around the hood of his car to the drivers side.

Once we've driven a little while in silence, I feel obligated to speak, to explain some shit before we get to his house. "Wesley, I'm only coming to your place for a drink, maybe two. If you want to talk about the internship that would be great, I'm excited. I was... Umm, nervous about it - well, I'm still nervous, but..."

His laughter cuts my rambling off. "I wasn't talking about the internship when I said we had shit to talk about. Yes, two drinks. Maybe three. What I have to say... Well, we're both going to need more than the two little drinks served at Chained."

I try to swallow and it turns into an audible gulp.

Shit!

"Ahh, okay. Maybe three. What is the topic you'd like to discuss, exactly?"

His chuckle causes my skin to break out in chill bumps. "After drink one, yeah?"

"What? You have to get another drink in me before even telling me the topic?" I scoff mocking scandal.

"Hell fucking yes, I do." He shakes his head with the devil's grin dancing across his face. A few moments later, he flips the blinker before pulling into a parking garage directly on Park fucking Ave. I can't help it. My jaw falls into my damn lap.

"What you need to pick something up from Hermes?" I ask looking around and laughing but not being funny *AT ALL*.

"What?" He glances over and looks at me like I've lost my damn mind. "Hermes? Hell no. For one it's ten thirty at night and the only fucking thing I have in my closet is Armani."

"Oh..." I tug up my dress.

Fuck yes! The damn girls are spilling out again.

"My dress came from Saks. Well, the discount rack at Saks."

Now his mouth drops open. "Saks?" Then the cocky bastard mouths 'Wow'.

42

"Yes, fucking Saks, why?"

"I just… I don't know. It looks like it was handmade for you. That's all." He shrugs and pulls into a parking spot. Before my mind can register what the hell I'm doing here - with him - he has my door open and he's pulling me from the car by my hand.

When we make it to… hell, I don't know - floor three hundred and seventy-five? The top floor, of course - the elevator doors part to reveal his 'home'. If that's what you can call it.

We enter the main entrance and walk onto the marble floor of the grand foyer where he unloads his keys, wallet, and cell phone on a long table. When I glance past the foyer and see plush white carpet, I kick my heels off which causes Wes to look over his shoulder and down at my feet before laughing.

"What?" I ask confused but more embarrassed over my knee jerk reaction.

Who sees white fucking carpet and doesn't kick off their shoes? Well, if you don't you're either an asshole or your shoes are brand fucking new.

"Nothing." His hand grasps mine before pulling me forward. "Your feet are cute as shit, that's all. What do you drink?"

I let him pull me past the living room, through the dining room and into another sitting area with a bar. Yes. A full bar. Liquor bottles lined up—the whole nine.

He pulls a bar stool out - again, yes. A barstool. I said the whole damn nine - I scoot my bottom up onto the stool as ladylike as possible. "Ms. Reese? What. Would. You. Like. To. Drink?"

"Oh, wine." I smile up at him behind the bar and watch his eyebrow lift up.

"Any particular wine or can I just grab the old box of Franzia from the back of kitchen pantry?"

My face scrunches up at the mention of Franzia. "White Zin, Riesling or Moscato. I like sweet wines."

"That I can do." He nods, pouring himself a scotch after he

43

hands me a glass of Riesling.

He literally drains his glass of scotch - less than three sips - swear to God. That, in turn, causes my nervousness to reappear and I follow suit by downing my glass of wine.

When I look back at Wes, he has that damn grin across his face that as a child I dreamed of and pined for, directed squarely on me.

"God-fucking-dammit, Stella. You are so beautiful." His brows furrow before he looks down into his empty glass.

"Thank you?" I duck my head embarrassed at the way I ended my statement with a question.

What the hell is wrong with me? He is just a man. He is a human. He is not a God, he is required to shower, shave, and brush his teeth just like every one else in order to remain healthy...and attractive.

Fuck, he is attractive too.

I let my eyes roam over him. My fingers itch to run through his short dark brown hair. My eyes could gaze into his bright green ones for hours. His wide shoulders cause my mind to wonder how it would feel being under him, surrounded by him. And his face? Holy cheese and crackers. It's just as beautiful, if not more now with the smile lines around his eyes and on both cheeks where his dimples hide.

"I need to talk to you about something. Before you react..." Wes's eyes stay locked on mine as he rounds the bar and makes us another drink, never pausing in his speech. "...I need you to hear me out. I don't want you to speak until I've finished. Is that understood?" I nod, too afraid to say yes in case he meant from the moment the words fell from his lips.

"Good. I hope that you understand, or it has dawned on you why I was at Chained tonight. Has it?"

My head nods yes again and I maintain eye contact.

"Good. So you understand that I am a Dom. I am dominant in every aspect of my life, my sexual life included. I have, over the last year, dated—well, not so much dated, more like fucked—strictly vanillas. In my mind, if they were kinky enough to allow me to be in total control, allow me to act out my fantasies, as well as feed the sadist within me, there was no reason to visit Chained or seek out a long term Dom/sub relationship. I've gone through hundreds of vanillas and quite frankly, Stella, I'm still a fucking starved man. Do you understand?"

Again, I simply nod.

The hand holding his tumbler of scotch stops on its way to his mouth and he points a finger at me around it.

"You, Ms. Reese. I want you." I watch somewhat fascinated as his lips press against the tumbler before sipping his drink. My eyes follow his hand as he sets his drink down. When he clears his throat, it causes me to quickly look back up into his eyes.

"So. Here's how this is going to go. I will test you. I will bend you. I will push you. Much further than you've ever been pushed. Not only on a professional level and a personal level, but sexually as well. My question is: Do you think you can handle me? All of me? Everywhere. I will be inside your mind, your soul, I will scratch so fucking far past your surface that you will be flayed open, exposed to only me." He picks his drink back up and pauses before taking a sip, keeping his eyes locked on mine over the rim of his crystal tumbler.

He sets his glass down and walks until he's standing directly in front of me. Using his thigh, he nudges my legs apart first before sliding his hips between my open thighs causing my dress to ride up so high, the question of whether or not I'm wearing panties is clearly visible. His huge hands cup my face before tilting it back until our mouths are only inches apart. His green eyes pierce mine as he declares, "I'm going to consume you, devour you - mind, body, and soul... You will be so immersed in me that I will be the only thing you see, feel, hear, taste, and smell. I'm going to fucking ruin you, Stella, so I ask—are you ready?"

Anxiety is already running through me, and every word falling from his mouth is making me more nervous, causing it to become so much harder for me to be able to concentrate.

"Wesley, I'm not—well, first of all, I'm not a sub, or a

45

submissive." My eyes dart around the room, assessing it for those slider bars, riding crops, and crosses that I read about in my books. However, my eyes can only see so much with both of his huge hands still holding my face. His eyes continue staring into mine, patiently waiting for an answer.

"Stella, have you even considered the possibility that you are?" His hands cupping my face begin to glide down my neck, brushing their way across my chest as they slide over the top of my breast. His large, calloused palms slide over the silk of my dress until he reaches where my skirt is pulled up. The beautiful devious grin he flashes me has me nearly begging for him; all of the promises he laid out moments ago whirling through my mind.

A moan escapes my throat and my head lolls back as his hand slides between my legs until he is sliding over my drenched swollen pussy and sinks a long deft finger inside me. He pulls out and sinks two fingers curling them up as his thumb circles my clit. "Holy. Fuck. Ohmygod." I whine, instantly on the verge of begging.

"Mmmm," His nose nuzzles my ear before he sinks his teeth into my earlobe. "Fucking wet little cunt wants me doesn't it, Ms. Reese?"

"Shit. Wow. Holy shit." I sputter. I can feel it already begin to pull as lights blink into my vision.

I have only ever cum on my own. It never comes at me this fast. EVER.

His fingers and thumb increase their pace and pressure. His husky words roll from his lips as they brush across the shell of my ear. "That wasn't an answer to my question, Ms. Reese. Now, you've let two of my questions go unanswered."

I'm there, I'm at the precipice and I'm throwing myself over, letting go, ready to be pulled under.

Suddenly his hand is gone, yanking me back from the edge. I blink at him in confusion, watching as he steps back away from me. He brings his hand up to his mouth and his eyes stay locked on mine as he slowly begins licking his two fingers around his damn beautiful devious grin. "Mmmm, if divinity ever had a taste, this

46

would definitely fucking be it."

He continues stepping away from me at the bar until he reaches a large, dark brown leather chair. He sits before sinking back and resting his elbows on the arms of the chair. His eyes narrow on mine over his steepled fingers before he continues, "That tight little cunt of yours was clamping down around my fingers hard. Now...would you like for me to explain why I didn't allow you to cum, Ms. Reese?"

My mind is in a haze of ecstasy, my vision is so blurred I can hardly see him, hell I'm barely able to make out his words and it takes me a moment to make sense of them. When I do, the haze clears and my vision blurs; but not from ecstasy, it blurs red from my rage.

What in the hell did I just allow myself succumb to?

"Wait—What? What the hell just happened? No—What the fuck is wrong with you?"

I abruptly stand from the barstool and before I can yank my dress down, my fucking knees buckle and I'm on the damn floor.

Wesley is instantly there helping me up.

Well that wasn't embarrassing or anything.

"You know what the fuck is wrong with me, Ms. Reese. I just explained it. It may not have been very clear, but I did explain myself."

My trembling hands push my hair behind my ears. When I gather enough composure and I'm able to speak, I spit my words at him, "Wesley you don't know a goddamn thing about me. You have no idea what the first seventeen years of my life consisted of; what I've had to do to get to where I am today. I am not a submissive or a sub or whatever. I am a fucking fighter. Because absolutely everything I am and everything that I possess, I've had to fight like hell to get."

I turn quickly to leave, but before I step out of the bar-slash-sitting area, I spin back around and narrow my eyes on his before I spew my parting words. "You can't be a submissive or peek into the lifestyle, not when the only sexual encounters you've ever experienced were rapes and molestations by father, after foster father, after foster brother from the time you were a toddler. There, there's your goddamn answer, Wesley. Good night."

I slam the door, stumbling from his penthouse to the elevator doors.

Chapter 9

Fucking Answers

WESLEY

Huh. Well, that's never happened before.

I'm stumped. Yeah, at a loss for words. I've never been put in my place and I've never been hit by a curve ball.

Dumfounded, I slouch back into the chair and let her words run through my mind over and over. I'm trying to convince myself I'd misheard what she said before she slammed out.

Surely I didn't hear her right. Right?

"...the only sexual encounters you've ever experienced were rapes and molestations by father, after foster father, after foster brother from the time you were a toddler."

"Jesus fucking Christ." I lean forward resting my elbows on my knees before rubbing my hands over my face. "That's what she fucking said." All I can do is shake my head in astonishment.

I'm pissed at myself for shoving all my shit at her. I'm pissed at myself for honestly thinking I could talk her or force her into being my sub. And I'm seething pissed at myself for thinking I had any right to even lay a finger on her, much less in her.

"I'm such a fucking asshole! Son of a bitch!" I leap from my leather chair and storm out of the room.

Before I know what I'm doing, I'm in my office calling Derrick, the best PI in NYC who's been in charge of any aspects of my life that I should call the police for, but don't.

He answers before I sit behind my desk, plowing my hands through my hair. "Speak."

"Derrick, I need some info and I need it by Monday morning."

"'Kay, you know the surcharge on expedited information. Name?"

"Stella Jolie Reese. The file I have on her barely brushes the surface. Foster kid from the age seven. Shit load of foster homes throughout Louisiana. I don't have the names of all the cities - and all my secretary could find were two foster homes - but there is mention of more."

"You want the full monty? Or are you just looking for answers during certain time frame?"

"Full fucking monty, man. That'd be great."

"All right. I'll have everything to you by Sunday night, Wes."

After I hang up, I sit in my office and stare at absolutely nothing for hours. My mind keeps splintering over and over as her words run their course on a loop in my mind.

"You have no idea what the first seventeen years of my life consisted of. What I have had to do to get to where I am today. I am not a submissive... I am a fucking fighter. Because absolutely everything I possess, I've had to fight like hell to get."

"You can't be a submissive or peek into the lifestyle when the only sexual encounters you've ever experienced were rapes and molestations by father, after foster father, after foster brother from the time you were a toddler. There, there's your goddamn answer, Wesley."

I have a fighter on my hands.

A shattered, damaged, little fighter.

Once I get my answers, I'll modify a stratagem.

Just because I lost this little battle, does not mean I intend on conceding.

I will readjust my tactics. Then I will fight a broken fighter.

And I will fucking win.

On Sunday night the file is faxed over from Derrick.

The shit I see, the fucking shit in that file, comes extremely close to causing the scotch I've consumed to make reappearance.

Stella Jolie Reese

DOB May 10, 1988

Female

Caucasian

Height: 5'7

Last documented weight: 134 lbs

Hair color: Brown

Eye Color: Hazel

Marital Status: Single

Mother: Unknown

Father: Fredrick Reese- found murdered at age 31. Police files indicate seven year old daughter (Stella Reese) was the only witness. All evidence points to the child committing the homicide in an effort to evade her father's sexual abuse. Charges were never filed and child was placed in therapy. CPS placed child in the foster care system where she was placed in a foster home.

Other living relatives: None

During an exam immediately following the incident, the SAFE RN documentation states the following was found upon assessment:

Over six broken bones noted via X-ray that appeared to go untreated. (See below):

Both clavicles, mandible, maxilla, left femur, right humerus.

The nurses' notes also state there were multiple abrasions, lacerations and contusions. Some of which appeared to be recent as well as healing injuries.

Also documented and photographed: Numerous bite marks

covering the patient from neck to knees, most of which were located on the patient's anterior thighs, genitalia and rectum.

There was significant scarring as well as recent in appearance due to redness and swelling lacerations consistent with repeated sexual abuse. During sexual kit collection, speculum placed for assessment. Fluid noted at cervix specimen obtained, labeled at bedside and entered in to kit evidence. Blue dye spray applied during speculum exam for small tears unable to detect with naked eye. Pubic hair combed, stray strands collected and labeled, entered into evidence kit. All patient's clothes removed per protocol and entered into specimen kit.

Foster Parents:

1) Mr. & Mrs. Blake Sims (1996-97)
Pine Bluff, LA
Child was admitted to the ER in Pine Bluff in 1997:
Documentation states:
Patient was brought into ER via EMS on a stretcher after students found patient (9 yo Stella Reese) in the bathroom of the school unconscious with copious amounts of blood around the patient. Upon assessment, after removing tampon and several pads 4th degree vaginal and rectal lacerations were noted consistent with extremely severe sexual abuse and rape. Patient stabilized with eight units of PRBC (packed red blood cells) infused per protocol. Social Services were consulted. Patient was discharged after three weeks per Child Protection Services to State of Louisiana. Charges against both Mr. and Mrs. Blake Sims were filed by the DA of Pine Bluff. Mrs. Sims charges were dropped due to lack of evidence. Mr. Sims was charged with rape of a minor. He served five years in Louisiana State Penitentiary.

2) Mr. & Mrs. Jonathan Temple (1997-1999)
Alexandria, LA
During a therapy session between the child, Stella Reese, a Social Service Counselor, and a licensed psychiatrist in 1999, the patient, 11 yo Stella Reese admitted to being repeatedly molested by Mr. Jonathan Temple. Charges against Mr. Jonathan Temple were filed by the DA of Alexandria. Mr. Temple served three years in Louisiana State Penitentiary.

3) Mr. & Mrs. George Long (1999)
Ruston, LA
During a therapy session between the child, Stella Reese, a Social Service Counselor, and a licensed psychiatrist in 1999, the patient, 11 yo Stella Reese admitted to suicidal ideations. When asked to verbalize the reasons behind this behavior, patient immediately began showing signs of PTSD. Pt was removed from Mr. and Mrs. Long's residence and placed back into child protective services until a foster family becomes available.

4) Mr. & Mrs. Joseph Smith (2000-2001)

Shreveport, LA

Stella Reese's whereabouts remained unknown from July 4th 2001 until January 3rd 2004.

In 2004, 16 yo Stella Reese was found living in an abandoned home on Texas Street.

Documentation states 16 yo Stella Reese admitted to living in both the abandoned home as well as sleeping some nights in her high school library she'd been attending without knowledge of the State of Louisiana.

CPS filed for a warrant to retrieve the following medical files: July 5, 2001- Time: 0018:

911 phone call:

"Hey there's some chick passed out by Cross Lake." — background unknown female voice—"Steve she isn't breathing! Tell them she's not fuckin' breathing!"

Male caller: "Umm... my girl says she isn't breathing. I would stay, but I can't be late for my curfew."

911 dispatcher: "Sir, I need you to remain where you are. Do you or your friend know CPR?"

—Phone call ends. July 5, 2001- Time: 0020.

Medical Records/ Doctors dictation notes/ Nurses notes:

Dr. Cole- Dictation notes of patient currently known as Jane Doe (age unknown):

Received patient via EMS to ER 1. Upon admission, patient status is unstable with a weak and thready pulse noted. EMS documentation states that patient was resuscitated via CPR and defibrillation. After patient stabilized, doctor assessment yields asphyxiation as well as first and second degree lacerations noted in and around vagina and rectum consistent with rape and/or sexual abuse. Lacerations were sutured using a 2.0 chromic suture times 2. Patient remains stable. Will continue to monitor. (Patient signed out Against Medical Advice less than nineteen hours after admission.) Prior to patient signing out AMA patient refused rape kit.

Patient's printed name and signature: Stella Reese

Stella Reese

Medical Records/ Doctors dictation notes/ Nurses notes of September 30, 2001:

Patient received to ER via EMS with symptoms of hypovolemic shock caused by an ectopic pregnancy gone without treatment and resulted in left fallopian tube rupturing and hemorrhaging. Patient Name: Jane Doe.

DOB: Unknown

Allergies: Unknown

Labs drawn yielded patient is AB+ blood type. Drug screen negative. All cultures, including STDs were negative.

53

Patient prepped in OR for Left Salpingectomy. Procedure performed without incident. Patient remains stable. Will continue to monitor.
Prior to patient signing out AMA patient refused rape kit.
(Patient signed out Against Medical Advice once awake, alert and oriented—50 minutes after anesthesia.)
Patient's printed name & signature: <u>Stella Reese</u>

<u>*Stella Reese*</u>

I can't fucking read any more.

Sam Smith, he was one of my buddies. I fucking hung out with him that summer. That was the summer before I went to LSU.

Oh my fucking GOD!

Memories, all of them, begin flashing through my mind.

Her at the lake fishing with us.

Her tagging along to baseball games, parties — Parties. I was... MOTHER FUCK! I scan back over the date and re-read the medical notes.

I was at that party. I manned the keg at that party.

Jesus Christ! I remember wondering why Sam brought his kid sister.

I lean back into my chair and let my eyes reread the file until almost three in the morning.

I want to know who the fuck did this shit to Stella. Every single motherfucker that laid a finger on her, I want their blood soaking my hands.

I'm fucking proud as shit of my little fighter, dammit. There is no reason for her to be the beautiful person she is today, inside and out. Not one fucking reason.

A Masters from Columbia? What the hell—Who does that? Who goes from where she was to where she is? And I know without a shadow of doubt that her childhood is what prevented her from getting into those other programs.

And I'm fucking glad, too. Now that I have my answers, I'm fully prepared to seize the fuck out of this opportunity I've been bestowed.

I may have to woo her, charm her, and fucking fight her the whole damn way.

But Stella Reese will be mine. In every goddamn way possible.

Chapter 10

Fucking Questions

"Trina?" I ask on my way in the kitchen, "Don't fucking lie, and keep your eyes on mine so I can tell whether you are or not. Does this outfit in any way say sexy, fuck me, I'm weak, or 'here just run me over'?"

She blinks at me.

"Well?" I grab my on-the-go coffee cup and take a sip of the piping hot heaven. I look over the bar at Trina... Yep, she's still fucking blinking at me. "Say it, bitch."

After she clears her throat she says, "You look like a professional, no-nonsense, confident, and highly capable sexy beast—That gives good head!" She falls into a laughing fit and I roll my eyes at her on my way toward the door.

"Wish me luck. I'll grab some wine for us on my way home, sis. Love you!" I call out before leaving.

By the time I get to Jacobs Publishing on Madison Avenue, I am a nervous wreck! I wish I could calm down and stop fidgeting. I brush my hands down my black pencil skirt for the seventh time and straighten the matching jacket. I'm in the middle of tightening my ponytail when the elevator doors open.

Head high, bitch. You own it and you know it, now show it. You've gotten this far all on your own. And after today, you only have three hundred and sixty four more days to go.

I waltz in the offices of JPH exactly like I did the last time I was

56

here. BOSS. BITCH.

I smile at the pretty receptionist and watch as she turns from pretty to an ugly skank right before my eyes. "Hi Rachel. Is Wesley in his office?"

Skank sneers and in a saccharine voice replies, "Don't you mean Mr. Jacobs?" My smile never wavers as the words 'Fuck you bitch, don't let me catch you in an alley' flit through my mind.

"He said to call him Wesley." I head towards the double doors of his office.

"It's a quarter to seven, he isn't expecting you, Ms. Reese."

I call out over my shoulder still smiling, "Yes he is, Rachel. Don't play dumb, it doesn't look good on you."

My palms meet the smooth dark mahogany of the doors before opening them.

Wes looks up from a file in front of him and snaps it closed, quickly putting it away. "Ms. Reese, you look absolutely stunning this morning. And your promptness..." His eyes glance at his watch, when they settle back on mine, they're smiling. "...I appreciate it immensely." The smile that slides onto his face makes my knees weak and I blush as the thoughts of what occurred between us the other night crowd my mind.

"Well, I should easily be able to keep you pleased then. If there is one thing I am, it's prompt."

My skin breaks out in chill bumps from his deep chuckle. But it's my hardening nipples that embarrass the fuck out of me. I know if he looks, he'll not only notice, he'll comment too. I'm in the middle of praying he keeps his eyes on mine when he replies in a deep sex laden voice, "Stella, you already know exactly what I want, what gives me pleasure. And you and I both know that you have never been just one thing, not once in your whole goddamn life."

Shit! I'm instantly bombarded with Friday's little parting disclosure I so gallantly delivered before storming out of his house.

"Yeah, umm...about what I said Friday; please don't give it any thought or, better yet, just don't even remember it. It kind of just

57

fell out before I could find my filter. I was pissed, and honestly, a hot mess after we... after you, well you know." My face is begging him not bring it up.

"Completely understandable. And I haven't thought of it once, until you mentioned it." He smiles again before nodding to the chair in front of his massive desk. "Have a seat, we'll be going over our schedule for today with Rachel in a moment."

Oh. Yay! Fan-fucking-tastic! Just the mention of Rachel causes me to have to stifle a gag.

"Perfect." I say cheerfully attempting to make myself comfortable for this wonderful upcoming torture session.

"If I may, I would like to apologize for the way I acted as well. In all honesty, it has been – shit, I can't even say it's been a long time. I can't remember a single time when I've wanted something as badly as I want you. However, I'm sure that is neither here nor there."

His dark green eyes pierce mine and a flutter of butterflies spring to life in my gut. But it's his next words that just down right fuck my mind up. "Unless...You would be willing to go to dinner with me next Saturday. Just dinner."

"Just dinner?" He nods.

Of course the bitch decides on this moment to interrupt us.

Rachel comes into the office and hands the schedule to Wes. "Here you go, Wes." She remains standing directly beside him, her eyes scan the paper in her hand. "Okay, we'll start at nine with that unknown author that wanted to meet with you, after that we have a meeting with the—"

Wes holds his hand up before saying, "Rachel, stop. Before you continue yapping on about shit I can clearly read, go and get Ms. Reese a copy of the schedule. She and I will go over it. You just answer the phone. I would say that I find this change in your behavior amusing if the reason behind it weren't so obvious."

Wow. Bitch you just got served.

I have to bite my tongue until the taste of metal fills my mouth to keep the smile from my face. My professional bitch look does not waver. Thank God.

"But, Wes. We always go over the schedule in the morning. And I don't under—"

"Rachel, I have an intern directly under me that needs to learn every single minute detail of JPH. I can't do that with you in my way parading around like you're the damn VP. I need you to do what I hired and pay you to do. Be a secretary. Besides, three's a crowd and I will not have Ms. Reese or her education get lost in the shuffle. She is my number one priority. Understood?"

She storms out of the office muttering a "Yes, sir." under her breath.

After the door closes behind her, the words fall from my mouth. "Well. You certainly pissed her off."

"Fuck her." He smirks. "Dinner, Stella. We were talking about dinner."

"Ahh… Sure. It's just dinner. I like to eat. Sounds good."

His laugh is so sexy and so damn sinister all at the same time, I almost fall in love with this motherfucker—Again.

"Right. Just dinner. You keep telling yourself that."

My first week seems to fly by. I've always been a quick learner, and since reading and writing has been my obsession for as long as I can remember, it's extremely easy for me to throw myself into every aspect of Jacobs Publishing House.

I soak up every single detail of what Wesley says while teaching me, every piece of information he hands me is a pearl of wisdom that I cherish. I absolutely revel in his compliments and the verbal praise of my adaptability and eagerness to learn.

Regretfully, Rachel and my relationship remains at a stalemate. I know… It breaks my heart to pieces too.

It's Friday and Wes and I are the only two souls left in the entire building. It's nearing nine o'clock at night but I don't mind. I could listen to him talk about his authors and editors; the marketing aspect of publishing— All of it. I could listen to him explaining it to me in his southern drawl that reminds me of pure milk chocolate mixed with bourbon. Don't ask me why my mind uses that combination of tastes… You know damn good and well your mouth watered thinking about it.

Wes' enthusiasm and love for what he's done with his company is so evident, it practically radiates from the pores of his skin. He fucking inspires the hell out of me, and that's saying something because I haven't been inspired by anyone—Ever.

To say I'm confused about what is going on between us is putting it mildly. I can't make myself go back to where I was mentally or emotionally before he touched me. I've never, EVER hungered for a man's touch. I've never had a physical relationship with a man that I've found attractive.

And holy Christ, Wesley Jacobs is the sexiest fucking man I've ever seen. He's tall, we're talking 6'4" at least. His dark hair is kept short and always appears as though fingers have been run through it during a good fuck session.

And his olive complexion against his stark hunter green eyes? Shit. Throw a fucking dark gray Armani suit on top, pfft… I stand about as much of a chance as a snowball in the ninth circle of hell.

"After we've met with new authors for the last time and all the negotiations are agreed upon and the legal paperwork has been filed, we usually start by requesting their last manuscript or their work in progress. YOU, Ms. Stella Reese, are going to take Jude Preston's MS when I receive it and you are going to make that bitch your baby. Tell me, what did you think about the author himself when we had our conference call with him?"

Through a yawn I answer, "I liked him, loved his ideas. For a guy that has practically sold his first two books on street corners and oversaturated the social media avenues available. Shit, what's not to like? His drive alone excites me."

Wes looks down at his watch, "Shit! Jesus, Stell it's past nine! I'm sorry! We didn't even eat lunch! You want me to drive you home? We can stop by one of my favorite little Italian bistros on our way to your place."

At his mention of food and home, exhaustion and I run into each other like a head on collision. "Yeah, sounds great." I motion to Mr. Preston's paperwork and his most recent manuscript. "Can I take these and get caught up on my new baby over the weekend?" I ask smirking up at him.

"Yeah, sure. Take whatever you need. I'm going to go grab my coat and shit from my office, then we'll leave."

We stop at a quaint little mom and pop Italian restaurant that holds maybe ten tables. The lighting is low and each table has a feel of seclusion or privacy from the surrounding grape vines climbing the walls and hanging from the ceiling.

Wes' large hand on my lower back leads us to a table snuggled into a small nook off to the side of the restaurant. After he pulls my chair out and I'm seated, he grabs the chair on the other side of the table, bringing it side by side with mine—and that sneaky grin of his doesn't once leave his face.

"Ms. Reese, you don't mind do you?" He asks before sitting.

"I don't." The smile on my face is the reflection of my excitement.

But that excitement ebbs when I briefly wonder as I look up at him from under my lashes if things would be easier for me if I'd lived a normal life. If every piece of affection I'd received from the opposite sex wasn't a direct warning of the impending pain and evil defilement I would, yet again, be forced to endure.

Wes rouses me from my thoughts when his hand brushes the hair from my face. "Hey, don't do that, Stella. Do you hear me? You're with me, you stay with me. I don't want your thoughts or your attention on anyone else." I try to just nod but that just spurs his voice to become more stern. "No, Stella, I want you to say it. Tell me that you understand."

"I understand. But, Wesley, I don't think you realize what type of woman you are dealing with." His hand covers mine and the smile on his face is so sad it causes my heart to break. And in this moment I want so badly to be pure for him, normal for him. I'd give fucking anything to be unbroken.

Women like me, women that have been shattered as many times as I have, there are no pieces remaining. All that remains is only sand...

And, like sand, our presence is never anything more than the fleeting moment we slip through your fingers. For that is all we can ever really, truly be.

"Signore Wesley, what a lovely surprise. And this bella ragazza!" His face alights with happiness. "Madam you merely gracing us with your beauty." He kisses his fingertips with his gray moustache covered mouth, "Piacere, Signore."

He returns his attention to Wesley, "Signore, your antico, no?"

"Please, Luciano. Grazie." Wes nods and smiles before directing his attention back on me. After the waiter leaves to put our order in, Wes turns his body towards mine before running a finger along my jawline from one ear to the other causing me to shudder.

"Stella, how do you prefer me to approach this subject? In life, wait... Let me start over. You are a strong woman. When I watch you walk into a room, your shields of armor are so impenetrable that everyone except the ones you love startle at your fierceness. However, the only reaction I have is an intense desire to... Well, for lack of better words, crack you open and see what's on the inside. So, back to the original question, shall we beat around the bush a little longer, or would you like for me to cut to the chase?"

Hmm... Sometimes beating around the bush does seem the better option. However, in the end, it all falls down to the bottom line.

Coughing to clear my throat, I follow my gut. "Hit me... let's do this fucking shit."

He lowers his voice a few octaves. "No, hit is something that I will never do. Slap that sexy ass until it turns red, fuck yes. Take my cock and slap your face with it as I cum, definitely. Hit? Never."

Chapter 11

Beasts Crave Beauties

WESLEY

Well, that image has fucking derailed my train of thought up more than I originally planned.

I can't do this this slow shit. I want Stella, yesterday, last week... I NEED her, now. Right fucking now.

"I want you to try... We'll start off slow. Well, as slow as I physically can without spontaneously combusting. Stella, I'm going to explain to you the reason I believe that you can do this." Smiling at her, I slowly raise my hand and tuck a piece of hair behind her ear.

"You don't flinch away from my touch." My hand brushes against her cheek before tracing the line of her beautiful jaw and neck. "Your body instantly reacts from the feeling of my hands on your skin." I let my fingertips whisper over her breast before leaning forward to block my illicit demonstrations from the restaurant. I grasp her breast in my hand before running my thumb back and forth causing her nipple to harden.

The moan that escapes her causes me to chuckle before I continue, "You soaked the cuff of my sleeve while I finger fucked that tight little pussy of yours Friday too, didn't you, Ms. Reese?"

"Mmhmm." Her breaths are coming in raggedly. One of her hands grasps my shoulder before clenching the fabric of my suit jacket in her fist.

I slide my hand down further until I reach her bare crossed legs. I pause my hand below the end of her skirt. "Open your legs for me, let me feel how wet that cunt is." Stella's head lolls back at the same time her legs part. I skim my middle finger over her wet pussy lips and growl, "Just like I fucking thought."

I slide the hand I'm palming her thigh with more in between them, nudging her legs further apart. I rub my hand against her wet flesh then I sink my finger into her hot wet pussy until I'm knuckle deep, then curl it finding the right spot. Her moans and pleas are coming out in labored gasps as her lips and breath caress my neck and ears. She whispers between her breaths in a husky voice, "Please, please Wesley." Her hips are bucking violently against my hand.

I'm lost gazing at her. Her body moves against me sensually as she transforms into raw sex personified. Her face and neck are flushed, her head thrown back. A sheen of sweat coats the skin of her face, neck, and chest. Her top teeth sinking hard into her puffy bottom lip, her beauty almost shatters me.

My voice is harsh and dark, "What, Stella? Please what? You want to cum?" My thumb circles her swollen clit faster before I delve a second finger into her tight pussy, thrusting them into her harder before growling into her ear. "You need to cum, angel? Then right here in this restaurant, I want you to bite down on my shoulder right this second and fucking cum all over my hand like a good little cumslut, Ms. Reese. Right. Now."

God-fucking-damn! As Stella's cum soaks my cuff from nothing more than my verbal command alone, I know - more than I know my own goddamn name - I know that there is a sub buried beneath the scars of Stella's broken façade.

I cannot keep my mouth from consuming hers, swallowing her loud moans and pleas of pleasure. I slowly withdraw my hand from between her legs, and pull her trembling body close to mine, our kiss never losing rhythm.

Once her shuddering stills, I lean my face back to look down into her drunken andalusite eyes before smiling at her and whispering, "You're going to be mine. It's time for you to accept it." I pause and wait for the orgasm-induced fog to lift and for understanding to cross her face.

After it does, I continue, "We can go slow, but I need you to know I'm going to push you, in more ways than one. I'm going to push and push until you are certain you're going to break, Stella. But you never will, will you?"

I sweep my lips against hers and nip at her puffy, swollen mouth. "Even with all the hell you've endured, you have never truly broken. But my plan is to force you to the verge. I plan on ruining you... destroying you. And you will come out on the other side better for it, because that which doesn't destroy you, Ms. Reese... Only makes you stronger."

After a few minutes, during which time she chewed on that bottom lip of hers and I contemplated shoving her beautiful face in my lap making her take my aching cock between her swollen lips, she finally speaks—Hell yes my mind is still saturated with images of her lips around my cock! "I'll try, Wesley. Shit, I can't believe I'm even saying this, but yes, I will try. Just don't expect anything from me. Because I make no promises. I'll never make you any promises."

Bull-fucking-shit. I'll get your goddamn promises—I'll have you on your knees begging me to listen to your promises.

"I accept nothing less from you, Stella."

The drive to her condo is quiet. Honestly, I feel like a weight, a burden that has had me shackled down for as long as I can remember, has finally lifted. As soon as the words 'I'll try.' fell from Stella's lips, they snipped the albatrosses tethered to my soul.

I haven't felt hope like this since before she came into my life again and I don't know what it is, I can't pinpoint why, however I also don't give a fuck why. All I want is to fall into everything that Stella embodies and I never want to go anywhere else but inside of who she is.

I've said everything I felt needed to be said and I won't push her any more than I already have tonight. As far as I'm concerned, what the fuck I just conquered in Luciano's was an impossible feat. I bent her will and common sense inward against themselves and they molded to my commands like soft clay.

Check. Mate. I've already mastered Stella Jolie Reese, and she's already submitted...she just doesn't realize it yet.

I pull up to the curb outside her place and quickly hop from the car to open her door and help her from my R8. Her little hand slips into mine as she looks up smiling at me as we walk to her door.

"Wow. I didn't expect to find a gentleman in you, Wes." Her laughter bounces off the sidewalk and buildings.

"I'll do my best to keep you surprised." I slide my arm around her waist when we get to the door of her building.

"Thank you for dinner. It was ahh... quite becuming." Her eyebrow lifts and a conniving grin appears when she enunciates the cum in becuming.

"It was. Tomorrow night's dinner should be as well, if not more becuming. I'll pick you up at eight." My fingertips tilt her chin until our eyes meet. I trace the bow of her top lip and pout of her bottom lip with my fingertips.

"Yes. Eight is perfect." I brush my lips over hers and pull her body flush with mine.

"You did very good tonight, Stella. How does it make you feel when I say that?"

"It feels good." She whispers.

"Good. Have a good night, angel."

I kiss the palms of her hands before stepping back and letting her out of our embrace.

"You too."

I remain where I am standing long after she's made it inside the building. Completely fucking dumfounded and unable to move, I have to force myself to turn around and walk back to my car.

As soon as my car pulls away from the curb, mad crazy fucking shit starts battering itself into my mind.

It's fucking insanity.

Goddamn primal on every level.

Every instinct I possess is screaming at me to turn around and demand for her to get her ass in my car and never fucking leave my side again.

The alpha inside me viciously howls for me to claim her.

The Dom residing in me adamantly demands that I bend, break, and control Stella—mind, body and soul.

But it's the uncivilized beast within that ruts and growls insisting that I fuck her into oblivion.

Chapter 12

When Beauty Fights a Beast

There is blood all around me. As the screams pierce my eardrums the blood soaks into my clothes. I'm so cold. I don't remember how I ended up on the bloody living room floor. I was asleep in my bed. Tomorrow's a school day and even though he was not home I still set my clothes out for tomorrow, bathed, brushed my teeth and set my alarm for in the morning. The last thing I remember before waking up here is falling asleep in my bed. I run my blood soaked hands over my body trying to see if the blood is coming from me. When I realize it isn't, that it's his blood I move to see if he's alive but stop myself before touching him. If he isn't dead and I wake him I won't like what happens. The screams continue getting louder. If they don't stop then I'll be the one that pays for it, he'll come after me again. I don't think I can handle more broken bones or other forms of agony he forces me to endure, not on top of all the bloody carnage I am having to witness. I cover my ears to stifle the shrieks but blood smears into my hair and on my face. I try to scream at them to shut up! I need them to shut up… When I try to yell at them to stop I realize the screams bouncing off the bare trailer walls are my own. Immediately I shove my fist into my mouth in an effort to smother my screams. As soon as the metallic taste of blood hits my tongue I gag around my blood soaked fist heaving up what little supper I ate.

I'm jerked from my nightmare by Eve lightly shaking me and whispering, "Stell. Stell, wake up, sweetie. You're having another nightmare, wake up."

"Hey, sis. I'm okay, I'm up. Sorry." I sit up and hug her neck, immediately I feel her tears on my shoulder and gently stroke her fine blond hair. "Sis, hey. Don't cry. I'm okay." I pull back and smile at her. "See, it was just a nightmare, babe."

"I don't know how you do it, Stell." She sniffs before wiping the tears away from her almond shaped blue eyes. "I know you don't cry. I know you're strong, but the shit you scream in your nightmares scares the living hell out of me. You don't always have to be strong. If you wanted to talk to—"

"Eve. Stop that fucking crazy thought train right now. I spent my whole damn life in therapy—on antidepressants and group meetings up to five times a week. It didn't help then, and it won't help now. The shit that I've been through is shit that I talked about and rehashed until I was blue in the face. There comes a time when you leave the past where it belongs, accept that life is shit, accept that it's up to you and you alone to make YOU… ME happy. And I have, sweetie. I'm fine." I smile again trying to convince her that I am okay.

"Have you thought about… Have you wanted to cut, Stell?"

I answer as honestly as I can, "If I have I quickly reminded myself that I'm not a coward. And THAT is the easy way out. I'm just fine on the path I'm on right now."

"I love you, you're like a sister me. I just don't want you in hell all alone." She looks at my pleadingly, and I can't help the sinister laugh that escapes my chest.

"Sweetie, you couldn't handle my hell. You just stay where you are, stay honest and pure, stay beautiful and untainted. Smile for the photogs and do your damn thing girl. Because THAT makes me happy. Too see you happy, makes me happy, Eve. Okay?" I smile to reassure her.

She nods before hugging my neck. "Here, your bed is drenched in sweat again. I'll throw these in the wash and be back to help you make your bed up."

"Okay. Hey, I didn't wake anyone else up did I?" I ask.

"No, Bo is still passed out from drinking too much during the Jets pre-season game. Trina's still in her room asleep."

70

"Whew, okay good. Thanks sissy."

After she helps me get my bed made I lie awake looking at my ceiling until the sun rises the next morning. My thoughts are all over the place. Wesley, I don't know what the hell is going on between me and him.

It's hard as hell for me to deny him anything he wants. And, Jesus Christmas I love to make him proud, or happy. Shit I get butterflies just from making him smile! The 'good job.' Or 'damn you're a quick learner.''s I get from him make me smile like a damn love struck fool.

From the moment his hand circled my elbow at Chained and he lead me to his car I'd let any and all reservations I previously had where Wesley Jacobs was concerned just float away. Well, except for when he sat back like the devil and refused to give my body what it was dying for. But even then I was far too intrigued by him to not play the devil's advocate.

If I may… Without sounding to cliché, just fucking listen to me. Woman to woman. Friend to friend. I've never allowed myself to even be interested enough in a man to do more than kiss me. I am a twenty-six year old, red blooded American woman who LOVES reading smut, reading how the characters feel, not just emotionally but physically. And when I had to walk away from Wes's penthouse that night, it fucking hit me like a mack truck! Goddammit I am starved… For him, for his touch, his words, his smile.

Now, with that little epiphany comes the question. Am I ready as well as strong enough to try to do what Wesley wants me to?

Umm… Fuck yes.

And before you ask if I'll be able to make it through, even if it does end badly and I'm left heart broken, your answer lies within the following statement: Bitch have you not been reading? This, Wesley fucking Jacobs is an ice cream sundae compared to savage and violent hell I've lived in, been forced to endure, and made it out of alive.

71

"Oh my fuck, seriously? Jiminy Crickets it's a damn date, bitches. Not my wedding day!" I am literally being tagged teamed with makeup, high heels, and perfume by Trina and Eve.

"Stell, please at least try the eyelashes. I will glue those bitches on so tight it will take a month for them to come off!" Eve's coming at me again with glue and lashes.

"Hell no!" I shoo her away and look up at Trina through the mirror, she's holding up a black sleeveless dress and a nude satin number with a plunging neckline. "Ahh... Nude?" I ask with a shrug.

"God-fucking-damn straight nude! Eve! Shit! Stop!" Trina yanks the glue and lash compact from her hands and tosses them in the trash.

Trina hands Eve our two glasses of wine. "Here, go fill those fuckers up." She kisses the air before telling Eve, "You know I love you! Right?"

"You only love me when I'm being your wine bitch." Eve mutters on her way towards the kitchen.

"Stell! Okay, so where are you at with this guy? I mean I know about your date last night. Or dinner, what the fuck ever. But... Here's my question." She holds up a pair of black fuck me stilettos in one hand and a pair of brown wedges in her other. "Shoes? Your answer will answer mine."

"Going with the black ones, sister."

Trina squeals and jumps up and down like a damn fan-girl screaming, "Hell YES! That's my girl!"

After I'm dressed in the nude dress with its pencil skirt hitting just below my knees, as well as the plunging neck line—That required double sided tape. I stand in my six-inch black peep-toe stilettos holding my clutch on the curb at 7:40 waiting for Wesley to show up.

A shiny black sports car I've never seen before pulls up to the curb outside my place and before I notice it's him he's out of the car opening the passenger door for me.

"Fucking hell, Ms. Reese. How in God's name do you expect me to make it through dinner without slamming you up against the nearest stable surface with *THAT* dress on?" He growls through his gritted teeth.

"You'll make it, well... Maybe you will." I grin before slipping into the low seat and sighing in anticipation.

I have no fucking clue what I'm doing. I don't know how to flirt, or be funny without it sounding completely ridiculous and forced.

I don't know what this night holds in store for me, nor do I know what Wesley has planned.

But what I do know... Is that I'm ready.

I've been fighting to stay alive, remain sane and in control for as long as I can remember. And tonight, whatever lies ahead. I refuse to fight it. As I stare outside the window, a quote I read at some point in my childhood that has always stayed with me, strikes me with a new meaning...

Come what may, but take thy with a slow

grace... For I no longer have what it takes to fight

such things without a face.

Chapter 13

And So the Lion Fell For The Lamb

WESLEY

She said I'll make it. I almost lost my shit with that spoken absurdity! If she had any... ANY goddamn idea how close I came to abducting her sexy ass last night, 'You'll make it,' would not be her choice of words.

NO! No. Do not ask me if I returned like a stalker last night and watched her building. And no. Don't ask if I checked and in return found her building's door, locks and security being so inadequate, I actually *coughs* pushed the process of acquiring said real estate.

Hey. Don't judge me.

I stop the Lotus in the valet line, pull the emergency break up, and step from my car, tossing the keys to the valet guy before I rush over to open Stella's door.

"I'm going to go out on a limb here... You like Italian food?" She laughs while looping her arm in my crooked elbow.

"Yes, I guess you can say that." I chuckle leading her through the stained glass doors to Antonino's Italiano Cuisine.

Stella and I are sat in a secluded area I reserved for us last Monday. I immediately spew our order in Italian to the waiter to get it over with and supply us with some privacy for the inquisition I have planned for Ms. Reese.

"What in God's name did you just order?" Her giggle sounds like music to my ears - which is quite odd because I hate it when women giggle. I've always found it irritating and childish. That's not the case with Stella, though.

I lean towards her until my mouth is next to her ear, "I promise you'll enjoy it, my Stella." I whisper before sucking her earlobe into my mouth and grazing it with my teeth, causing her to shudder.

"I thought about a lot of things last night after I dropped you off. Mostly thoughts based on you. More specifically: where, when, and how I will acquire you. Do you understand?"

After she ducks her head I watch a faint blush creep up from the low neckline of her dress and over the top swells of her breasts. HARD. My cock is hard enough to drive nails because of that blush.

"I thought a lot about you as well, Wesley. More than I am willing to confess. However, I can say that I'm certain whatever is happening between us, I like and I'm ready to see where it's going." I witness her determination as she gathers and pulls it up around her like a cloak. "To answer your question, yes, Wesley, I understand."

Good girl.

Have I mentioned I find it downright appalling and annoying as fuck when my questions are not directly answered? If not, then you've been duly noted.

"I want you to stay the night with me, Stella. I want to begin this..." I motion between us before settling my hand on her bare thigh just below her skirt, "...Us, tonight. I will push so hard that you are going to want to both run to me and away from me. I'm going to twist your emotions and mind into nothing more than a cluster-fuck. If you are able to withstand my diabolical methods, if you remain a good girl and please me without pissing me off too many times, then after I fuck your mind, I'm going to fuck you—past the brink of insanity, exactly where you've left me waiting since I first laid eyes on you. Understood?"

She nods emphatically, "Yes. I do, I understand."

My hand tightens on her thigh. As my other arm slides around her waist and pulls her to me, my mouth slants over hers.

Our tongues war between our teeth biting and licking one another's mouths. I swallow her moans and mewls. When her hand moves over my raging hard on and squeezes, I feel pre-cum leak from the tip of my cock and it causes me to jerk back, looking from her swollen, pouty red lips to her ever changing hazel eyes.

My thumb pad swipes the corner of her mouth and with my other hand, I remove hers from my cock before I tsk her, "No. That is not acceptable, Ms. Reese. You. Do. Not. Touch. Only when I tell you, are you allowed to touch. Understood?"

"Yes." Her tongue sweeps over her lips before she looks anxiously down at her clenched hands in her lap.

"Good." My fingertips pull her chin up until our eyes meet. "Good girl. I'll show more tolerance towards your little missteps than usual. That's how important it is for me to own you." I smile and lean into her lips for a quick kiss before the waiter is at our table with wine and appetizers.

"Wow." Stella's eyes light up at the appetizers I ordered. "This looks...Wow. I forgot to eat today, I was so excited. This looks delicious, Wes." When she smiles at me like she is right now - like a kid on Christmas morning ready to open their first gift ... over forty measly bucks worth of appetizers - crazy shit starts happening. For one, I'm proud. My chest splits with pride knowing I made her smile that way. Then I feel an overwhelming need to protect, keep her safe and hidden from anyone or anything.

I just stare at her gobbling up calamari, fried ravioli, and stuffed mushrooms and somewhere in my awe, I fall a little more for Stella Reese.

I fall more than I've ever fallen in my entire life... I fall more than I ever intended on falling.

After dinner, we drive to my penthouse. We walk into my foyer and I notice Stella kick off her shoes. Around a chuckle I tell her, "Stella, leave your heels on." Her eyes fly to mine, blinking at me for a moment before slipping her little feet back into her high heels.

"Okay." She says quietly.

"I think we should start by you removing everything except the heels, Ms. Reese." She balks at me and I shake my head before walking into the living room and taking a seat on my high, winged back leather chair. I lean back in the chair to rest my left foot over my right knee and steeple my fingers before narrowing my eyes on her still unmoving at the edge of the foyer.

"Do not make me repeat myself, Ms. Reese. Everything but the heels."

She swallows several times before moving into action. The entire time she chews on that damn pouty bottom lip of hers. Once her clothes are removed she is standing before me in nothing but a pale pink corset and black stiletto high heels. NO Panties. FUCK.

"You are fucking stunning, Ms. Reese. Absolutely exquisite, breathtaking. Even though you've yet to do what I demanded, you've still made my cock so hard, it throbs. Now, after you've finished doing as I said, I want you to tell me how what I just said makes you feel."

I watch as her trembling hands begin unbuttoning the corset fumbling several times with the buttons. A sardonic grin slithers its way onto my face when the pale pink material flutters to the floor in front of her;. Standing before me, the embodiment of seduction, her pale creamy skin is the epitome of perfection. Her breasts are pale and tipped with perfect light pink pebbled nipples, her pussy completely bare and ravishingly mouthwatering.

I feel like a famished man; one that has been neglected of sun, water, food, even life. For the first time, I'm granted a taste of heaven, feasting on the woman every single woman before her paled in comparison to.

I didn't think it was even possible, but I fall even more for this Aphrodite, this enchanting little temptress, more than I ever thought possible. I fall for her right then and there.

Once I've somewhat gained a grasp on my quickly slipping reins of control, I clear my throat before speaking. "How do you feel standing in front of me completely bare knowing that I would give almost anything to bend you over that foyer table and fuck you until you passed out from pleasure alone?"

She fidgets on her feet, chewing on that goddamn lip of hers again and I watch uncertainty skate across her features. "I don't know how to explain it… my mind is all jumbled up with words and feelings I don't understand. Can I have a minute before answering?"

"No. You may not have a minute. I want you to tell me, Ms. Reese, does it make your pussy wet? It's obvious I make your body shudder. I can see your body quivering from here. Now, answer the question, is your pussy wet?"

A blush creeps from the tops of her perfect perky tits up the delicate arch of her neck and settles high on her cheeks. "Yes, sir."

"You want to be a good girl for me, don't you, angel?" I ask.

She moans before answering, "Yes, sir."

The beast within me snaps his shackles and batters his way through, instantly causing me to stand and stalk towards her. I stand towering over her tiny frame, my six four stature dwarfing her. "Put your fingers between your legs, rub that pussy for me, Ms. Reese. Right. Now."

Her chest is heaving in breaths, making her breasts rise and fall over and over as her hand slides in between her legs and barely brushes herself before moving her hand back to her side again.

"No. Stella, rub your fucking clit until I can hear how wet you are, then finger your goddamn pussy. If I wanted you to slide your hand over it, I would have used those words. Now, if you want to make me proud: Finger. That. Pussy."

Her blush deepens, staining her cheeks darker than I've yet to see on her beautiful face. As she does as I demanded, pride swells in my chest and blood swells my cock. I step back before unbuckling my belt then unbutton my slacks and release my cock. Slowly, I stroke it watching her from hooded eyes as she shudders.

When she looks down her eyes grow wide and she gasps before licking her lips and moving her hand faster. "Good girl, Stella, now—finger your cunt."

She does as she's told while I step back a few steps until I feel the back of my knees hit the chair behind me, I sit down and lean back, widening my knees and continue stroking. Stella's eyes are clenched closed, her chest is rising and falling faster, and I know just by the quivering of her body's muscles, she has brought herself to the brink of orgasm.

Bearing in mind the last time I kept her from release, I caught hell as well as created a set back for us, I slowly, softly tell her in the most authorative voice I can muster. "Stop, Ms. Reese. Remove your fingers, don't you dare cum."

Her eyelashes flutter open and confusion flashes across her features. "Huh?" She blinks rapidly but removes her hand.

"You want to be a good girl for me don't you?" I ask again.

"Y-yes."

I release my cock before raising my hand and crook my finger, "Come here, Ms. Reese." She sways a bit before staggering forward, stopping when directly in front of me.

I smile up at her before instructing her, "Grab a pillow and set it on the floor between my feet." I point to the couch covered in pillows, spurring her into action.

Once she has the pillow placed, I nod towards it, "Knees on the pillow, hands placed one on each thigh, understood?"

"Yes, sir."

And then it happens, right fucking here people - it happens - and if I weren't already sitting down, my knees would've buckled and I would have landed on my ass.

Stella Jolie Reese settles into an almost perfect sub stance, her knees hit the pillow, legs bent putting her ass on her feet, her hands land softly, one on each of my thighs. Stella keeps her head down but I still see her smile around chewing her bottom lip.

I whisper to her in an even tone, "You have no idea how happy you make me. You doing okay?" Her head nods but I tilt her face up with one hand and grasp my cock in the other. When her eyes meet mine I tell her, "Words. From now on, Stella, you use words, not gestures, understood?"

"Yes, sir. And I'm fine. I promise." Her hazel eyes are almost hunter green and completely clouded in lust.

I glance down at my cock in my hand then look, narrowing my eyes on hers, "Put the fingers you almost covered in cum inside my mouth."

She brushes my lips with her two fingertips and I suck both in all the way to the knuckle before swirling my tongue around each one, licking her fingers clean. My eyes roll back into my head and close, a groan escapes my chest as her taste floods my mouth. I suck both fingers dry before releasing them.

"Finger that sweet goddamn cunt of yours again until you coat your fingers in cum, Ms. Reese."

She immediately does as instructed, my fist tightens around my cock, stroking it faster as I watch her bring herself to orgasm, bucking against her hand wantonly. Her face chest and breasts are flushed... Her eyes never wavering from mine throughout the entire life altering moment.

I have to clear my throat before speaking, but the words still come out husky, "Put your cum covered hand around my cock." I grab her hand forcing it to grasp my cock and watch as she awkwardly holds it before expertly running her thumb around the rim then over the slit collecting the pre-cum seeping from the tip.

"Have you ever had that pretty mouth of yours fucked before?" I ask.

She shakes her head, "No. I've... No." The lust in in her eyes wars with uncertainty for a brief minute.

"Mmm... Good girl. When I ask you who you belong to, what are you going to say?"

"Y-you... Yours, Wesley's." She keeps her eyes on mine.

80

A salacious smirk curls my lip, "Goddamn right you're my good girl. Now wrap that cum covered hand around the base of my shaft, open those pretty lips and lick my cock from root to tip. When your tongue gets to the tip, swirl it around the rim then wrap your beautiful fucking mouth around my cock and suck. I want you to suck so hard your cheeks hollow, understood?"

"Yes sir." She immediately tongues my cock, licking as instructed, and when the heat of her mouth consumes my cock, I almost blow my load. I bite a hole through my cheek trying to keep myself from cumming too soon. As the metallic flavor hits my tongue, Stella continues sucking my cock into her mouth until the head hits the back of her throat.

"Yes, FUCK yes, Stell. Goddamn it, baby." My fingers thread into her hair at the base of her skull and clench fists full of her long, dark loose curls. On their own accord my hips thrust up, but Stella never loses a beat. "Fist my cock at the base, pump your hand in rhythm with your sucks. FUCK. FUCK YES! Goddammit, I love your mouth, Stella, Jesus Christ."

Over and over again the head of my cock pushes against the back of her throat before slipping past the ring of muscles in her throat. I vaguely remember her gagging, and tears streaming down her face, but I'm beyond rational thought. Using my hands I tighten my grip in her hair before using it as leverage. My hips thrust into her mouth, as my fists yank her face closer. I fuck, literally fuck Stella's mouth...

When finally, by the grace of God, I come to my senses and make myself release the death grip on her hair, she sucks until the popping sound signals the dreaded release of my cock from her mouth.

I look at her completely dumbfounded as she wipes the tears from her face. And I'm certain shock has consumed my features, "What? I did it wrong?" Her brows knit.

"Ahh, hell fuck no you didn't. Only certified cock inhalers suck cock like that, what the fuck, Stell?" I harshly demand.

"I read books, well..." She shrugs as shy as a school girl. "Smut

81

books, I read smut books a lot. They can be... very descriptive." She looks back up at me with a grin, "I took notes, just in case..."

"Took notes? The fuck, did you study them morning noon and night too?" I ask before shaking my head, "Never mind. Don't. That's not important." An exasperated sigh is released from my lungs. "I'd ask if I'm going slow enough for you." I shove the heels of my hands into my eye sockets, "But I swear to Christ, if I went any faster, I'd swallow you whole right this second."

After I move my hands from my face, I look down and the sight of her on her knees looking up at me from between my thighs starts doing crazy shit to my chest again. It twists and constricts almost cutting off the words trying to come out.

"Ms. Reese, have you ever heard the term 'safe word'?" I shove the question out with more difficulty than I anticipated.

"Yes, sir." She nods.

"I told you I would push and bend until you break. However, though I want to break you, I would rather die and spend an eternity in hell before shattering you. So, to avoid that, you give me a word, no more than two syllables, a word that you speak only before you shatter and lose yourself. Ms. Reese, I need you to give me your safe word."

"Rust." She says with such evident determination I have to bite my tongue from asking the meaning behind her choice of words.

"Rust it is." I stand before gathering both of her hands in mine, pulling her to her feet and leading her to my room.

Chapter 14

What a Stupid, Scared Lamb

I can do this. I can do this. I can do this.

My internal rallying is cut off when Wes leads me through the heavy double doors and into a bed room that closely resembles the one used by Jonathan Rhys Meyers or Henry VIII from The Tudors.

A huge massive four-poster king size bed resting on a raised platform takes up most of the far wall. Dark gleaming hardwood floors peek out from around plush area rugs strategically placed throughout the room. Off to the side a small bar is sounded by a sitting area with furniture in the same dark reds, browns and gold colors the rest of the room holds.

The sound of Wesley's shoes clunking on the floor draws my attention to where he now stands beside the bed. I watch in utter fascination as he slowly unbuttons his dark gray dress shirt, his eyes never leave mine, but my nerves keep me from being able to maintain eye contact. Once my eyes slide to his hands I can't stop them from devouring every inch of the tan skin he reveals, inch by inch, button by button.

After his shirt is completely unbuttoned he makes quick work of his cuffs before his shirt flutters to the floor and the weight of his belt causes his pants to do the same.

Son of a FUCK. The man is absolutely beautiful. No, not just beautiful, I mean he is the epitome of male perfection. Look! Count them! 1, 2, 3, 4, 5, 6, 7, 8— You get that ladies? Eight pack. Jesus

Christmas, I thought the V was a mythical thing; a photo shopped, or spray tan, an optical illusion. No. No. I gladly. Fuck gladly, I emphatically, enthusiastically, announce it is absolutely not. They do exist. I know I'm gawking, running my eyes from his broad freckled tan shoulders to his narrowed waist over and over but shit, I can't help it. It's like Twitch, Remy, and Jesse all tossed their DNA together, and I get to ride the result!

"Come here, Stella." His husky command causes a shudder to convulse throughout my body before I instantly move forward.

Out of pure instinct my head remains lowered, I'm uncertain if it's because I'm trying to hide my excitement or something else altogether.

When I'm standing in front of him it places his cock directly in my field of vision. Damn, even his cock is beautiful. Every fucking thick rigid inch of it. I lick my lips as the memory of tasting him floods my mind.

I hear Wesley tsk me before feeling his fingertips touch my chin and tilt my head back until my eyes meet his. His husky voice causes my thighs to clench together on their own accord, but his words have my eyes rolling back into my head before moaning, "As much as I love fucking that pouty mouth of yours, angel, I will lose my goddamn mind and blow this entire thing if I allow your lips anywhere near my cock right now."

His hands span my waist and he hauls me up causing me to yelp before gently lying me down on the bed. He walks around to the other side until he's at my head, "Arms, angel." I raise my arms and lay them above my head. His fingers circle both wrists before I feel silky material slithering around them and tighten, binding them together then anchoring them securely to the bed.

The position pulls my shoulders further back into the mattress, pushing my breasts out to a Russian salute. I close my eyes and listen as his bare feet pad across the hardwood floor.

When I feel the silk material being tied around my right ankle and then anchored spreading me open it evokes panic to jolt through me and thrum through my veins. The panic causes me to struggle for breath.

The palpable change in me seems to go unnoticed by Wesley, his movements never pausing as he continues binding my left ankle to the opposite side of the bed, spreading me even wider.

He walks until he is standing directly over me before a smile curls his lips, "Perfectly splayed— bare open for my eyes to see, and visually worship every delicious curve and line of your exquisite fucking body."

I can barely make his words out around the sound blood rushing in my ears.

A mantra, or chant starts battering it's way around inside my mind: *I can't do this. I can't do this. Make him stop, tell him to stop. I can't fucking do this, say it! Scream it goddamn it! RUST!*

"Shhh... Ms. Reese, open you eyes and look at me right this second." I clench my eyes tighter, and pull my lips into my mouth before biting down on them and shaking my head back and forth. My chest is heaving, my nose flaring, I can't breathe. There isn't enough oxygen.

I can't do this. I can't do this. Tell him to stop. I can't fucking do this, say it! Scream it! RUST!

SMACK! My eyes fly open and I gasp, pulling blessed air into my lungs. He just slapped the fuck out of my... "Did you just slap my pussy? Did you just open-palm slap the fuck out of my pussy?!"

His face mirrors the devils with that wicked damn grin dancing across as he slides his hands from my ankles to the inside of my thighs before he looping each thigh over his arms and bringing his face an inch away from my core. His hands rest on my abdomen and he glances down before his shoulders nudge me completely exposed, "It fucking worked, didn't it? You piped the fuck down." He growls through his teeth before licking me, splitting my bare folds wide open.

"Holy shit!" I cry out. My head pushes into the mattress and my neck arches bringing my back clear off the bed. His fingers link across my lower belly and his hands still my lower half from bucking away from his talented tongue. He shoves his tongue inside me before swirling it around and lapping up the wetness caused by his brilliantly skilled mouth. When his teeth and lips clamp down around my clit and suck it into his mouth my vision fucking tunnels.

I vaguely hear myself moaning the words, "Oh my God!" His finger slides inside of me knuckle deep and crooks, thrusting in sync with the rhythm of his tongue sucking and flicking my sensitive clit.

"Gawddammit!" The scream rips from my throat as sheer, unmitigated euphoria swallows me whole, pulling me further under than ever before.

Seconds, minutes, hell hours could've passed before I feel myself surfacing. However long it was, it was long enough for Wesley to release me from my silken restraints and turn me onto my stomach.

His fingertips bite into the flesh of my hips before he raises my ass up, "Jesus fucking Christ, Stella." He groans before shoving his head between my legs from behind, I feel his nose between my ass cheeks as his tongue swipes, lapping up cum from my pussy. His hot breath puffs against my swollen wet flesh, "If pussy were a food, and I could live off cunt alone I would never leave this fucking table, I swear to Christ."

He moves, standing behind me to his full height before leaning down, "One more fucking taste," He licks me from clit to asshole then grasps my hips, bruising them with his massive hands. "Now." His hands slide from my hips and smoothly circle each globe of my ass before running them slowly up my back, his tongue follows in his hands wake circling and tracing each of my vertebrae until his hands meet my shoulders and grip them tightly.

His mouth stops between my shoulder blades and he roughly whispers against my skin, "Now, Ms. Reese," his stomach muscles tense and I feel his cock slide between my ass cheeks before thrusting back and forth. When he stops he uses his torso to align the head of his cock at my entrance, "I'm going to fuck," He wraps my hair around his fist and pulls my head back, "The goddamn hell out of you. Understood?"

The head of his cock pushes in only to immediately be pulled out. "Yes." I try to nod but his grip in my hair tightens as he wraps it around his fist a second time. "Y-yes, sir." The words fall out as I moan and try to push myself back against him.

I barely have 'sir' out of my mouth before he slams into me to the hilt. A piercing shriek is ripped from my throat causing him to still, the hands fisted around my hair and gripping my shoulder allow me no room for movement. I'm shocked when I feel tears bite the back of my eyelids. Wesley's lips brush kisses between my shoulder blades before whispering, "You've been bent, but you've not yet broken, angel. Yes or No. Rust?"

Around a ragged moan I reply, "No, fuck no rust." I rock back against him as much I possibly can trying to urge him to move.

I've never felt so utterly complete in all my life, at the same time completely split in two.

Pain and pleasure blend their colors, pride and humiliation lose their importance. All I care about and all I ever want I have right now in this moment, and I'll beg to keep it, "Please, Wesley, baby, please." I push back with every ounce of strength I own trying to create the friction I need and it causes the hairs to snap from their roots at the nape of my neck.

"You trying to fuck that cock, angel? Huh? You better not be trying to twist control away from me." He removes the hand he has my left shoulder gripped in before landing an open palmed slap across my right ass cheek. "Now—I fucking break you."

He grunts pulling almost completely out before thrusting back in, slamming into me over and over. "So fucking tight, angel. Fucking hell, yes. Goddamn it, you're so fucking tight." Both hands release their hold on me causing me to fall forward, and before I can get my hands under me to push up he circles my wrists with his fingers, bringing them both to the small of my back, he uses them as leverage and commences fucking the ever living hell out of me.

Instantly I feel the beginning tugs blur into forceful pulls, pushing me towards the edge. "Oh God, yes, Wesley, fuck that feels so good."

With one hand he anchors both wrists securing them behind my back before bringing his other hand up to grab my shoulder. He growls the words between his uninterrupted thrusts, "You." Thrust. "Do." Thrust. "Not." Thrust. "Cum." Thrust. "Until." Thrust. "I." Thrust. "Say." Thrust.

Speaking is beyond my scope of abilities. The pulls of ecstasy increase into yanks and shoves over the brink… I know he expects me to not only speak the answer but to obey his command, however my overwhelming disability has me in a position to conquer neither feat. Moans and mewls are all that I'm capable of as stars and Christmas lights spot my vision. I feel my body begin to convulse and use the last wisp of strength I possess to refrain but almost instantly I feel it snap, hurdling me over.

Wesley's hands slide up and tighten around my throat, my back arches from the sheer force of his thrusts. When I realize he's choking me, cutting off access to much needed oxygen panic seizes me, and my hands fly to his at the same time he yanks me up onto my knees, stabbing into me harder and faster, I claw at his hands not caring that I'm breaking skin. The wetness of blood makes it difficult but still I continue attempting to claw his hands from my throat.

"I will fucking choke you out before you cum if I have to, but you will NOT cum until I SAY you cum." His hips are lunging erratically and his hold around my neck tightens. "NOW. FUCKING BREAK GODDAMN YOU!"

His control is snapping, so much it's tangible, I can physically feel it snap. I somehow gasp a breath in and slam my body back at him, meeting him punishing thrust for punishing thrust. I stifle the orgasm barreling its way through me and with my last reserves of strength and dignity I spit the words out, "I DON'T BREAK, MOTHERFUCKER!"

BAM! I'm instantly on my back being jerked to the edge of the bed, Wesley yanks my ankles on to the top of his shoulders before gripping my waist and impaling me onto his cock.

His mouth crushes mine, each of his hands delicately cup my jaw as our mouths and tongues devour each other, he continues pounding into me as if his very life depends on it.

His green eyes lock with mine and he harshly growls, "Fucking cum on my cock, you little cumslut. NOW!"

My body responds urgently to his verbal demand and I throw myself, plunging over the precipice. Shutters rack through me causing my frame to convulse inside and out. I cum. HARD.

Wes slams into me balls deep... I hold onto to him, my nails scoring his back and cum again around his cock as his arms shake. I use every muscle in my pussy to grip and milk every drop of his hot cum inside me.

Only one thought flits through my mind before consciousness abruptly leaves me.

I'll be damned... I may be a shitty sub, but Wes was right— A sub I am.

Chapter 15

Monsters in the Dark

Monster

I have watched from the shadows for as long as I can remember. As a child I watched for nothing more than a cure for boredom and dejection. Friends and family never held much importance with me. I tired very early on in life of daydreaming and people watching at nearby parks.

The picnics and tug of war I'd yearned for while watching families and friends interact had lost their appeal when I finally, at the ripe young age of eight, gave into the sadistic demons that had lived just below the surface since my very first memory.

The more I fed the demons the more their hunger expanded.

I started slow and small. Tricks and traps set up for my intended victims. Vaseline on the top step as I sat still in the shadows to watch as my forth grade teacher's feet slip out from beneath her before falling hard down the stair well. The great thud sounding out after her screams stopped signaling the end.

Tricks and traps didn't feed the demons for long. They wanted blood and they wanted it badly.

As a young boy, I never spoke and made sure to always blend in. If one were to ever recall my presence or a memory at best, they might recall a quiet boy in the background reading—nothing more.

Honestly, the only person that knew I wasn't mute was myself. Sometimes even I had to hum for less than a second while utterly alone in order to verify that I indeed had a voice. It was just one I didn't see any need for.

When the neighbor's brakes gave out and she barreled into the busy intersection at the end of our street. No one noticed the boy hiding in the tree watching as Ms. Wilson was pulled the rest of the way through her windshield, practically in pieces.

That was my first attempt at jerking off in a tree. That day was a win-win in more ways than I would have ever imagined.

The demons basked in their fulfillment as I went to read and study anything and everything I could get my hands on.

Astronomy, Geography, History, Biology and Algebra—They were my friends. I saw no need for human friends. Humans do nothing but take from each other. My friends, they did nothing but feed me, inform me, I gained more from my friends than you have ever gained from yours.

Though I loved my friends, it was Anatomy and Physiology that truly stole my breath away. When a ten year old boy stumbles across something as astounding as Anatomy and Physiology, something unexplainable occurs. For me, while reading and studying the subjects, learning the incredible give and take, cause and effect in its most fundamental state—the epithelial cell, the nerve cell, the muscle cell, the blood cell, THEY were the gospels in my mind. And Anatomy and Physiology were the bible.

I devoured any and every book affiliated with human science until I was certain if given the chance, I could end one person's life with the knowledge I'd acquired and revive another if I truly applied myself.

And then? I studied even more.

I was somewhere in metastatic cancer, wholly enthralled with this cell, this singular fantastic cell that belonged with all the other cells, and no matter its cell ranking, be it an adipose cell or a neuron cell, it stepped out of line and walked away. It altered its course and went from just a cell to an abnormal cell, recruiting other dying cells to revolt, to begin a revolution in the form of a malignant tumor. All they would have to do is reach the lymphatic system, and then…checkmate.

It was her sad laughter that pulled me from the cell spell I was under. Her laugh was so incredibly melancholy it tore at my heart. After hiding my books away, curiosity led me from my window to the roof, where I continued hopping from tree limb to tree house and settling in the shadows and low hung branches atop the old abandoned shed in my backyard. Her hair was the color of real maple syrup. It was long and shiny, the breeze brushed the strands from in front of her face. I'd never seen anyone beautiful before, not even once in all my eleven years.

She was beauty embodied. Her face held an expression of despair veiled with fierce anger and agony laced together, covering her and creating an enigma.

Her voice, though child-like, brimmed full of desolation as she sang a somewhat familiar tune. In an effort to grasp the lyrics after she turned her back to me, I leaned over the edge of the crooked shingle roof shed, out of the shadow's security to hear her words.

I may be mad

I may be blind

I may be viciously unkind

But I can still read what you're thinking

And I've heard is said too many times

That you'd be better off

Besides...

As her voice carried off into the chorus, she turned. Instantly, I lurched back for cover, trying to fall back into the shadows. Instead, the shingle under my foot slipped, becoming unhinged from its spot. My feet shuffled to gain tread only to come up short and kick the shingle from the old roof and land at beauty's feet causing her eyes of every color to clash with mine.

If I were forced to ever explain my fervent need to expend, delving into the subject of English. Reading every written word known to mankind, searching adamantly for the words to piece together to help me interpret the thoughts and dormant emotions she evoked. If I were ever asked to name my muse behind mastering English Literature, it would be her...

The beauty with eyes of every color.

Chapter 16

Pawn to Rook

WESLEY

After I move Stella's sleeping form up on the bed, I pull the sheet up to cover her before sliding into bed and curling her body around mine. I grip her thigh and hike it up over my waist, my lips settle on top of her head and I inhale the scent of her hair before kissing her.

God, she smells like a crisp winter morning.

I run my fingertips up and down her arm and cannot keep the ridiculous smile from my face any longer.

I look down at her through the darkness and whisper, "You don't fucking break, angel?" I chuckle, "No, I guess you don't my little angel that fights. But you sure as fuck submit."

I have felt true pride in my life maybe a handful of times. Actually, I can fucking count the times on one hand and not use all five fingers.

My first touchdown in peewee football. My ma was cheering her ass off. I was supposed to be a backup fucking kicker. Well, that didn't last very long. The coach's kid, along with half the rest of the team, came down with a stomach flu. Yep. As much as I hate to admit it: My life was completely altered by a stomach virus.

See, at that point in my life I was nothing more than a poor kid whose mom had once been a *VERY* well known, well... whore for my schoolmates' lack of better words. So to say I didn't have any friends was putting it mildly. Now, on this fateful Thursday night, because of my height and my 'unnatural' ability to throw the perfect

94

spiral at six years old, I led the remaining shitty half of our team out onto the field as quarterback. The phrases 'hitting them in the numbers.' And 'threading the needle' where whispered in excited shock throughout the entire game. However, when I was three quarters down the field facing my touchdown line and every kid on my team was either already on the ground or in the middle of being brought down... I tucked that ball under my arm and ran like the hounds of hell were snapping at my heels in the fourth quarter, last play of the game. I literally flipped my ass over the touchdown line being blocked by kids that were three and four years older than me. The moment the parents on both teams stood in unison to cheer and clap and my eyes landed on my ma and saw her smiling, beaming with pride as tears fell down her face - That was the first time I tasted pride.

The night I took my high school football team to state champions and won that motherfucker practically one handed. On the way out to the car, I had my arm around ma's shoulder and her excited chattering went on and on until it was stopped by a gentleman asking to take us to Western Sizzling for a steak. He said he wanted to talk about my options, yeah... My *options* for which college I preferred.

That man was the assistant coach and head scout for LSU. He not only said that I'd get a free ticket to and through college, but that they wanted me in quarterback position for LSU before my Junior year in college. They also said that my mom's living expenses would be paid as long as I played ball. That is probably one of my fondest memories as well as my proudest moments to date.

The third and last time I was swelled with pride was also tampered down with the knowledge that even though I'd taken control of JPH and turned it into a highly successful 'smut rag' publishing company, (my father's words, not mine) and in less than two years turned the Jacob's fortune from millions to billions. On the other side of that victory, that feat, was knowing either way the old fucking bastard that had left me and my mother in a shit town when I was a kid would forever reap any benefits of me kicking his ass at his own game of publishing monarchy.

So, now that you know about the few times I've felt pure pride

95

in my life, hopefully you'll understand that when I'm struck by the revelation that Stella did indeed submit - fighting the whole damn time - but she submitted, the pride I feel astounds me. The resounding effects of the unadulterated pride swelling inside my chest for the fourth time in all my thirty-one years, leaves me baffled and utterly confused.

At first, I wonder if it's because I've finally tapped that, but quickly I discredit the thought. That can't be it. I tried tirelessly for over six fucking years to get that bitch Rachel in bed. And it turned out little miss 'No-I-don't-think-so, Boss' was just as irritating and 'bamboo shoots up the fingernails' torturous as all the other bitches I'd fucked within the first thirty minutes of meeting them.

I lay here looking down at Stella in my arms asleep with her body curled up against mine, my fingers twirling the ends of her chestnut hair that reaches the top of her ass, when an intense feeling of happiness fills me, the urge to protect her and keep her happy overwhelms me—it doesn't scare me. It doesn't irritate me. It fucking intrigues me.

These are all very new emotions for me. I am so deep in uncharted territory that it should scare the fuck out of me, but the only emotions I feel are curiosity and excitement.

At least until thoughts of her past come crashing in on my happy thoughts. Then irritation and seething anger mix with my need to keep Stell safe.

And I will keep my little fighting angel safe.

I only hope when I get bored with her, and I will - look at my track record for Christ's sake - that Stella doesn't end up hurt because she does something foolish like falling in love with me. She's had enough heartache in her life, and I refuse to add any more.

Somehow, not anytime soon - this thing between us is too new - but at some point, we'll need to have a little talk and I'll let her know that falling for me is a no-no. I don't necessarily want to put an expiration date on what we have, but I definitely need to let her know what we have is *NOT* forever and will never lead to wedding bells and two point five kids with a sappy happily ever after. It's not in the cards for me. Hell I don't even want those cards in my deck!

I don't think I was born with the DNA responsible for a man to fall in love and be with the same woman forever. I'm not sure if I missed out on those because of my mother who never married, or my father, the asshole that only married to acquire a nice piece of life long arm candy.

I really like Stella, a lot, don't get me wrong. I'm just not that guy, I never have been. And I'm really hoping that she's not that girl. Because if she isn't that girl, then this thing we have, could be fucking incredible! It could very well be the time of our lives, not forever, but definitely something neither of us will ever forget.

I wake up and immediately panic seizes me, choking me when I see Stella isn't there. After I pull on some boxers I dart through the house looking for her. Once I reach the main sitting room I hear her in the kitchen growling before saying, "For an expensive looking coffee maker, you certainly are a piece of shit. How the hell?"

I walk into the kitchen to find her staring at the Italian stovetop moka pot on the counter with her brows furrowed and a look of both confusion and pissed off on her sleepy, pretty face.

My laughter causes her to look up and the smile that follows lights up the whole damn kitchen. "Are you already fighting my kitchen appliances? What's next, accosting my building's door man?"

"You have a door man I can accost? What in God's name am I doing fighting your coffee maker for then?" She laughs.

She's wearing nothing but my dress shirt from last night. Jesus Christ! Just like my damn drunken vision. Only this time, when I reach out to touch her, she doesn't disappear... I pull her to me before sliding my arms under her bare ass and scooping her up,

"Good Morning, Ms. Reese." She giggles before brushing her lips against mine.

Her legs wrap around my waist as her arms slide around my bare shoulders. "Good mornin', Wes. I hope you slept well." Her lips are still smiling when she leans in to kiss me. My tongue traces the seam of her pouty lips seeking entrance. She immediately grants me access and I groan into her mouth as our tongues dance and slide around each other like we've been kissing for a thousand years.

"You want me to make you a cup of coffee, an espresso, or a cappuccino?"

Her eyes widen, "You can make that piece of shit do *ALL* of that?" She asks mocking disbelief.

"I don't know if I'd call it a piece of shit, but yeah." I chuckle, "I can make it do *ALL* of that."

I smack her ass that is still resting on top of my forearms. "Hop down, angel." Her legs unlock from around my waist before she slides her body down mine. "So, what'll it be?"

"Coffee, black. One Splenda. Think you can manage that?" She says over shoulder before reaching the opposite counter top and hiking her little ass up on to it to sit, perched while watching me move around the kitchen.

"I'm pretty sure I can."

After I have the coffee brewing, I turn to face her and lean back against the marble counter top before crossing my arms and narrowing my eyes on hers. "It's Sunday. You stayed the night, which if I may be honest here, that's a fucking first. So... What do you have planned for the rest of the weekend, Ms. Reese?"

She smirks and crosses her own arms as her left eyebrow cocks up, "From angel to Ms. Reese already? I must say, you are quick to shift gears, Speed Racer." She sighs running her fingers through her hair before she continues, "I looked over Jude Preston's manuscript a bit yesterday. I barely even scratched the surface though. I planned to have the whole damn thing read before tomorrow, so *THAT* will be at the top of my priorities for the remainder of the weekend. Cool your jets, Mario Andretti, I'm only still here for a cup of coffee. After which I'll be out of your hair."

I'm directly in front of her in only two strides cupping her face in my hands and studying her eyes. After a moment, when I see both the disappointment and sadness in her eyes that I was hoping I wouldn't find it dawns on me that she isn't just being a bitch; she's actually being serious and it makes something in my chest constrict right before it cracks.

"Angel, that is not what I meant, not by a fucking long shot. I don't want you to leave."

Actually because of your buildings inadequate security I prefer you stay— at least until I can find a safer place for you.

Thank fuck for small miracles. That would've made shit awkward had I let it push its way out.

She blinks up at me for-fucking-ever. Finally, she clears her throat and looks down before speaking. "Well... Thank you for saying so, Wes, it was very nice of you. But I don't really think I would get much of anything read, much less retained around you." Her sad laugh takes whatever in my chest cracked and shatters it. "I'm gonna go hop in the shower, babe." She looks up at me as she scoots off the counter. "Then coffee, and then I have to get home."

She stands on her tip-toes and kisses my chin before hurrying in the direction of the master bathroom.

Well, fuck. What did I say? All I asked was what she was doing today. Right?

Stella left over thirteen hours ago. I've been in my office playing chess with myself for the last ten. Well, not really playing more like trying to figure out where the hell my mind has gone. Insanity seems to be taking residence where my usual no nonsense rational thought process once resided.

The mere thought of initiating the 'talk' with Stella causes me to become physically ill. Not because I fear her rebuttal; It's the thought of her agreeing I can't accept. Her reciprocation of that which I endeavor, *THAT* is what chills the marrow of my bones.

I slide the white pawn to rook, ending the game; and as my middle finger tips the black king over, I announce to the empty room, "Checkmate." I lean back in the chair and rest my chin against my linked, steepled fingers while glaring at the chessboard.

The complete and utter irony is not lost on me.

It isn't lost... but that in no way means that I know what the fuck to do with this conundrum I've somehow found myself in.

Chapter 17

Disappointment Causes

"Trina, I promise. If there was something, anything to tell you, I would." I lie through my teeth. "But other than I slept in the guest bedroom, his house is ridic, and he has an Italian coffee maker that spits out cappuccino AND espresso, I got nothing, babe."

My one and only best friend stands there in front of me with her jaw hanging to the floor and her bulging eyes blinking at me. After a moment, she regains her composure and starts searching for hints of deception.

"You spent the night with *THE* Wesley Jacobs and all you have to report back is fucking *COFFEE!?*" Yeah, the last part of that rant was more along the lines of a shriek or a high-pitched dog whistle... In case you were wondering.

I walk into my room with Jude's manuscript in hand and fall face first on to my bed before rolling over and releasing the exasperated sigh lodged in my throat. Trina aka I-smell-a-bone-and-intend-to-find-it, is hot on my heels.

I slyly cross my arms behind my head in an effort to hide that both hands have fingers crossed. "T, I swear on my life, nothing happened." I bat my eyelashes giving the most sincere look I can muster and ask, "You do know who you're talking to right? Why would I keep anything from you?"

She sits on the foot of my bed sighing. "I don't know. Ask

101

yourself that question, Stella. Why aren't you telling me?"

"Honestly, Trina I don't know what to make out of it, hell I don't even know what IT is. Hey," I kick her shoulder with my toe. "I promise, whenever I figure out what the hell is going on, you'll be the first to know, 'kay, sis?"

She stands and on her way out the door concedes, kinda. "Fine. You have two weeks! And if I don't start getting answers by then, someone will get their ass kicked."

Shit. A girl can't keep anything to herself these days without pissing everyone off?

I pick up Jude's manuscript and get busy. I have three hundred and forty pages to read by tomorrow morning.

I'm not sure what time I passed out reading 'Twisted Obsession'. And no, the fact that I passed out has nothing to do with the books capability of maintaining my interest. I was enthralled from page one. I'm so excited with my first project, it sure beats the hell out of children's books. Sorry, nothing against children's books, I just don't like children.

After I've showered and dressed, I tell a grumpy Trina bye and head off to work.

I walk into JPH at a quarter to seven. When I see Rachel missing from behind her desk it makes my day instantly better.

Hopefully she called in and isn't just late. Hey, I'm a wishful thinker—I'm just fucking with you, no I'm not.

I'm less than a foot away from Wes's office door and startle as it flies open. Rachel steps out of Wes's office wiping smeared lipstick from around her mouth and when she looks up and sees me a sinister smirk crosses her face.

"Oh," she closes the office door. "You're early." Her giggle resembles razor blades along the ear canal. "Either that or we must have lost track of time again. Sorry."

You little fucking bitch. It is ON!

The 'I-don't-give-a-fuck' smile on my face doesn't slip once. "That's quite alright, Rachel. One day, when you grow up, you'll learn being a whore is different than knowing how to fuck and suck like a whore." I pause and mock deep thought. "Actually, no. If you're *STILL* having issues telling time, there's no hope you'll ever learn the difference." Mentally we're in an alley and I just surprised the bitch with my shiv two seconds before shanking her ass. I'm more than a hundred percent sure the smile on my face reflects my lovely thoughts.

"Oh, honey... You didn't really think you ever had a cha—"

Okay, so I snapped. Okay, so I *may* have my hand around her neck and I *may* have slammed her against Wes' office door. I snapped, sue me!

I find myself close enough to Rachel's ear her hair brushes my lips as I speak. "Oh, honey... You ever *EVER* make the mistake of talking down to me again it *will* be your last words. I come from nothing, I have nothing—except a rap sheet, but you already know that. Here's a piece of advice for you, Rachel, never fuck with someone who has nothing to lose. You will *ALWAYS* end up with more than you bargained for."

Using the hand I still have locked around her neck, I jerk her away from the door and open it, pausing before walking into Wes' office. "Stay out of my way, Rachel. I'll only warn you this once."

Even with everything that just occurred, I somehow still effortlessly waltz into Wes' office like I own that bitch. He will never know that in this moment I am falling to fucking pieces inside. I smile brightly at him as I take my usual seat across from him before crossing my legs. "Good morning, Wes."

I pull 'Twisted Obsession' from my satchel and lay it on his desk. "I have four words for you." I point to the manuscript. "Holy fucking shit! Wow!"

He leans back in his seat and I feel an intense urge to punch

103

him in the throat to see if the smirk on his face can be choked off by a crushed esophagus. "That good, huh?"

I nod, "Better than good. Honestly, Wesley, I haven't read anything like it before."

I decide right that second, rather than dwell on whatever the hell happened between Rachel and Wesley, I am going to throw myself into Jude Preston's novel and do all I can to assure it becomes a best seller.

Wesley has made it more than obvious that what happened between us on Saturday night was nothing more than a one-night deal.

And if I can be completely honest, okay, half-ass honest, I'm relieved. It sucks when you're trying to concentrate on the important priorities in your life and you have personal problems bubbling over onto them. Now, I can wipe all that shit from my mind and stop worrying over nothing.

"Stell, I'm happy for you. I'm glad I was able to give you an author whose work you appreciate. But keep in mind that they won't all work out so well. I'd rather blow my fucking brains out than read a book with a female Dom as the main character." His laughter is infectious. Like stomach flu infectious and I'm forced to smile while smothering the bile rising in my throat.

"Yep! I am totally amped about Jude and his unconventional unique writing style. Anyway, so is there anything else you need from me? I'm going to go get started on this and call to set up a meeting with him about cover art ideas." I grab the manuscript while slinging my satchel over my shoulder before standing to leave while internally injecting ice into my veins.

I brightly smile at Wes, but before I can attempt to turn and leave, I'm stopped in my tracks at the look on his face.

"Just what the fuck do you think you're doing, Ms. Reese?" he asks and my false bravado falters. I blink rapidly before straightening my spine, however my mouth starts opening and closing like a fish on the bank.

"Ahh…I'm sorry. Excuse me? I just told you what I was doing, Mr. Jacobs." My hands fist the satchel straps at my shoulder and my eyes lock on his, preparing for battle. "Did I miss something?" *You know, other than your morning blow job by your talented secretary?*

As soon as the thought crosses my consciousness his eyes narrow on mine. Shit! Can he fucking read minds?

Sitting forward to rest his elbows on the massive mahogany desk before him, his face adjusts from my Wes, last week Wes, to complete asshole Wes with an even bigger asshole smirk.

"You want me to beat around the bush or get straight to the point?"

Are you fucking kidding me right now?

"By all means, please, get straight to the point, Mr. Jacobs." My tone is drenched drips in as much acidic saccharine as the smile on my face.

"We'll start off with today's schedule. I've already told you, Jacobs does not start work nor do we start meetings without having gone through the schedule and organizing the day ahead." His left eyebrow rises in smugness.

It takes me zero point seven seconds to mentally shut the fuck down, extinguish my emotions, and ready myself to square off with Wesley Jacobs—Yeah, I've been conditioned that well, peeps.

You walk into enough situations where you are the one that bears the brunt of the conflict, simply because you walked into your house after school, you learn to compartmentalize really fucking quickly. If you don't, instead of cutting to feel, you cut to never feel again.

"Mr. Jacobs—" His right palm flies into the air and halts my speaking.

"Call me by my father's name again and I will have you escorted from this building. Do you fucking understand me, Stell?"

Okay… So, now I'm not only trying to compartmentalize, but also stifle my seething rage. And it's probably a good time to mention that I don't cry when I'm sad, I don't. Never have. I don't cry when I'm in pain or pissed either. Conditioned people... I've been conditioned to not shed tears since before I was fucking two years old.

However, when I'm pissed and find myself unable to adequately express the depth of my anger, I do cry.

With that being said... who is blinking away tears right now? Yep. Me. Now... guess who passive aggressively tells her boss and last Saturday nights wonderful fuck the following, "Wesley, how about you take care of your business and I will take care of mine. As far as I'm concerned, my orientation ended on Friday."

I spin on my heel and stomp from his office towards my little cubbyhole office on the opposite side of the building. *AWAY* from Wesley fucking Jacobs.

However, before I can get out the door and close it, his parting words are the last of that conversation. "Angel, your orientation is nowhere near being over and I've just begun to fuck you senseless."

In an effort of self-preservation, I pretend I didn't hear any of what he just said. Walking by Rachel's desk, I tell the cock-sucking whore, "I'll be in my office. Heed my advice, *Rach*, and stay out of my way."

After my nerves have settled and the demons are asleep, I feel the tension release itself from my muscles and bones. Exhaling a long awaited pent up breath, I pick up the phone and dial Jude.

Jude was stuck out of town for his manuscript meeting, some family emergency, so I'm excited to finally meet the man behind 'Twisted Obsession'. His PA, a cute petite blonde named Sarah attended the meeting while he was on speakerphone.

When he answers the phone in a husky voice, "This is Jude." I glance up at the clock. Shit! Seven forty eight! I should've waited until after eight!

"Oh! Hi, Jude. This is Stella Reese with Jacobs Publishing, I hope I didn't wake you." I am so proud of how professional I sound.

Jude doesn't even attempt to smother his yawn, causing my confidence to dwindle and immediately begin scrambling for an apology. "Shit, I did wake you up. I'm so sorry. I can call back, I was just trying to see if you would hopefully be my date to... No, have a date. No, no. Meet, have a meeting. Dammit. Are you available this afternoon, say around lunchtime? I'd like to set up a meeting with you and go over a few things." I laugh through more than half of my spiel. I mean, when you sound like an idiot, own that shit and laugh at yourself. There really is nothing else you can do.

"Ahh... Yeah, like noon, one, or two o'clock lunch, babe?"

Oh, hell no.

"Thank you very much for the endearment, but it isn't necessary. Actually, it's sort of a pet peeve of mine. So if you wouldn't, I would greatly appreciate it." My eyes roll on their own accord when he chuckles.

"Babe, time. And get used to it, because it's also a pet peeve of mine. It's called being friendly."

Really?

"Ahh... We'll address it at lunch. Is noon okay?"

"Yeah, noon is perfect. You're on Madison Ave, right?"

"I am." I begin to rearrange my pens for the second time during the conversation.

"Awesome. There's a deli a few blocks from you, they have the best steak clubs. It's called Steinburg's, you know the place?"

"Yes."

"Perfect. I'll see you there at noon, Stell. Can't wait to meet ya!"

The line goes dead.

Ooookay. I'm pretty sure I have a damn—*another* damn flirt on my hands.

"Well, hell, if you can't beat 'em, join 'em."

If Jude Preston is even somewhat attractive, I will return the flirtatious banter. I think it is well past time for me to get out there and at least check the rules and stats on the dating game.

My lack of experience has been made more than apparent by Wesley...Again. And quite frankly, I'm sick and tired of being that girl, the one on Amazon 1-clicking over fifteen times a week in search of my next book boyfriend. And I can thank Wesley for that. Him and his big beautiful cock.

I grab Jude's manuscript and, starting from the beginning, I go through every sentence looking for possible revisions.

I have no idea how much time has passed, just like the first time I started 'Twisted Obsession' I was sucked in by the collage of fragmented characters and Jude's intertwined story line. The main character is easily the most intriguingly sinister motherfucker that has ever been created. He has me on the verge of committing fictional homicide on one page, and wishing I was at home with my B.O.B. the very next.

I am flushed and soaking wet when I'm interrupted by a knock on my office door. I have a slight panic attack and glance at the clock to check the time. 11:47.

"Shit!" I call out, "Come in!" And start shoving my files, revision notes and the manuscript into my satchel. I sling it over my shoulder and grab my purse before looking up to watch as Wes closes— And locks the door behind him. "Wesley. Hey, I'm just on my way out. I have a meeting with my author at noon."

I walk from behind my desk and try to move around Wes to get to the office door. But before my hand can touch the doorknob Wes yanks and tosses both my satchel and purse over my desk and into my chair. "Wesley, what in the..."

WHAM! He has my body shoved up against the door. Immediately, one hand fists into my hair arching my neck back and forcing my face to his. His other hand jerks my skirt up around my waist before shoving his thigh between my legs and roughly rubbing it against my clit.

I feel his teeth sink into my earlobe before slowly scraping it until he releases it from his mouth to whisper into my ear, "The fuck you doin', angel? Huh?" His hand replaces his thigh and his fingers sweep between my folds before stroking me hard and fast.

108

"Wes, no. Please. I can't do this shit again. I get it. And I'll be fine. Just." I shove both palms against his shoulders and knee him in his balls, sending him crashing back onto my desk. "Just leave me the fuck alone, okay? I got what I wanted. You got what you wanted. Now, we're done. Finished."

I spin around to leave without all my notes just in attempt to get the hell away from him. My hand grasps the door knob before he growls, "No! Fuck no, Stell! I am nowhere near finished with you. You are mine. I fucking possess you. Do you understand me? Mine." He growls.

"One more sexually harassing statement like that, Wesley, and I will file charges. I don't belong to ANYONE, and if you think you that can use this internship as a way to corner me into being your submissive or your fuck toy, YOU, sir, are sorely mistaken. I will walk out of this building and never come back. The only reason I am here is for decoration on my resume."

I slam the hell outta that office and storm from the building.

Chapter 18

Rectify a Betrayal

WESLEY

"Son of a bitch!" I roll over groaning in agony, trying my damndest to keep from losing my coffee all over Stell's desk.

What. In. The. Hell. Has gotten into her? She walked in my office this morning like a goddamn ice princess. Her defenses so impenetrable you could practically see the steel shutters in her eyes... directly behind that fake ass smile painted across her face.

After I somewhat squelch the pain and nausea, I drag myself off her desk, only to swipe my arm across it in a fleeting fit of rage. I sink into the chair in front of her desk and rake my eyes over the shit I just strewed everywhere.

I made it clear Didn't I? Saturday night and Sunday morning, I am certain I made it crystal clear. She is mine. Period. I made her coffee, there was a slight misunderstanding, but I straightened it out. Right?

I lean my elbows forward resting them on my knees and shove my hands into my hair. Guilt floods me as I look at all the files and paperwork on her floor.

"I don't need this, hell, I don't want this shit! Pussy doesn't have a name, or a face. Pussy is nothing more than pussy."

I'm uncertain why in the hell I ever thought otherwise.

It takes a while before I am able to physically move; once I do, I quickly pick up the mess I made on the floor of Stell's office.

I stalk back to my office and bark at Rachel, "Get Mr. Preston on the line. Forward him to my office."

My office phone starts ringing as I sit behind my desk. I snatch it up, cradling it between my ear and shoulder, "This is Wesley."

"Wes, what's up man? How are you?" The noise in the background makes it difficult to hear him.

"Excellent. I've just finished with the meeting that ran over, I'm headed your way now. Did Stell already order for me?"

"Ahh... no she didn't. I was under the impression Stell was taking control over 'Twisted'. She's doing an awesome job. Adorable as shit too." His chuckle pisses me off.

"No, Jude, she's an intern. She isn't taking control of shit. Not until she has a job at a publishing house. Until then she is under me. Understood?"

"Huh, okay... Well what do you want me to tell her to order for you?"

"Y'all are at Denmon's right?" Hell yes I'm guessing.

"No man, we're and Steinburg's. The deli a few blocks down. Where the hell did you get Denmon's?"

"Secretary must have written down the wrong restaurant. I'll be there in a few." I hang up the phone and haul ass out of my office.

"Rach, call downstairs and have my driver waiting for me." I push the elevator button and the doors slide open.

"This is good, Travis." I jump out as soon as my driver pulls the car up to the curb.

Walking past the restaurant on my way to the entrance, I catch sight of Stella and Jude through the window. Stella has her head thrown back laughing. One of her hands is hovering over her laughing mouth and the other playfully shoves at Jude before settling on his shoulder.

When I see her lean in close to him so he can tell her something in her ear, my entire system switches from dumbfounded to furious.

Is Stella Reese flirting? With Jude? Her author? She has lost her goddamn mind!?

I shove my way through the restaurant and before I know it, I'm towering over the laughing couple. The palpable seething anger rolling off me causes Stella to look over her shoulder.

When her eyes meet mine all the blood rushes from her face and she stares up at me in shock. "Glad you're enjoying yourself, Ms. Reese." I look over scowling at Jude. "Jude." I nod towards the table. "May I?"

Stella scurries from the booth where moments ago she was practically falling into Jude's lap. Her moment of shock must have been short lived; now she appears flustered and pissed. And from the blush staining the skin of her neck and her face, I'm willing to guess she's also embarrassed as hell.

"Wes, what are you doing here?" She snaps. Huh, maybe the blush is from her being pissed off.

"Why wouldn't I be here, Ms. Reese? You're an intern for Jacobs Publishing and I am Wesley Jacobs, correct?" I smirk at her and slide into the booth. "Sit, please, don't let me interrupt your lovely lunch date."

"It isn't a— Gahh!" She whips her little ass into the booth...right next to me.

Good Girl.

"It isn't a date. It's a meeting. A lunch meeting." She growls through her teeth.

"Well, you certainly could've fooled me." I look over her head and wave a waiter over to our table.

When he reaches the table, he tries to hand me the menu. I

shake my head refusing to touch the filthy thing.

"No, thank you. A Johnny Walker on the rocks." I turn my attention back to Jude but am interrupted by the waiter clearing his throat. "Is there a problem?" My eyebrows touch my hairline.

"Yes, I'm sorry, sir, but this is a deli. We have Yearling on tap, soda, or coffee. That's all we serve."

"A Yearling will suffice."

"Oh my God." Stella whispers beside me, covering her face with her hands.

"Stell? You alright?" I ask her around my smirk before looking back over the table at Jude. "So, where are we?"

"Actually, Stell and I have covered everything. We were just enjoying the rest of our lunch before you got here." He smiles at Stella. "Weren't we, babe?"

Babe?

Oh. So...this son of a bitch wants to die.

"Babe?" I look between Stella and Jude, noting the blush blooming across her face and the cocky expression across his.

"Ms. Reese, 'Babe' is not an endearment commonly associated with professional behavior. Tell me that you've conducted yourself better than it seems." I narrow my eyes on hers, pinning her to her seat.

Jude's voice interrupts the thoughts crawling and scratching their way around inside my head.

"She's done a splendid job. I adore, Stella. Her ideas, her opinion, everything she proposed today during our meeting was fresh and directly in tune with the direction I originally saw 'Twisted' headed in." He pauses to lean forward and glare across the table.

"I was nervous about handing my manuscript over to Jacobs. In all honesty, had the family emergency not kept me from our meeting last week, you, Wesley would have received the third degree. However..." He nods his head towards Stella, his glaring

113

expression sliding away with an extremely pleased one settling in its place. "...As soon as I laid eyes on Stell and she opened her mouth, any doubts I had instantly vanished." He slouches back into the booth before looking over at me with a smug smirk. "And yes, while it was business time, she was the epitome of professionalism. But we're at recess now and it's playtime. Merely a lunch shared between two close friends."

From under furrowed brows I look back and forth between the two of them. I'm pissed. I'm confused as hell. And most of all, I want some damn answers. However, if I ask any questions or start demanding answers from Stell, it will only make me look like the slimy bastard I'm trying to paint Jude as.

Dammit. Son of a bitch.

The waiter sets my beer in front of me and I have to calmly refrain from snatching it up and chugging it down. I take a slow small sip and set it back down before clearing my throat.

High road. I need to take the high road...but first, I gotta find the damn thing.

I have no idea where the words which fall from my mouth come from. Without thinking them, processing them, or filtering them they are already said.

"Stella is an exceptional addition to Jacobs. I plan on keeping her long after her internship is complete." Wait. What? Damn it! That is not what I meant to say.

I grab my beer from the table and tilt it back, swallowing half the contents then slam it on the table a little harder than I intended.

"What?" She looks at me like I've lost it. And I have. "What does... Wes, we've never talked about... What exactly are you talking about?"

I lay my hand on top of hers and smile at her with every drop of charm I possess, "We'll talk about it later tonight."

Stella's jaw unhinges and hangs open. I drain my beer and wave the waiter down. "Well, I believe playtime is over." I hand the waiter a hundred. "I apologize for my tardiness. I'm glad Stella was here to solidify your faith in JPH. I wouldn't have let her begin the meeting without me if I'd thought she was incapable." I nod towards Jude before motioning for Stella to remove her ass from the booth. "Ms. Reese. Shall we?"

She moves quickly, scooting from the booth and stands. She turns toward Jude smiling and holds her hand out. Jude, still slouched back in the booth takes her hand; and instead of shaking it he brings it to his mouth and brushes his lips across it, maintaining eye contact with Stella the entire time.

She ducks her head, smiling, but quickly looks back at him, "It was a pleasure to finally meet you, Jude. I am ecstatic at the opportunity to work with such a talented writer." She slips her hand from his before grabbing her bag and purse. "I'll call you once I finish the revisions. Sound good?"

"That sounds perfect, babe. You have my number. Call anytime. Business or play." He smirks.

"Jude." I nod towards him before sliding my hand to the small of Stella's back in an act that screams possession, "Stell, my driver will take us back to work. We're already running a bit behind."

She smiles again at Jude before moving toward the restaurant's exit. My hand does not waver from the small of her back.

Once Travis is headed back towards the office, she breaks the silence, gritting her words out. "What in the HELL was that? Jesus, Wesley! Why didn't you just start circling my feet and pissing on me?"

"No, Stell. I will ask the damn questions. Can you explain to me why MY intern was flirting with one of MY authors?" I roar across the backseat.

She sputters, shaking her head. "You are absolutely ridiculous. I refuse to even answer your absurd question." She turns her body and looks out the backseat window.

I have to lock every muscle in my body to keep from jerking her little ass over my lap and whipping the shit out of her.

Travis parks in the parking garage in front of the private

115

elevator leading directly to my office suites.

I climb from the vehicle and hold the door open for Stella as she slides across the backseat and steps out. The doors to the elevator have barely closed before I shove her face first against the elevator wall with one of my hands, cuffing both her wrists, pinning them at the small of her back.

When I feel the elevator ascending I hit the emergency stop button before yanking her skirt up as far as it will go. I thrust my erection against her ass growling into her ear, "You need to get this straight right goddamn now, Ms. Reese. You belong to me. Your pussy belongs to me. Your mouth belongs to me." I slap my palm across her bare ass. "This ass belongs to me." My hand connects with her other cheek before snaking up her spine and sinking into her hair. I grab a fist full to pull her head back forcing her eyes to mine. When our eyes lock, I continue. "Your submission, flirtation, your motherfucking everything, belongs to me. If I have to fuck you stupid to fuck you straight then I will."

My knee replaces my hand at the small of her back keeping her pinned in place. I quickly unbuckle my belt and pull my cock out. I circle her wrists with one hand again as I stroke my cock in the other. Sneering down at her, I ask, "That pussy of mine wet, angel? Or does it need to be spanked like that little ass of yours too?"

"Wes, stop trying to intimidate me. It won't work—." My hand snakes around to the front of her before shoving her legs open and slapping my fingers against her bare, wet pussy until I feel her clit swell. I move my fingers rubbing her slick swollen clit rough and fast, easily evoking moans from her. Moans my ears have starved for since Saturday night. "Oh, God." She cries out.

I feel her weight shift as her knees buckle but keep her held up, pinning her to the front of my body using the hand I have between her legs as leverage.

I release her wrists and palm her thigh, roughly squeezing its tautness before pulling it up and folding it against the wall of the elevator. I raise the hand I'm working her clit with and slap the drenched skin of her pussy twice, then immediately delve my fore and middle fingers into her.

116

Once I'm knuckle deep, I curl my fingers and fuck her hard with them.

My teeth sink into her earlobe. Between my clenched teeth, I tell her, "My pussy. You know how I know that pussy belongs to me, Ms. Reese? Because it fucking weeps for me."

"Son of a— Oh, shit. Ohhhhhh God!" She constricts and convulses around my fingers.

"Don't you dare cum. I will tear your ass up, do you hear me?" I thrust my cock between her legs, sliding it through her wet pussy lips. "You cum on my cock when it's buried inside you, or you don't fucking cum at all. Is that understood, Ms. Reese?" I rub her clit harder then scrape my middle fingernail over the tip quickly, causing her to yelp. My finger pads roughly circle her clit again while my other hand continues finger fucking her, bringing her closer and closer to orgasm.

Bringing her to the brink.

Through clenched teeth, I demand, "Is that understood?" I would demand her answer if I didn't realize she's too far gone, incapable of speaking anything coherent; incapable of nothing except the moans and pleas she cries out through her ragged breaths.

She's on the verge when I pull my hands away from her pussy and hook her legs over my forearms. Standing behind her, I brace both hands against the wall quickly lifting her up and splitting her wide open. Using my torso, I thrust my cock into her balls deep.

The orgasm barreling its way towards her has her pussy already convulsing around my cock, clamping down so hard my eyes cross. Pummeling into her pussy, I growl, "Cum. Cum on my fucking cock, NOW!" Increasing my pace, I fuck her, stabbing into her deeper and deeper until my cock is battering against her womb. "I fucking said CUM!" I roar at her.

Her cum instantly covers my cock and the tops of my thighs. And as her pussy pulls me deeper, tightening around my cock like a fucking vise, I shout, "GODFUCKINGDAMN IT! Pussy's so fucking tight, angel. FUCK! FUCK YEAH!" I grunt, pumping and filling her full of my cum.

Something primal snaps in my psyche, causing me to shove my cum deeper and deeper inside her until I'm utterly drained and she is completely full.

My arms ease her legs down slowly, one at a time sliding around her waist. In a fit of eagerness to suck on the skin covering her neck and shoulders, I tear her shirt open in the front sending tiny pearl buttons scattering across the floor as I pull the offending material off one of her shoulders.

Keeping one arm around her waist, my other hand clenches the material of her shirt as my mouth falls to the sweat slicked skin of her shoulder.

I cover the top of her back in kisses, nips and tastes before settling my sweaty forehead between her shoulder blades and whisper against her skin, "What the fuck are you doing to me, angel?"

Chapter 19

Pieces

Wesley's words, "What the fuck are you doing to me, angel?" pull me from the haze of lust I was contently drifting in.

When lucidity settles in, I briefly assess my current state and immediately burst out laughing. I'm standing · – barely - with my cheek resting against the cold steel of the elevator wall as mine and Wesley's cum leaks down my legs and seeps into my high heels. My skirt is ripped and hiked up over my ass and at some point my shirt was torn open and dragged down to my waist.

"Wesley Jacobs. If you think I am walking into that office, past the receptionist that swallowed your cock for breakfast, to sit behind a desk for the rest of the day, in my current, very obviously been fucked state, you have lost your damn marbles, baby." I chuckle.

His large warm hands cover the top of my bare shoulders before turning me around to face him. He stares at me with confusion, bringing his hands to cup my face and tilt it back. "Who swallowed my cock, angel?"

I shake my head and try to pull it from his hands to no avail. "Nothing. It doesn't matter anyway." I exhale a long sigh. "It's none of my business what happens between you and Rachel, Wes. However, know this. As long as there is a you and Rachel, there will be no you and I. No fucking, no flirting, and none of this 'Mine' bullshit. This," I motion at my appearance. "If this ever happens again. I'm done. Mark my words, I will walk away from Jacobs

Publishing and I won't look back."

His expression remains confused. "Right, okay. But who the fuck swallowed my cock? Or supposedly swallowed my cock? Excuse my confusion and repetitive question, but the last person who swallowed my cock was you, Ms. Reese. So, please enlighten me. Who. Swallowed. My. Cock?"

I blink up at him dumbly for several seconds before responding. "Rachel. This morning. She met me right outside your office before I came in with bitch, slut, and lipstick smeared across her face. The only thing she was trying to wipe away was the lipstick."

"She didn't suck my cock! I'd rather choke the bitch with my hands to shut her up than with my cock. What the hell are you... Did she say she sucked my cock?" He growls the last part out.

"Oh my fucking God! Wesley, seriously? It doesn't matter." I slap the emergency button and hit P for parking garage. After I yank my skirt down and my top up, I wrap my top around me and cross my arms under my chest. Facing the elevator doors I shove the words out around the pain splintering my chest, "Just, leave me alone, okay? I thought I could handle you. Hell, I was even excited to get the chance to. But Wes, you and I are too much. Way too much." I look over my shoulder at him as the doors open. Before walking out, I whisper, "Let's just stop before one or both of us isn't able to walk away from this alive."

I grab my bags from the floor and quickly walk to my car. As soon as I close my car door and lock them, my face falls into my hands.

And I cry...for the first time in my life, I sob as my heart shatters.

Before I can get all the way into our apartment, Trina is practically suffocating me with her mother hen clucking. "I have been beside myself! At wits end worrying where in the hell you were! Wesley called from the office saying you were upset." Her eyes scan me from head to toe, widening more and more until landing back to mine. Behind the hand she has covering her mouth, she whispers, "Jesus Christ, you were raped? Again?" 'Again wasn't a whisper, it was more of a shriek.

"No, sissy. I wasn't raped. Again. More like thoroughly fucked, 'Love in an Elevator' style." I smile sadly at her and squeeze her hands. "I just need a shower. And a bed. I'll be fine, T. Promise."

I walk around her and head towards the bathroom, when the saint I will love for eternity says, "I'll pour us some wine and meet you in your room with a cup full of olives."

Don't ask about the olives. For as long as I've known her crazy ass, Trina has been popping olives between her sips of wine.

I feel a thousand times better after my shower. With the tears, cum, and most of the self-loathing washed away, I step into my boy shorts and slip a cami on. After I brush my teeth, floss, and pile my hair into a bun, I walk from the bathroom making a beeline for my bed.

I walk into my room and see Trina sitting on the foot of my bed. She tosses a green olive into her mouth. Before she bites into it, she talks around it. "Wine's on the table, baby girl."

I scoop it from the table, taking a couple sips before setting it on my nightstand and flopping into bed. "This day sucked ass."

"Ready to talk about it?" Her eyebrow raises.

"Okay, so I lied. Or crossed my arms behind my head while crossing all my fingers at the same time I crossed my legs, blatantly in front of you, as I made a solemn vow. I'd apologize, but really, in all fairness I would've known exactly what you were doing AND I'd have called your ass out on it." I give her a cheesy smile before telling her, "I love you! I really, really, really do. But I'm not ready to talk about it."

She continues staring at me over the rim of her glass. "I'll be ready to talk about it when it isn't too painful for me to even try and put it into words. Better?"

"Honest?" She counters.

I make a show of nothing being crossed, "Cross my heart and hope to die."

"Alright. As soon as it doesn't hurt though, I want all the deets. Full disclosure. Every single damn thing, you hear me, sis?"

"Absolutely. Thanks for understanding. You don't know how much I appreciate it, T."

She sighs before standing up and making her way out of my room. "Get some rest. You've been fucked beyond all common sense. Believe me, rest is exactly what your poor little self needs." Before pulling the door closed, she smiles at me, "Night, Stell."

"Night." I whisper before rolling over. Instantly unconsciousness steals over me, and at three forty five on Monday afternoon, I fall to sleep.

Chapter 20

Monsters Under the Bed

MONSter

When you're eleven years old and feel love for another human being for the first time in your inadequate young life, you descend effortlessly into a web of obsession.

The demons scratching just beneath the surface of my exterior no longer sought blood. Instead, they pleaded for glimpses of Beauty.

Beauty sadly smiling. Beauty dolefully singing the song I learned, listening to religiously, and hummed myself to sleep with every night.

Anywhere Beauty was, I could be found in the shadows, if one were to ever look or pay attention. Thankfully by eleven, I'd mastered the art of concealing myself.

And because the demons and I loved Beauty, and my social skills left much to be desired, I reverted to the only thing I knew ... I watched.

I watched Beauty more than I watched the back of my own eyelids.

I watched Beauty more than I studied my Anatomy and Physiology bible.

When I wasn't watching Beauty, I had my nose in English Lit book after English Lit book... trying in vain to find the confidence, the depth of my feelings, and the words to convey both...only to fail and give up, time and time again.

I stopped sleeping in my bed the very night that followed the day I heard her sing and I slipped on the roof trying to get closer to her.

Every night from that day on, I took my pillow and a blanket and hid them under her bed. During her bath time, I would stuff toys and clothes under my comforter and mold them into a child's sleeping form. Then, before Beauty was finished with her bath, I would slip beneath her bed and become the epitome of still silence.

Some nights she slept peacefully. Most nights she screamed and sobbed, speaking broken hushed words of blood seeping, of blood covering, of blood dripping from her hands. And she screamed, begging for the screams to stop.

Every single night she screamed and shook the bed frame above me, I fell more in love with my Beauty.

Now that I've told you the first time I fell in love with Beauty, allow me to tell the story of the first time my love twisted into stained hate.

Chapter 21

Talk

WESLEY

Two days. I've done nothing except pace my office, stalking back and forth, wearing the plush carpet thin for two days.

Sleep evades me. Motivation to do anything other than concentrate on the burdens racking my every thought is nonexistent. I strike out at anyone and everyone that dares address me. I came within inches of removing Rachel's head yesterday when she spat at me in a sneering tone. "I cannot believe you are letting that disgrace to society needle her way under your skin. What is wrong with you, Wesley? Have you finally lost your damn mind? Is that it?"

She left after I explained that every time I looked at her all I saw was how much of a leech and failure of a decent human being she truly was.

And she hasn't returned. Thank God.

I should go home. I should shower. I should probably eat.

Instead, I pour myself a tumbler of scotch and dial Stella's number.

"Ello?" Trina answers before shuffling the phone around. "Shit, damn, hell. Sorry! Hello?"

"Everything all right?" I ask.

"Oh, hey. Yeah, dropped the damn phone. She's asleep. In case you were wondering. I know you aren't calling for my stellar conversation skills." She laughs.

"Of course I am, Trina. You sell yourself short, love. However, now that we're on the topic, is she okay? Has she said anything? Is she coming to work tomorrow?"

"Jesus Christ, Wes. Pipe down on the third degree for a second. Yes, she woke up around lunch. I managed to get a cup of broth in her and extract the words, "I'm going to work tomorrow." But that's it. So no, she hasn't told me jack and I have a shoulder, actually two available if you feel the need to pour your heart out. And... Sorry, Wes. But I don't know if she's okay, to be completely honest with you."

A sigh escapes my mouth and I nod before saying, "Thanks, Trina. I appreciate you talking to me. Let me know if y'all need anything."

After I hang up, I contemplate on continuing to stalk or head home. Shit. I really do need a shower and a shave. Plus, I've gone through all the scotch I had hidden in my office.

I drank my weight in fucking Johnny Walker last night when I got home. I showered, shaved, and sat in my huge oxford leather chair and commenced drinking until I drowned the sniveling voice in my head that constantly begs and urges me to snatch Stella from her apartment and fuck her so stupid she can't think straight. At which point, I would be made to care for her until my dying day.

Which is complete and utter absurdity.

I roll - literally roll - until I fall from my bed landing on all fours and crawl to the bathroom.

I shower again, however it does nothing to clean the scotch from my sweat glands. I grab the phone in the master bedroom and call Myrta, my housekeeper that stays during the week. "Mr. Wesley, good morning, love. How are you?"

"Hey Myrta, not so hot. I need you to have a Bloody Mary

made for breakfast. Oh, and make sure Travis will be on time to drive me to work today too."

"Ohhhh, Mr. Wesley." She tsks. "Youth does not sit in your corner for long. Why do you continue to spat in her direction?" Her English isn't broken, however her Spanish accent twists and cuts the words making them sound as Spanish as the Mexican town where Myrta was born. When she's pissed? Her capability to speak English is thrown out the window.

"I don't recall spitting at anyone." I chuckle. "I'll be down soon."

God bless Myrta's soul! She had one Bloody Mary on the kitchen counter and another in my to-go coffee thermos.

I walk into my office sipping the cure to my hangover and smile when I see Rachel isn't here. I hope our little tiff will cause her to quit. Without a two week notice. After I put a call in to my business manager requesting a temp secretary, I set the phone in the cradle only to pick it directly back up when it rings. "Wesley Jacobs."

"Wes, what's up man? It's Jude."

"Jude? Is there something I can do for you?" I ask as I sink into my chair.

"Umm... Maybe. Have you heard from Stell?"

Speak of the devil and she will appear.

Stella walks into my office smiling. The urge to toss her across my lap and spank her little ass to kingdom come is one I am barely able to restrain. "Nope. Sure haven't. Now, is there something that I can help you with?" I say, enunciating the 'I'.

"Damn. I've been trying to call her since Monday evening. Well, when she comes in, give her a message for me, yeah?"

Hell. No.

"Sure thing, buddy." I smile like the devil across my desk at Stella.

"Just have her call me. That'd be great. Thanks, Wes." Click.

127

I gently set the phone down without removing my eyes from Stella's or allowing the devious smile to slide from my face.

She nervously sinks into her chair while tucking her hair behind her ears before she whispers, "Hey."

"Angel, you look beautiful today. Did you know that?" I stand slowly from my seat keeping my eyes locked on hers until her nerves cause her to glance down and break eye contact.

"I didn't. But thank you for the compliment. Wesley, I can't do this." Her voice pleads and her eyes connect with mine as I round the corner of my desk. In two quick strides, I'm in front of her and sinking to my knees.

"Shh..." I cup her face in my hands and brush my lips against hers before pulling back and looking into her eyes. "Listen to me. I want you. Only you. I don't know nor do I give a fuck what Rachel said or did to make you think otherwise. Now, this is the important part. You are to remain silent and hear me out. I let you get your rant out, even as preposterous as it was. You will allow me the same. Understood?"

She nods before speaking. "Yes, I understand."

"Us - we are going to be hard work. We're both so fucked up that no one wants or understands us. And the ones that are ignorant enough to believe they do, we immediately discredit their obtuse asses. So yes, WE are going to be hard, WE will go at each other like ravenous beasts overcome with anger, with passion, with hate, with love and do you know why angel?" I continue without giving her a chance to answer. "Because that is the breed of people we are. Everything which is important to us we give of ourselves hundred percent. Opinions are important to us, being right is important to us, and WINNING is important to us." I slide a hand from the side of her face and bury it in her hair, fisting and pulling, "Oh yes angel, we will fight.", I mutter crushing her mouth to mine.

Our tongues circle, our mouths swallow, while our lungs breathe each other's breath. And just like every time I'm with Stell, weird crazy shit starts running through my mind. Chasing away ideas of ever letting her go.

128

When her teeth sink into my lower lip before sucking it into her mouth, I moan and pull her lips open with my thumb on her chin. Devouring her mouth.

I pull away from her swollen lips and smile. "We will fight, angel. We'll fight hard. But it'll be worth every strike below the belt, every spiteful word uttered . When we love, when we fuck, when our passions rip through us with wild intensity, it'll obliterate all of the bad. I want all your hate, Stell just as much as I want all your love. This, Us, is going to happen angel and there isn't a damn thing you can do to stop it, angel."

I stand and kiss the top of her head before tipping her head back with my fingertips under her chin. "Is that understood?"

She nods, swallowing and whispers, "Yes."

After I'm sitting behind my desk, I clear my throat steeling myself for 'the talk' although every atom in my body is screaming trying prevent my words, "I'm not asking you for forever, Stell. Honestly, I don't think I'm made for forever's; but I don't want to put limits on us either. You and I are like a candle burning at both ends, or a star blazing through the fucking night sky, so we'll just let this - let us - burn and blaze until there's nothing left."

"I...I like that. It makes it less scary somehow."

I smile at her, elation fills my soul, happiness saturates me from the inside out. "Good girl."

Our little talk on that Wednesday seemed to clear up all of our misunderstandings. She's spent every night at my place since. I was only able to keep myself pinned behind the desk for thirty minutes before I had her pinned over the desk, riding her sexy little ass straight to kingdom cum from behind.

Stell and I have been going pretty strong for the last few months. Just like I predicted, we fight like cats and dogs. But Jesus, Mary, and Joseph... When it's good? It is the best damn good anyone has ever felt.

I knew from the beginning Stella had a submissive nature under her façade of steel.

Tonight's agenda is a charity dinner I must attend and although my father is also attending, the fact I'm going with my angel has me smiling in the mirror. After I tighten my tie I sit on the dressing chair to slide my feet in my dress shoes.

I'm not sure why but anxiety is tingling through my nerve endings. I pour a scotch and walk over to the desk in the corner of my room. I dial Myrta while sipping my scotch slowly as I sit behind my desk and pull out Stella's file. I flip through the pages over and over, rereading each note and connotation. There is something, something Derrick missed or deemed not important, which has been niching, hovering in my mind like mist. I sense the dread of it while reading her pages and attempt to zero in but it's gone as quickly as it appeared.

"Ola señor Wesley. Are you stashing for your party?" She chuckles at her joke. Because it's Saturday and Myrta's usually gone by noon, I know without a doubt she's tapped into the wine cellar.

Laughing at her I say, "Myrta, I hope stashing is not what Stell thinks when she sees me, but I'll make sure to fill you in if she does. Is the limo ready?"

"I say stashing. Like handsome, draper. You know? No? Oh, yes, the limo is here. He can drive me after you are at party, sí, Mr. Wesley?"

"Ahh... It's dashing and dapper. And absolutely, Myrta. In fact, you should grab yourself a bottle of wine from the cellar to take home with you." I sip the last of my scotch before standing and buttoning my suit jacket. "I'm headed downstairs, Myrta."

I'm by the door slipping on my over coat, when I catch something out of the corner of my eye causing me to look over my shoulder. I see my tipsy housekeeper half walking half staggering toward me. "Senior Wesley, so dashing you look this night. If I didn't know you were the Diablo in an ángel's disfrazar, I show you mi Maria years ago."

130

I laugh realizing how tipsy she truly is. Note the mixture of Spanish and English. One more glass and Myrta will be lashing her Latino tongue at a rate that I have no chance at understanding. "Thank you. However, I'm uncertain if that was a compliment or an insult." I kiss the top of her salt and pepper head. "I'll tell the driver to make sure you make it home. No more cellar juice, sí? I want you at least to remember the ride home..." I narrow my eyes on her clouded ones "and make it to bed, safely. Understood?"

"Sí, sí. You have pasarlo bien, buenas noches, señor Wesley." She pats my shoulder and pinches both cheeks before walking err...wobbling away.

By the time the limo pulls up to Stell's, I need another damn drink I'm so nervous. "Stan? You picked up the long stems from the florist, right?"

He hands me a long gold rectangle box through the divider. I open the box and scoop all twenty-four purple and lavender colored long stem roses wrapped in silver satin. After I look over them and shake them around, slapping a few crinkled leaves and get thorned for it, I shove the stupid box at Stan. "The hell did they come in a box for? That's the dumbest shit I've ever seen, Stan."

"Sir, you asked for the most expensive purple roses. Expensive roses come in a box. If you prefer, I can just swing by Kroger and grab a ten dollar bouquet wrapped in cellophane."

I shake my head in disgust and climb out of the limo with my... Stell's... now unboxed purple roses.

Chapter 22

Cinder-fucking-ella

"I don't look like a whore?" I ask scooping my tits into place before sliding my hands across the fine black delicate lace covering the nude silk of the dress visible beneath.

"Nope. You look like that hooker... What's that movie all you damn white girls loved in the 90's? Pretty Slut, no... that's not it. OH! Cinder-fucking-ella!" Trina tips a little too far in her chair before her equilibrium can catch up with her erratic hand motions that are commonly associated with... Well, Trina's drunk off her ass.

I smooth 'Barely Nude' by L'Oreal on my lips and tell Trina through the mirrors reflection. "It's called 'Pretty Woman' and don't act like you didn't cry when Vivian told Kit she was going to San Fran at the end."

I pucker my lips and quickly assess myself from head to toe in the mirror. Trina pinned all my dark tresses up, leaving strategically placed wisps and curls framing my face.

My dress? Fan-fucking-tastic! I don't even want to know what T had to do to acquire it. And the nude designer stiletto peep toes on my feet are another question I won't ask for fear she'll tell me she either sold a kidney, robbed a bank or both.

"So what, it was a movie I related to, Stell. Sue me." She's in the middle of rolling her eyes when the apartment buzzer goes off, her rolling eyes become wide as her smile lights up her adorably inebriated face. She scurries from the bed calling out over her shoulder . "Time, sis? How much time you need?"

Staring at my reflection I inhale deeply. As I exhale, I mutter, "There is no time left. Lord knows I can't fight this shit any longer."

As soon as I see Wes standing in my living room, with a bushel of purple roses wrapped in silk, butterflies take flight in my stomach, my pulse quickens, and I can hardly catch my breath. I realize how beautiful Wesley Jacobs is as my eyes drink him in, standing before me in a classic black on black suit and tie.

Once we are in the limo whisking our way to a charity ball Wes cornered me into, I whisper, "Wes, what exactly is my roll tonight? Am I your intern or your date?"

His expression is nothing short of salacious cockiness covered in hot sex. His husky voice carries through the darkened limo's interior. "My thoughts precisely. You, in either way, shape, or form, are mine. My intern. My date. My pussy. My ass. My smile. My laugh. Any and everything that is you, Ms. Reese, is mine."

He leans forward. bracing his elbows on his knees, and drains the drink in his hand before setting it off to the side. Wes' eyes stay locked on her mine, watching... I feel my heart jolt as I begin fidgeting from the intensity of his glare. I feel as if my nerves are going to leap from my skin.

During our silent ride to the charity function I sit looking out the window at New Yorks skyline. The limo glides in front of Rockefeller Hall, I catch sight of celebrities lining a red carpet as they move inside and I glance at Wes nervously realizing he's sliding beside me. His capable arm circles my waist as he pulls me close tucking me into his side. "We don't have to do the red. If you prefer, I can have Stan drive us around the back, angel."

My gaze doesn't leave the topic of conversation, "What will happen if we go in the back? I thought being seen was the important part of these things."

"Yes, it is however, it is the number of zero's on the check I write which is the most important." He nuzzles my neck and jawline before whispering into my ear, "Stell, you look absolutely beautiful tonight. Let me show the world how lucky a man I am. Would you do me the honor of walking the red carpet with you by my side?. Do it for me, angel."

Shit!

"Shit!" I roll my eyes just as Stan the limo driver pulls us up to the circus of flashing lights and chaos.

The door of the limo swings open and I freeze, I sit in the car and look out at the extended hand in front of me and simply blink at it.

"Ms. Reese, take the man's hand.." Wes, so close to my ear his lips brush my skin, finishes his command and nips the skin on the back of my neck spurring me to action.

I grasp the gloved hand and smile the brightest smile I have as I step from the car. As soon as Wes is out of the limo, he tucks me back into his side. I love it when he holds me like this. I feel sheltered, protected, and loved. Even though I'm a billion percent sure my smile looks like it belongs to a crazed person, I refuse to let it slide from my expression. I smile dammit, and even when my cheeks hurt, I still don't stop smiling.

Once we're in the party hall, our coats are taken and our drinks are served. Wes leads me around the circle of guests introducing me to everyone as his 'angel'. I'm on the verge of either kneeing him in the balls to shut him up, or playing like I'm a narcoleptic...mostly for entertainment reasons, but also to get out of smiling and shaking hands with everyone. Wes seems to sense my rising tension.

"I know, Stell. I'm over this shit too. Come on, we'll go find our seats." Wesley's hand settles on the small of my back and we begin heading in the direction of the tables when we are quite literally tag teamed. Wesley takes an older couple to his left, I take a young hot author to my right. Absolutely! Between the two of us, I definitely came out ahead in the situation.

"Jude!" I smile as he rushes towards me with a dazzling smile. I can't help giggling when he lifts me and spins around. But before setting me back down to the earth, his arms lock around my waist keeping me less than an inch from his face.

I blush trying to turn my head away from his direct and blatant flirting but his words have my eyes seeking his again. "You look utterly breathtaking, babe. Wow. I mean, WOW. That asshole forget to tell you I've been calling you all week again?"

"Jude, put me down. This is probably the most scandalous I've ever felt. People are staring, please put me down." I whisper-scream.

Wesley's booming loud voice has every head turning our way. "Motherfucker, she already asked you once. I won't wait for her to ask again. I'll just mow your ass down right here in front of everyone. Understood?"

I'm dropped to my feet and a whoosh of air leaves my lungs before Wesley turns towards the couple he was talking to. "Josephine." He nods at the thin somewhat older woman dripping in diamonds and fur before turning his attention to the older gentleman. "Father."

Wait. Hold the phone! I'm meeting the folks? Son of a bitch!

"I'd like for you to meet my angel, Ms. Stella Reese. She and I have been dating for several months." He grins looking down at me. "And if I were you, I wouldn't piss her off or get in her way. I would, however, get used to her, because she isn't going anywhere - not if I have anything to do with it."

I tap the arm mine is looped around. "Oh my, Wes! Would you shush?" I turn to Josephine with my hand out, "Josephine, it's lovely to meet you." I smile and watch as she shakes my hand (if you can call it shaking) only touching it with the forefinger and thumb of her right hand with a look of disgust on her face.

I quickly yank my hand away and maintain my composure, extending my hand again only towards Wes' father. "Mr. Jacobs, it's nice to meet you as well." He shakes my hand – correctly - and smiles. I pause briefly as I notice how much Wes looks like his father.

But, not too much to deny the bitch that lies within me who wants off her feet.

"I do hope you two have a lovely evening, please excuse me, standing in six inches is quite unnatural as I am sure you would agree, Josephine." I smile my friendly viper smile and wink. Looking up at Wesley I ask, "Wesley, are you finished mingling, dear?"

"Well past ." His hand never leaves the small of my back as he leads me to our table. Once we are seated he bursts out laughing waving a waiter over for water. His eyes smile at mine over the rim of the glass and after he sets it on the table he picks up my hand to rest it in both of his. "If you don't stop being so adorable, I'm going to fall in love with you, Ms. Reese and if that happens, so help us God, we're all in trouble."

"Don't threaten me. It's your fault for dragging me through the throng of paparazzi and stuck up heifers. I'm surprised I didn't chew someone's Gucci covered arm off. I'm starving to death!" I mutter.

When I glance across the table at Wesley, he's looking over my shoulder with a scowl so menacing, it causes me to shiver.

"Wes, are you okay? What is it?" I ask.

Before he can answer, Jude's voice floats over my shoulders at the exact moment his hands slide and settle on top of them. "You two wouldn't mind if I intruded would you?" I look up at him over my shoulder and smile patting the table at my side.

I kick Wes under the table as I notice his hands fist and knuckles blanch. "Absolutely not, Jude. There's plenty of room."

Wesley clears his throat and leans forward, but before he can speak, I dive into conversation with Jude about his work in progress and the recent overnight hit 'Twisted Obsession' has become.

A little more than an hour goes by when I finally see my two best friends, Eve and Bo, arrive. Eve is from ridiculous old money. When T and I first inducted her into our little family circle, every chance we got the three of us would get girly-excited and dress up to go with her to these fancy parties. It didn't take long for them to lose their luster though. Me and T stopped going, but poor little Evey still had to go. Especially with her modeling career taking off.

I squeal clapping my hands like a school girl when she gets close enough to the table.

I've kept Wesley to myself for the most part. Besides talking to Trina about our relationship, I don't. So, needless to say I'm a tad bit nervous yet excited to finally introduce Wes to Eve and Bo.

After the introductions are made, we all sit at Wesley's table chatting while the dinner courses are served. Everyone seems to be getting along great – well, almost everyone. If Jude would stop with the innuendos and straight out blatant flirting with both me and Eve. I swear to Christ. This guy has the biggest damn ego.

He bounces between flirting with me and Eve, oblivious to the fact that every time he flirts with me, his life is in the balance and Wes holds the cord. And when he flirts with Eve, his life is also in the balance, except Wes hands Bo the cord.

We're eating dessert when the music starts and I begin feeling sick. I blame the stress and anxiety over dinner for the sudden nausea. My nerves feel as if they've been hooked up to electroshock, suddenly Jude's hand grabs mine and he stands saying, "Have the first dance with me, babe." Every nerve ending fires with a jolt of electricity sending my dinner back up.

I leap from my chair and mutter, "Excuse me." Before covering my mouth and quickly making my way to the ladies room.

After having lost my dinner in a cacophony of ralphs, I make my way from the bathroom stall to the sink without looking up.

I wet my face and am patting it dry when I hear a sinister cackle behind me, "Just like his whore mother. I can't say that I'm surprised. The Jacobs boys seem to have an affinity for impregnating the female dredges of society."

My eyes snap up to meet hers in the mirror. A smile dances across my lips as I quietly respond, "Josephine. Cynicism does not become you, love. And you can cool your rumor jets, I went through enough abuse as a child and teenager to guarantee that I will never conceive. So unfurrow your brow, witch." I spin on my heel and slam from the restroom.

Chapter 23

That Which Belongs to Me

WESLEY

I'm at my breaking point. I'm a seething melting pot seconds from bubbling over when I see Stell flying towards our table, flustered and pale as a ghost. She looks fucking horrified. I'm out of my chair and halfway across the room before my mind even registers how scared my angel truly appears.

When I'm within reaching distance, I slip one arm around her waist and the other over the top of her shoulders before tucking her tightly to me. "Angel, what's wrong?" Her entire frame is trembling and I feel the hairs on the back of my neck stand on end.

I'm barely able to make out her whisper, "Wes, I don't feel well. Please take me home. I'm so sorry." I see Josephine step from the bathroom. The same bathroom that Stell just came running from like the hounds of hell were nipping at her heels.

"Tell me by home you mean mine and yes, we'll leave immediately." I probably should've coaxed her a bit more gently into that proposal, and I fully intended to, but the insane surge of possessive emotions, along with the physical ache to protect Stell, causes the words to fall from my mouth.

Is it because Jude was all over her most of the night? Possibly.

Stell nods against my chest and whispers, "Yes. Let's go home, Wes."

And that's all I need. Moments later, I have Stell still tucked tightly to me as we slide into the limo. Once Stan pulls the car from the curb, I pull her onto my lap and cradle her against my chest. I remove the pins from her hair before running my fingers through it with one hand while gently scratching her scalp at the base of her neck with the other. At some point during the ride home, she falls asleep.

The limo parks outside my building. I step from the car and scoop Stell up, looping one arm under her knees and the other behind her back. Once I stand to my full stature, I tell Stan, "Hey man, grab her shoes and hand them to me." With the hand under her knees, I wiggle my fingers indicating where to place the shoes. As soon as he hands me her shoes I turn and carry Stell up the stairs and into my building.

Once we're in my penthouse I walk into my bedroom and gently lay Stell down on the bed. After I have her dress off, I grab a t-shirt from my bureau and head back stopping dead in my tracks. I was concentrating on removing her dress, not paying attention to what lay beneath. Biting down on the inside of my cheek doesn't prevent the groan that escapes my throat.

Her body is encased in a satin nude corset cinched around the waist by boning sewn into the material. Between her pushed up, cupped breasts the corset plunges to her navel and laces from just below her breasts down. The light pink nipples that I love barely peek out over the top of the corsets satin material. Hooked across her hips is a garter belt with silk nude hose clipped to the straps. My eyes appreciate silk, satin, and lace but at this moment they barely skim over everything to land on her beautiful bare pussy. Instantly I'm hard enough to knock on wood and my mouth waters at the sight of her.

With perfectly Saintly intentions I loosen the lacings which begin just below her breasts in the middle of the corsets plunge, and slowly untie until the corset opens like the gates of heaven. When I'm fingering the clasps holding her hose I find my face over my favorite place.

Once I have her garter belt and stockings off, I hook her thighs over my shoulders and run my nose from the back of her knee to her inner thigh. Even though I've just eaten a seven course meal, I'm suddenly famished. Dying for a taste of her.

140

I'm stopped on my decent into decadence by Stell's shrill ear splitting scream. The sheer terror in her scream causes me to jump and scramble up her body pulling her rigid frame on top of mine. "Shh... I'm here, angel. Wake up, Stell. Stell?" Her shrieking does not waver as I try to wake her. I can feel her body expelling all the air In her lungs , her scream pauses as she drags in another lung full of air before continuing to wail in horrified panic.

Fear and concern thread their way through me causing my arms to wrap tightly around her. I kiss her sweat soaked forehead and grab ahold of the tops of her shoulders before shaking her and shouting, "Stella! Wake up!"

She stops mid scream. Ragged breathing slowly quiets as the sweat covering her entire body turns cold.

I feel her begin to tremble as I grab the sheets and comforter and pull them tightly around us, kissing her face and the top of her head over and over until we are settled under the blankets.

My emotions are a damn whirlwind. Anger, panic, love and protectiveness all batter inside my chest for first place. Not knowing what the hell to do, I do nothing except continue holding her and running my fingers through her hair.

Time stands still but it feels like an eternity before Stell looks up at me and rests her chin on my sternum. "I'm sorry, Wes. I never wanted you to have to witness that. I hate that anyone has to witness it, but you... I never wanted you to."

"Wha—" I sound like a damn toad. I clear my throat before speaking again, "What were you dreaming about? Do you remember?"

She smiles sadly. "Yes, unfortunately I always remember." Her head ducks down and she rests her cheek back on my chest.

"Do you want to talk about it?" Before I can finish my question, her little head shakes. My chest feels like someone left a grenade in it without the pin and the explosion shreds me from the inside out.

"I can't. I'm sorry, I just can't. I've tried. The state of Louisiana had me seeing every damn counselor and psychiatrist in almost every parish. It didn't work then and it won't work now. I'm fucked up, Wes. And believe me, you don't want to know why, I promise."

My hand slides into her hair and hugs her face to me as my arm circling her waist tightens. "You're not fucked up, angel. You just have nightmares. That's all."

Her manic laughter sends chills down my spine.

"Just nightmares, huh? Don't fool yourself, okay? I've let enough of how fucked up I am slip for you to know that your statement is total bullshit." She chuckles. "Just nightmares."

I don't know what the hell to say or do. I do however note that speaking seems to be a bad idea. And she isn't pushing me away, until she does I refuse to let go of her.

So I hold her. I stare at the shadows dancing across the ceiling and continue holding her body to mine. After her breathing evens out and the tension wound tight in her muscles relaxes, I still don't loosen my hold on her in fear of not being there if another... whatever the *FUCK* that was happens again.

I can't honestly say this insane idea didn't stem from the sadistic bastard inside me. But sometime during the night and early morning hours, as my fingers traced the obvious self inflicted razor blade scars on her outer thigh, it dawns on me that she has stayed almost every night for three months and not once suffered a nightmare before last night. There is only one common denominator, in all of those nights over the last three months I have dedicated at least two hours to completely and utterly Dominating, bending, and shoving Stell beyond her boundaries. And she submits, every fucking time - effortlessly.

Last night was the first night we went to bed without our Dom/sub play. The first night the exhaustion from our intense chaotic love-slash-hate-slash-fuck storm didn't lull us into unconsciousness.

With that said, I believe Stella's submissiveness is the key to her nightmares.

Now, it's just a theory, and I'm going to need a little more information before I pull out the big guns and test my theory.

I slowly slide Stell from my chest laying her down before easing from the bed. I pull on pajama pants and head to my office, bare feet padding soundlessly across the hardwood floor.

Once I'm in my office, I call Derrick. Hell no I don't give a shit that it's seven am on a Sunday. "Speak."

"Derrick, I need something from you ASAP. No later than this evening. It's not foot work, more like finger work, scouring the internet kinda shit."

"I'd rather foot work. Whatcha got for me?"

"Check to see if you can come across any case studies focusing on the connections between reported sexually abused victims turning to the BDSM lifestyle once they reach middle to late young adulthood."

"That's it? You know you can just look Erickson up on Google, right? You sure you don't want to save yourself ten k?"

"Derrick. Has money ever been an issue for me? No. Do what the fuck I pay you to do or I'll go find someone that will without asking questions or tossing their two cents in." I hang up and immediately dial Trina and Stell's number. After a few rings, Trina picks up the phone and mumbles, "Hello?"

"Hey Trina, sorry I'm waking you, but we need to talk. Stell's fine, or well, physically. I wouldn't have called if I didn't think this was important. You still with me?"

She yawns and a split second later starts shouting, "Fuck. Shit. Motherfucker!" The next thing I hear is the phone crashing into something.

"Trina? The hell, you okay?"

"Sorry! Sorry! I tripped over my Kindle cord, and no I didn't enjoy my trip. It was painful. Okay, I'm all ears, what's up?"

"On average, would you say Stell has nightmares weekly, every other week, or monthly?"

"Fuck. It happened didn't it? She thought she'd, hell I don't know, found the cure to her nightmares by staying with you."

"I'm not willing to take that assumption off the table just yet. So, how often?"

"Before you? Like totally before you...I'd say weekly. After you, well, at first, probably every other week, but she hasn't had one in over three months."

Interesting.

"Has Stell ever mentioned why I was at Chained that night several months back?"

"Well, it doesn't take a rocket scientist. Has she gone into detail? No. Other than you being her... ahh real first. And that she likes you. Whatever y'all do between the sheets she claims fixes her, the part of her that's wired differently than everyone else."

"Hmm... That's what I'm trying to piece together. The scars on her outer thighs, how long has it been since she cut? Do you know?"

"Longer than I've known her. She doesn't talk about it, Wes. And I don't feel like I have a right to tell her to go back to therapy. I mean, shit, she's been in therapy since she was seven. She stayed in therapy until she was in her twenties. If anyone would know whether or not therapy helps, it's her, right?"

"Y'all have known each other longer than what? Five years?" I ask.

"Yeah, since Junior college."

"Okay. Well, if I think of anything else I'll call. Hey, Trina!"

"Yeah, what's up?"

"Ahh... Do me a favor, don't tell her I called asking all these questions. I promise you, I have her best interests at heart. And if I am her cure, then I need to know what I was doing to keep those fucking nightmares out of her head."

"I won't, Wes. But the first time you hurt her, I will remove your balls. *THAT* is the only promise you get from me. Period."

I chuckle at her confidence that she could take me on long enough to get to my balls, until appreciation for Trina taking care of my angel for all these years floods through me. My chuckle dies in my throat. "Thank you, Trina. For everything." I hang up the phone and look down at the damn file that's been mocking me since coming into my possession.

After a while the words in the file start dancing as I try to reread them and pinpoint what I'm missing. It's right in front of me. But I can't see it. Dammit!

I turn the TV on for background noise, hoping it will keep me up. When I realize that it's making shit worse, I stalk towards the kitchen to make a strong cup of coffee.

As I wait for it to brew, I go over the files in my mind again.

There is something I'm missing. And last night somewhere between Stell's nightmare and me slipping from the bed, something inside me clicked.

When it clicked, the double helix of my DNA took a twist and it altered the very foundation of the man I always believed myself to be.

If I can't protect Stella, every day for the rest of my life, I'll go completely fucking insane. And I can't make one hundred percent sure she's protected if I'm not the only man in her life, forever.

'The talk' has just become null and void. What happens next? Hell if I know.

The only thing I do know is Ms. Stella Jolie Reese will forever be mine and mine alone. I just need her to answer one question correctly.

Chapter 24

Rust

When I wake up in Wes' bed, the same smile I smile every morning curls the corners of my mouth. I reach my arms above my head before sticking my ass out and moaning through a wonderful full body, still in bed, 'damn that feels good' stretch.

I brace myself for the every morning pains that accompany the nights I spend under Wes' demand, held at the precipice by nothing more than a thread causing my every muscle group to constrict, clenching determinedly to assure that thread remains intact until Wesley designates that it's time to clip, snip, and break.

However, when my bottom is at the edge of the bed and I don't feel the familiar dull sting from the previous night's spanking or paddling, my smile slips from my face.

It's when I stand and felt absolutely no pain or muscle aches that alarm bells resound through my blissfully ignorant mind… Right before the nightmare ricochets into my consciousness.

After I close and lock the bathroom door, I turn and look at myself in the mirror. "Fuuuuuuck! WHY?!?!" I ask my reflection.

All I see is my father's eyes staring back at me. And that thought alone sends me on a collision course with the toilet, where the top of my head dunks. I'm thankfully able to rip the wet hair from my face before my gags and upchucking commence.

I brush my teeth prior to dragging myself into the hot spraying water of Wesley's shower that deserves a spot in Forbes. The entire time I'm under the pounding jets, all I can do is relive the events of last night in slow motion.

Why am I such a bitch? Every time someone is there when I wake from my ninth circle of hell, my defenses fly up and I'm a wretched bitch to whomever is there. Unless it's Trina. With her, I just follow like a weak lamb.

Once I've finished my shower, I pull one of Wes' LSU t-shirts on. Since it hits mid-thigh, I forgo a pair of his boxers. Besides, it's Sunday, Myrta isn't here.

I step from his room, but on my way to the kitchen, I hear a television at the other end of the hall and change direction heading towards the sound of Fox News Updates.

I'm thrown off guard when I find myself outside an open door leading to what looks like an office. I always assumed it was nothing but a locked closet. I step across the threshold glancing at the desk stacked with open files before my eyes move to the TV. "Wes? Baby?" I ask walking into the office. Once I'm a foot away from the desk, I resolve that he isn't here. My eyes sweep across the files open on his desk, but my instinct not to pry and do what pleases Wesley wins out.

I quickly leave his office and make my way back towards the kitchen. When I walk in to find Wesley standing there with two cups of coffee in his hands and completely lost in thoughts that mar his handsome young features, it cuts off the flippant joyful 'Good morning' resting on the tip of my tongue.

I freeze at the kitchen entrance and watch as a myriad emotions play across his features. Uncertain if I should high tail it back to his room and fake asleep or proceed into the kitchen and act as if the tension surrounding him isn't thick enough to choke me, I remain still and silent at the edge of the room.

I stand at the threshold indecisively for less than five seconds when his forest green eyes slam into mine, the intensity of his gaze steals my breath away.

He's so goddamn beautiful, his facial features soften and instantly his eyes are smiling, as if my presence alone extinguished

147

the agony that was wreaking havoc upon his mind. I smile back at him, whispering, "Hey," before tiptoeing my way slowly to him.

Wes hands me a coffee mug, "Good morning, angel."

I duck my head before gulping a mouthful of no Splenda added coffee. After I choke it down and cough, I look up at him in question. "What? We run out of Splenda, baby?" He shakes his head before he nods towards the Splenda canister on the opposite counter.

"You sure are acting odd this morning." I pluck the spoon from his cup and before I can open the Splenda canister, much less add Splenda, Wes has me shoved over the black marble countertop so swiftly that I don't have time to throw my hands in front of me to cushion the blow my cheek and hipbones absorb. The metallic taste of blood fills my mouth and suddenly, I'm wrenched back as Wesley's fingers capture my hair and closes into a fist. My face hovers above the countertop as he swipes appliances and canisters, clearing the entire surface with his forearm.

Canisters full off salt, baking soda, Splenda, and sugar crash to the floor sending grains and powder in every direction, settling in, on, and around the expensive appliances that crashed to the floor.

I feel his rough hands between my legs before a growl emerges. A split second later, he jerks his t-shirt over my head then uses his overwhelming weight to shove me back over the counter. When my breasts hit the cold marble, I gasp. His warm calloused palms brutally knead the skin of my ass. Suddenly the rough abrading stops leaving me begging for a touch, any sensation he will offer.

Instinctively, I bow my back seeking the harsh, warm caress of his hand. My reward is as masochistic as it is fulfilling when finally his open hand connects, striking each globe of my ass in a manic and crazed rhythm, alternating from one side to the other, yet somehow never striking the same spot twice.

I somehow manage to remain silent throughout the barrage Wesley rains down upon my bottom.

After twenty unexplained blows, he releases my hands and cages my body beneath his.

I should probably point out that before this moment, words like 'caged' and 'beneath' catapulted me into a downward spiral of panic.

For the first time when these scary words flit through my mind, panic isn't left in their wake.

It dawns on me, resonating its way through every molecular structure that these old fears are no longer fixations; they no longer yield the power they once used to keep me held prisoner.

Wesley's desires leave me second guessing everything I have always believed about myself and my life. The limitations and boundaries of my ability to withstand, where I always thought my breaking point was, the line drawn in the sand of my sanity - Wes smashes through all of it, dragging me past my comfort zones.

These ties that bind me, he breaks and replaces with restraints of his own; but Wesley's ties are not ones that bind, they're what sets me free.

Wesley's bare chest is flush with my back as he rests his scruffy cheek against mine. Both of his hands slide down my sides over my rib cage, my hips and then around the tops of my thighs, to stop between my legs, each hand cupping an inner thigh. "Angel, I'm going to ask you a question. And without thought, without hesitation, you're going to answer as honestly as you can using only one word, yes or no. Is that understood?"

I don't even think about my answer...there is no need to. "Yes."

"Do you think your nightmare occurred last night because I tucked you in bed without fucking you straight?"

Wait—No, I mean yeah, maybe, but no that's not why I have nightmares. Wesley doesn't cause my nightmares he just usually makes them go away.

"Wes—" His palm claps down over my mouth.

Against my ear he growls through his teeth, "I said YES or NO!" He removes the hand between my legs. A split second later, it slaps the already reddened skin of my ass.

I bite down on the hand covering my mouth causing him to jerk it away. "Wes, stop. Listen to me. I'm trying to explain..." Whack. His palm cracks across my flesh. The pain causes lights to flicker behind my eyes. Whack.

"Wes, please!" Whack. "I-I, Let me..." Whack. "F-fucking." Whack. "TALK!" Whack. I fill my lungs with as much air as I can struggle in and use it to shout, "RUST!" Closing my eyes as I feel tears flood them, I whimper against the cold black marble, "Rust.".

Instantly, not an inch of his skin is touching mine. Before I can turn around he has his t-shirt back over my head and I'm slipping my arms through the armholes. He walks to the other side of the kitchen and starts the coffee maker.

"I'm sorry. I just needed to explain, Wesley, and you kept pushing. Your question isn't a question that can be answered with just yes or no. It's much more, so much more than just yes or no, baby."

When his shoulders tense and he doesn't respond, guilt floods me. Its intensity feels like a physical blow to my chest. It hurts so bad, I can barely breathe around it. Tears continue stinging my eyes. "Wesley, please. I'm so sorry. I-I..."

"You broke." His words are hardly audible.

The weight of those words are so dreadfully powerful it causes crippling dread to invade my body. Agony and despair shred through my heart like shrapnel, so sharp and quick I gasp as tears stream down my face.

Something is happening, something profound and I can't stop it. It's flying at me like a freight train and there is nothing for me to hold on to, to brace for its impact. Nothing. It's going to hit and when it does, it will destroy me.

Nausea churns in my stomach causing my mouth to water. I swallow as quickly as I can to keep the bile down.

My back slides down the counter and I wrap my arms around my knees as my bare ass settles on the grit and powder covered floor. A cry escapes my lips, "Wesley. Please don't do this."

He doesn't answer, and if he tenses his back muscles any more, they'll snap. "Okay. I let you down." I nod at his back, "The least I can do is explain myself, answer your goddamn question the only way it can be answered. No. You are not the reason I had a nightmare. You are not why I have nightmares. My nightmares are caused by sick perverted men and usually star the sickest and most perverted man to ever live. Only he isn't alive in my nightmares. My father is dead and I am covered in his blood, trying to silence whoever keeps screaming, but I can't. Because they're my screams and in my nightmare, I can't make them stop."

I stand from the messy floor and dust my ass off before finishing. "But yes. Every time I fall asleep after you've whipped and wrung my mind, body, and soul out, I wake up happy and rested and so much farther away from my nightmares and past than I've ever been before you came into my life." I turn and make my way back to his room tracking sugar across the hardwood floor and plush area rugs on my way.

I shower and dress before leaving. On my way out, I see Wes still standing in the kitchen, completely unmoved from where he was when I turned around after screaming 'Rust.'

Chapter 25

The Desecration of Beauty

Monster

I conditioned myself at a very young age to function on as little sleep as possible. Even at four, I recall thinking that sleep was an unnecessary excuse to be lazy. At first, I attempted to go completely without it. After the seventh day, lucidness evaded me and simple conscious decisions blurred. It was the eighth day that I physically lost all control. Control of my bowels, my stomach contents, my mind—Everything. The last thing I lost control of was my eyelids. I fought those to the very end. And then I fell asleep.

Through trial and error over a period of several months, I mastered sleep. From that moment on, I only allowed myself two hours of sleep in a twenty four hour period.

This long practiced sleep pattern is what blessed me every night as I lay beneath Beauty's bed and listened to her terror.

She and I are so much alike. Except she is so much more destroyed than I ever have or ever will be. I liked to think her destruction was caused by her fighting the demons within, instead of welcoming them with open arms as I did.

My eyes literally starve when I am unable to watch her. Even after no more than thirty minutes, the physical effects begin crippling me. The longest stretch of time I've had to endure consisted of twenty-one hours, she'd gone several towns over to meet with a specialist and spent the night before returning.

By the time my eyes finally soaked in the sight of her, my vision was blurred from tears of agony and torment.

The last six hours of physical torture I was forced to endure because of her, all because she hadn't had the ability to cope with the demons; all because she had to fight rather than simply give in. I lay those last hours upon her bed and constructed her death at my hands in over a thousand different and beautiful ways.

But when I see her walking up the walkway through my swollen, teary eyes, all I feel is home and love in its purest, simple form.

The powerful emotion is so incredible that a giggle bubbles from my mouth before I can stifle it with my hands covering my lips. Her eyes of every color clash with my red swollen ones, halting her in place. Her brow furrows and she frowns. When she steps towards my direction, I run the other away and hide; but not for long, just long enough to be forgotten, then I'm back in the shadows watching my Beauty once again.

Later that night, I lay beneath her bed and listen to her breath as she sleeps ever so peacefully. After six hours of listening to her sleep, I allow myself to be lulled into REM sleep.

I'm jarred awake before the sun has risen, confused by sleep. My hand grips the frame under her bed and I move to slide out from beneath it, only to be stopped by her whimpering. Excitement surges through me. This is a wonderful turn of events. Beauty's nightmares usually happen an hour after she falls asleep. Never more than an hour. I'm euphoric and giddy with joy. A smile spreads across my face from ear to ear as I settle in and patiently wait for the orchestrated melody of Beauty's horror.

Her whimper causes my ears to perk up. The grunt that follows causes my smile to fade.

"Shh…If you be good, and keep quiet, I'll make sure to not hurt you too bad. I love you. Did you know that? Do you have any idea how long I've wanted you, baby girl?" The mattress above me groans, bowing from excessive weight. Movement in my periphery causes my eyes to dart to the other side of the bed where I see a pair of ugly feet, men's feet, with his gnarled, yellowed toenails curling around the tip of each toe, peeking out of the toe of his navy house slippers.

A grunt cuts through the room followed by Beauty's yelp before the mattress begins squeaking. The sounds, him grunting, her yelps and cries, and the mattress squeaking all interlace and sync into a morbid rhythm punctuated by a male's grunted words of love and praise. As I lay there listening to him praise her for her tight cunt, madness consumes me. Fierce hate for Beauty swells and unfolds, blanketing and snuffing out any love I ever possessed for her. Choking and killing any goodness I ever associated with my Beauty.

She is nothing more than a weak desecration.

And Beauty will pay for her abhorrent actions, she'll pay in the only currency I accept; blood - her blood.

Chapter 26

No Explanation

WESLEY

Why couldn't she just answer the question correctly? She not only answered it wrong, she fucking safe worded out. And for what? So she could explain? She took a very simple question and contorted it completely out of its intended context.

"Shit!" I turn from the counter and am forced to look over the mess strewn across my floor. "Thank God Myrta's coming tomorrow." I say to the empty room as I storm out of the kitchen.

As soon as I'm behind my desk I sit back down and read over the files again; chasing the same damn ghost. After reading and rereading the files, I snatch the phone up and dial Derrick. "Speak."

"I need more than what's in these files, man. Something is missing, something fucking huge. I feel it in my bones. Is this all you could get?"

"Ah...it was with the information you'd given me. But I can take apart each one and look for a lead. You originally wanted a timeline, or I assumed that was what you wanted from our conversation. You want me to break apart the timeline and extensively research it from every angle? Then yeah - whatever's missing, I'll find it. Gonna take a lot longer than days though, Wes. We're talking weeks. Month and a half tops. Her vagabond upbringing has her shit scattered across the state of Louisiana."

"Yes. Do that. And the quicker you get me the info the more your fee doubles. I don't want that shit wrapped up it a pretty bow either, send it to me in chunks. We'll both look over it. You got anything for me on this morning's job?"

"Oh yeah. I emailed it to you earlier, fax should be coming through."

"Thanks, D. I'll wire the payment immediately."

"Sounds good. Got anything else for me, boss?"

"Yeah. Fucking hurry up."

After the event that occurred Sunday morning. I honestly saw no other way to protect Stell than from a distance; at least until I can get this shit ironed out and I can pinpoint for absolute certainty what it is I'm missing.

The case studies that Derrick faxed over were all the conclusive evidence I needed. The key to curing Stella's nightmares is her ability to accept her submissiveness. That was where she failed; not me, but herself.

Instead of reacting to my Dominate actions, she hesitated. That hesitation tipped the domino that tipped the next domino and ended in a cascade of tipped over dominos all ultimately resulting in her denying me as her Dom; the trust that I mistakenly believed I'd already held.

Instead of using her strength to withstand the consequences of her actions, she did what I thought - what I believed with every fiber of my being - she would never do:

She gave up. She broke.

Out of weakness, she gave up on the only thing that could save her.

I wasn't hurting her. She'd withstood much more in the way of pain and self-discipline than a few swats to her bottom. So she didn't safe word out because she couldn't physically and emotionally take any more. She safe worded out because she panicked and refused to stay calm. In turn, she safe worded out by snipping any and all tethers tying her to submissiveness...to her cure.

She cut me off at the knees by saying that one syllable word. Rust.

I can't help her. She took my ability to help her away. And until she realizes it, until it resonates through her as clear as a bell and she returns to me able to express it without me giving her the words or coaching her into understanding, all I can do is patiently wait... And pray to God to help her see what I could not.

Stella called in sick every day this week, so when I walk into my office on Friday morning I'm caught off guard by the sight of her in front of my desk.

"Good morning. I didn't expect to see you here today." I set my briefcase down beside my desk before shrugging out of my suit jacket and sitting down.

"Yeah, I'm sorry about that. I must have a stomach bug or something. I can't keep anything down. I have an appointment with my doctor today at four o'clock, if it's alright for me to leave a little early?" Her bottom lip is pulled into her perfect mouth, her white teeth flash before chewing it.

"Absolutely, far be it for me to keep you from your health. I'm sorry to hear you've been sick too. I wish it was the reason I'd believed you called in sick." I grab the phone and dial my new secretary, Barby.

"Barby, Good morning. Do you have the schedule? Ms. Reese and I are ready."

"Yes, sir. I'm headed in now."

"Excellent." I set the phone in its cradle. Stella's fidgeting in her seat and I have to bite my tongue to keep from correcting her.

I could kiss Barby's face for her timing. Sweet girl. Not a mean bone in her body. Brunette, got a body on her that would normally have me pulling out my signature Wesley Jacobs charm. If the angel sitting in front of me didn't have me twisted up in emotional knots.

Barby was the one in the office when Rachel came in expecting her job to... well, still be hers. So she scored her first gold star by printing out the email I received from HR after filing her

157

termination paperwork. Barby said "I printed them out and handed them to her. After she stared at me for five minutes waiting for her glare of death powers to work, she huffed and stomped her foot then spun around and stomped her way towards the elevator, muttering curse words the entire time. When she tripped walking in to the elevator, I was thankfully able to hold my laughter back…Until the elevator doors closed, of course."

See, I told you. Not a mean bone in her body.

"Barby, what's our day looking like?" I smile at her and lean forward, resting my forearms on my desk.

"Good morning, Stell. Are you feeling okay?" She looks at Stella with worry knitting her brow.

Stella smiles at her, but goddamn if it isn't so sad, it causes my chest to ache.

"Not really, Barby. I have a doctor appointment this evening though. So, hopefully, they can find out what it is and I'll feel better soon. Oh! Can you add that to the schedule? It's at four."

Barby nods before marking the schedule then smiles at Stella, "Done! Now, Wes, you have a meeting with Melissa Wilson, the horror romance author you've been looking at, she's from eight to ten. I have conference room B set up for you." She looks back down at her legal pad. "Stell, Mr. Jude has been trying to reach you. I figured if you wanted him to have your number, you would've given it to him, so I didn't offer. I did, however, promise to book him for your first available meeting slot. He'll be in at eight, you two are set up in conference room D. I set the file on your desk that has his up to date manuscript and the new cover art he is looking at to give 'Twisted' a new facelift. I left two hours open for the meeting. At ten, you'll meet with Wes and five potential hires for the editor position." Barby looks over towards me before continuing, "After lunch you have a two o'clock meeting with Silver Marketing, then a four o'clock meeting with—" Her face scrunches up. "Sorry… Your father and the National Publishing House Society board members. The receptionist of NPHS said this was an annual meeting."

I nod feeling my temper rise at the mere mention of my father's name.

"Stella, I don't have anything on the schedule for you after lunch. I'll leave you and Wes to discuss whether or not he wants you in his two o'clock with Silver."

I stare at Stella over my desk before Barby interrupts, "Wes, did I leave anything out?"

I slightly smile at her before taking the files. "Nope. Excellent as always. Thanks Barby."

After she leaves me and Stella alone in my office, neither one of us speaks for a while. Stell's the first to break the silence.

She clears her throat before speaking. "Wes, I'd be happy to sit in on your meeting with Silver. I-I mean, if you want me. Err... I meant if you want, if you think I should." Her head ducks down and she coughs.

"You've sat in on plenty of meetings with our marketing companies. I don't see how this one would be any different than those. You're free to leave at lunch." I smile at her then look back down at Wilson's files.

"Oh. Okay. Well, I'll see you at eleven," She stands up and gathers her things. "Have a good morning, Wes. And I guess a good weekend too." She shrugs her shoulders and makes her way from my office. Every click of her heels is a fucking gun shot to my chest.

I stare blankly at the door she walked out, rubbing my chest and praying for Derrick to hurry up with some damn information.

Chapter 27

I'm Sorry...Fucking What?

Jesus, Mary, and Joseph. It has finally happened. I have wondered almost daily for as long as I could remember, how much longer my sanity would hold out. How much time I had before my cheese finally slipped right the fuck off my cracker.

And now I know. It wasn't the constant nightmares that did me in, it wasn't the horrid memories of being raped and molested by every father figure and a brother figure that cracked my marbles. No. Ugly and hate, perversion and vitiation are not the precipitators of my mental collapse.

Falling in love with the man I swore to hate, trusting him, being honest with him. Giving him absolutely everything that I could and watching as he walks away from it like it never mattered - in the end, love is what destroyed me.

I sit behind my desk staring blankly at the wall crying. Crying over a broken heart. I couldn't be more weak if I tried. I am utterly disgusted with myself. If I wasn't so afraid of the pain, or botching it and winding up a vegetable, I would put a bullet in my head just to save the world from the pitiful excuse I have become.

I glance at the clock. Shit! It's seven fifty two! After grabbing my purse I jog-slash-walk to the ladies room.

I splash water on my face then pat it dry. I'm digging through my purse, trying to find enough make-up to fix the current state my face is in, when Barby walks into the bathroom.

"Hey, girl." When I look up and she catches sight of me in the mirrors reflection, her smile vanishes. "Oh, shit. Oh, shit! I was hoping you were really sick. Oh, shit that sounds terrible. I mean..." She sighs as defeat takes over her features. "I know Wes has been weird all week. And the tension during schedule was thick enough to cut with a knife. I was hoping you were calling in sick because you were sick, not because there was trouble in 'Wes and Stell paradise'."

"Well, I hate to make it any worse. But I was sick, I am sick, and there is no 'Wes and Stell' anything anymore." I smile sadly at her before getting back to fixing my face.

"Well, shit! I'm so sorry, Stell. If there is anything I can do, please don't hesitate to ask."

"I won't. And thanks, Barby. You're cool as hell. You should come out with me and my friends sometime. You'll fit right in, girl."

"Hells yeah! That sounds awesome!" She practically skips into the bathroom stall.

I'm smearing on my lip gloss when she walks out and walks to the vanity to wash her hands. I toss all my make-up into my purse and sling it over my shoulder before smiling at her. "See ya later, girl."

Before I can get to the door, Barby says, "You know the best way to hurt the guy that hurt you is to replace him. Or rather, make him think you've replaced him." I look over my shoulder at her with an eyebrow raised and motion with my hand to keep going. "Just saying... Jude? Is hot as hell. And I know for a fact that he wants him some Stella Reeses cups."

"Oh?" I lean my shoulder against the wall and cross my arms. "And how do you know this?"

"I don't think I have ever seen an author willing to do the amount of changes or write a manuscript as fast as he does, just for the chance to see his publisher; much less, his publisher's intern." She winks. "Take him for a spin. Or at least make Wes think you are."

161

I nod as I absorb her rationalization behind this. Then I look back and smirk. "Alright, I will. What can it hurt? Right?"

"Exactly."

I shake my nerves out, pull my shoulders back, and hold my head up high as I open the door to conference room D. There sits Jude, leaned back in his seat, arm hooked over the back of the couch, legs spread wide. He's wearing his signature black on black suit and tie, his long sandy blonde hair is standing up on the top of his head as though a hundred fingers have plowed through his hair. The rest barely brushes the collar of his jacket.

Yeah, just as hot as I remembered. Can't say it'll be hard faking this. "Hey, Jude." I smile brightly on my way to him. Trying not to act so obvious, I hold my hand out for a handshake I know he's going to slap away. He always does.

His steel colored eyes snap to mine and instantly, his face lights up and he leaps from the couch before walking to meet me halfway. As soon as I'm in reach, he picks me up and hugs me tight, chest to chest, nose to nose. "Hey, babe. You look... Wow. Radiant. That's all I have. I know I suck. I should have more words than that. Your beauty makes me, the 'word master', forget how to use them." His eyes close and he breathes in a deep breath before setting me back down on my feet.

"Jude, you are such a flirt." I laugh for the first time in almost a week. "Don't you dare stop though, I need it. My self confidence needs it more than you know." I move around the conference table and sit.

Jude is right on my heels and he sits directly beside me. "So, I looked at the covers for 'Twisted'. I really liked two of the five, but I need to know which one you liked the best?" I lay each possible cover on the table, side by side, before looking over at him.

His face is smiling so sweetly at me. I hate that I fell for Wes. Why couldn't Jude have tried harder. Been more dominant and demanded my attention the way Wes did.

Dammit! Focus, Stella.

"I like whatever you like, babe. You tell me which one to choose. If 'Twisted Obsession' was yours, what cover would you want to represent it?"

I blush before ducking my head, hoping he doesn't see. I look at each cover, one by one. After I've looked at every cover, I pull the original two that I felt best fit the story away from the pack and point to the first one. "This one I like because the main character had so many conflicting emotions which in the end fractured his mind. His inability to speak, to voice what he was feeling, I believe was the main reason his sanity finally snapped, turning his love into a sick perversion or... 'Twisted Obsession'. When I look at this cover, even though it's a woman under the shattered stained glass screaming, I think it portrays the message behind the book perfectly. Who's to say even though Renee seemed happy that she was? She could have very well been just as broken, if not more than John was. We can't say because we only read his point of view. So, I think that concept ties this picture to the story as well. I see, man or woman—doesn't matter - someone in the midst of a silent scream to stop their fracturing sanity with the broken mosaic of stained glass representing said sanity." I smile at Jude waiting for his response.

He nods thoughtfully and stares at the picture for a long time before looking up and smiling at me. "That's deep shit, babe. I love it. You get this story on so many levels. I love that about you." He points to the second picture, "Now, tell me what you see in this one."

I look over the picture slowly and smile. There isn't any one thing about it that I can put my finger on or say to explain why I love it. In my opinion... I speak my rambling thoughts aloud, "In my opinion, it depicts the epitome of his obsession. Everything he ever wanted to touch, to see, but never got the chance." My eyes run up the curve of her spine. She's sitting on a bench, completely nude, with her arched back turned to the camera. Her hair is twisted in a sloppy French twist and her face is slightly turned, making her beautiful profile visible. In the picture, it looks as though she feels someone watching her and is just about to look over her shoulder in search of the person.

Staring at the picture, I whisper, "She is his 'Twisted Obsession'." I tap the picture with my finger, "Bottom line, it's so simple I don't need to decorate my reasoning. It'll only take away from the utter simplicity." I shrug sliding both cover pictures in front of him. "That's my two cents, babe."

His gray eyes flash to mine and I wink at him. "I can flirt just as well as you can, Mr. Preston."

He smirks, "Well, I'll be damned. You most certainly can."

Jude and I meet for lunch. He kept calling it our first date and I kept telling him, and anyone he said it to, it's just lunch. It was also exactly what I needed. He is always so much fun to hang out with. I forget all the problems plaguing my mind. And I laugh - constantly. Our lunch was so fantastic that when he drops me off outside my building and asks for a real first date tomorrow night, I don't bat an eye before wrapping my arms around his neck and squealing, "YES!"

However, now that I'm sitting in this cramped, God forsaken doctors waiting room... I don't feel so hot anymore. Actually, I feel like I'm going to be sick, again.

After sitting in the waiting room for a damn hour, the nurse opens the door holding a file. She finally, thank GOD, says, "Stella Reese?"

I walk towards her and smile half-heartedly. "Hi," I say when I'm close enough for her to hear.

She holds the door open and motions for me to walk ahead, "Hi, Stella." She points to the scales. "If you want me to hold your bags, I just need to get your weight."

"Oh, sure. Thanks." I hand her my stuff and step onto the scales.

Huh. You'd think without eating for a week I'd drop a few lbs.

"Okay. Follow me." She leads me to an exam room and points to the paper covered table. "You can hop up there. So, what's been going on? You told the receptionist you've been nauseated for... Oh, wow. Five days as of yesterday. What about today? Any

164

nausea?" She looks up at me.

"Yeah, earlier. But I did eat some soup and a few crackers for lunch and kept it down; well, so far." I shrug my shoulders.

"Hmm... Okay, let me take your vitals first." She opens a cabinet above the sink before setting a container beside it. "Then I'll need you to give me a urine sample. If that doesn't give us any answers, Dr. Thomas may want to draw some blood." She walks over and wraps a blood pressure cuff around my arm before shoving a thermometer under my tongue.

After the monitor beeps, she scribbles on my chart, removes the cuff from my arm, and takes the thermometer out of my mouth. "Your vital signs are perfect. That's good news." She smiles at me like I passed a test or something.

Yay! Way to go vital organs! You win again!

She hands me the container. "Here, follow me. I'll show you where the restroom is."

After she points to the bathroom and explains what to do with the betadine swabs - that I refuse to elaborate on - she says, "Just leave your urine specimen in the metal cabinet. Then head back to your exam room, room number five. The doctor will be with you as soon as he can."

I have scrubbed my hoo-ha with cold brown cotton balls, pissed in a cup that I wrote my name on and put it in a metal cabinet with two way doors, washed my hands and awkwardly - because I know that all these people know that I...just now, in that bathroom... scrubbed my hoo-ha with cotton balls soaked in brown stuff - walk back to exam room numero five.

Another thirty minutes passes and I'm on the brink of declaring to never, under any circumstances, return to any doctor – ever - when the doctor walks in.

Hmm... Isn't it ironic, don't you think?

"Ms. Stella!" The older man cheerfully announces. He's impressed with my vital organs, these things are always showing off, I swear.

"Doctor Thomas!" I mock his excitement.

He laughs and shakes his head before flipping through my chart. "Your vital signs are awesome. That's good. Urine came back okay, other than you're dehydrated, but with the number of days you've been sick, that's expected." He looks up from my chart and smiles before sitting down.

"Crap. So now you're gonna take my blood?" I really did not foresee me getting stuck today. My blood is fine, ask my vitals, they'll tell you.

"Ahh... Well, yeah. It's kind of standard protocol for your diagnosis, Ms. Stella." He sets my chart down on the counter before pulling his glasses off and setting them on top. He pinches the bridge of his nose for a second then looks at me with stark seriousness rather than the cheerful happiness that was there seconds before.

Fucking dread bathes me inside out. I suddenly become terrified of the words this man is about to say. I want to tell him to shush! Not to tell me. I'd rather live in ignorant bliss! I chastise my epic failure of an excuse for vital organs...for only behaving when the nurse is around.

Please, God don't let it be Cancer. Please, God don't let it be cancer!

"Ms. Reese, when's the last time you've had a well women's check-up?"

Wait. What?

I blink at him.

"An OBGYN? A woman's doctor... They specialize in women's health? Babies, menstrual

cycles...".

"Oh! Okay." I laugh. "Hell, doc. I don't know? More than five years, I think."

His nod and facial expression leads me to believe my answer isn't exactly sufficient.

"Is the reasoning behind that because you've just recently

become sexually active?"

Whoa! Whoa! Nuh uh, no damn way, doc. I know where this shit is headed and my stomach bug has nothing to do with my vagina or how frequently it bleeds.

My defenses have triggered and been raised. The therapy patient inside me flares to life and ensembles my use of closed-ended answers.

"Yes." I nod curtly.

"Well, that's certainly understandable." He smiles. It's awkward and fake as hell.

"Hmm." I respond, unsure if a yes or no is appropriate.

"Okay." He pulls a prescription pad from his pocket, gum wrappers that were also in his pocket fall and litter the floor unnoticed. "I'm going to refer you to a very good friend of mine. Best OBGYN in New York City. You'll love her." He says while writing something on his pad.

"Sounds fun." I lie with the same fake ass smile still on my face knowing damn good and well that God himself won't be able to drag me to see this 'friend' of his.

"Are you interested to know why I'm referring you to the best OBGYN in New York, Stella?" His voice is laced with authority and condescending tones that raise my hackles even further.

"Because you care about the health of my vagina?" It takes everything I have to not giggle like a damn girl.

"Stella, your urine pregnancy test came back positive." Exhaustion coats his statement.

Whoa! Wait! I'm fucking sorry... WHAT?!?!

"Positive? Positive, as in YAY! I passed?" I'm scrambling for straws over here, mister. Shit! Give me something!

Please let it be cancer, please let it be cancer!

Dr. Thomas stands and, before leaving the exam room, hands me the prescriptions. "This is your referral to Dr. Hughes." He taps the piece of paper. "And this one is a prescription for your prenatal vitamins. Congratulations, Stella. You're pregnant."

Ahh… Again, I'm sorry, Fucking WHAT?!?!

Chapter 28

Vengeance

Monster

When your world has been ripped from beneath your feet, when the only sliver of goodness, the one and only thing you've ever loved, the last snippet of purity, spoils before your very own eyes, it doesn't just leave you angry or disappointed…

…It rocks you to your very core, the fundamental cellular level that lies beneath. It churns curiosity fervently, generating a mere habit into a maniacal infatuation.

My demons are insatiable with Beauty. However, where I want Beauty's blood coating every inch of my skin, the demons only yearn to be the reason she smiles.

After the first night, she pleased Mr. Sims and apparently liked it enough to keep quiet as well as never mentioning it to friends in an effort to prevent the rumor mill from learning about her whorish behavior. Even with all the disappointment she laid upon me, I still made a vow to myself to always, no matter what, be there when she needed me. The problem with my vow was, nine times out of ten, the codependent is too confident to accept that they are indeed codependents or they are in denial.

Those key factors mix, preventing her from seeking out my help before she understands I am the only thing that can truly save her. Her lost pureness leaves nothing except stained Beauty in its wake.

At first, I tried convincing myself that her age put her at a disadvantage. I wanted so badly to believe her too naïve to understand what she was doing was unacceptable. And it helped

169

choke the anger out for almost a year.

Until it dawned on me one night as I lie there listening to their grotesque concert orchestrated with his grunts and her cries with the squeaking springs, she has done this before. Her dreams alone, the same dreams that lured me in, bewitched me into falling in love with her, are enough proof that she isn't naïve. No, of course she isn't. All along, this was Beauty's game... And I played right into it. Consuming any and every glance, smile, or sound I could gain for sustenance.

Like every man in the history of men starting with Adam and Eve, I've allowed myself to be blinded, used as an emotional puppet, pushed around on a chessboard by a mastermind that I – me - I was naïve enough to wholly believe and profess her beauty derived from her pureness.

A switch flipped inside me. Rage. Rage more potent than any other emotion I've ever felt surged and surged through my through my veins, driving forcing my sanity to its brittle brink.

I sat quietly concocting and strategizing the perfect plan. Watching. Weeks turned into months and I was patient, I continued to plan. Until the day came and I set the wheels in motion that would lead to Beauty's ultimate downfall.

Leading to my long awaited payment, my vengeance... Her blood.

The plot I created was easily enacted; A note placed here, a note placed there. An inconspicuous minute tattle tale whose weight was great enough to trigger a man into unleashing his ravaging beasts upon a girl.

I spoke. To another human. Once I knew my conspicuous notes had been found in the order which I'd intended, I muttered shyly with confusion apparent on my face the tiny tattle tale to Mr. Sims. "I saw her and her friends giggling and only caught a part of what she told her friends. "His is the smallest I've ever seen, I thought when boys grew to be men, everything else grows with it. It's so boring. I'll probably just tell the teachers or school counselor, so I won't have to pretend I'm not so bored anymore." All of her friends broke out into a fit of giggles." After I apologized to Mr. Sims for not knowing what she meant, I walked away smiling, swearing to never speak again.

I had to bite down on my own fist until I tasted blood to keep the cheers of delight from escaping me while I lay under the bed that night, listening to her horrified and agonizing screams—much like the ones from her dreams.

The best part, what coursed through me like a drug and made me feel high, was knowing that it was me responsible for every one of her tortured cries.

Chapter 29

Teacher Vs. Dom

WESLEY

Weeks have gone by since Stella shouted her safe word. I'm no closer now than I was then at understanding what I feel is missing. Or understanding if my course of action in response to her safe word was the correct path.

It sure as fuck doesn't feel right. I'm uneasy and my restraint is wearing thin. My control is slipping. I know I'm supposed to wait for her to understand. I know I can't have her or take her until she realizes that she is the one that holds the key. That it's not my Dominance over her, it's the submissive within that is the key.

The idea she might never understand this concept drives me fucking mad. It abrades the snippets of restraint and the reins I barely grasp for control. I spend my days talking myself into staying in check, maintaining the rule... And I spend every night talking myself into just giving in, let the threads of control just slip through my fingers. They aren't worth losing my angel.

I'm unsure how much longer I can withstand this torture. I've lost my ability to concentrate on *anything* that isn't her. In meetings, I have people - important people - standing directly in front of me speaking; however, I have no idea what the hell they're saying. Because every single part of my anatomy is honed in and focused on Ms. Stella Jolie Reese standing outside her office in a black pencil skirt, red silk blouse and those damn black stiletto's which I *know* lead up between her thighs to her naked pussy!

"Wesley!" I snap my eyes to my business manager. "Which one?"

Shit! Which one what?

I quickly flip through my mind searching for what this meeting was for. When all I come across are recollections consisting of Stella, I get creative and mentally search for Stella and meeting memories.

Ding! Ding! We have a winner!

This is why I am so adamant on morning schedule meetings. See how useful they are when you least expect it.

I glance at my watch. Nine-thirty. First meeting. Editors!

"I like Shane best. Of all the applicants, he's definitely the most suited for not only our team, but the company as a whole."

What? He really is. See? I have my shit together; I just have to go about finding it a little differently these days. It's called adaptation. Look that shit up, people.

"Perfect. We'll start the paperwork and I'll let you know when to expect him."

After we shake hands and everyone has left, I sink into my seat exhausted.

It's only nine-forty. Why the hell am I exhausted at nine-forty?

Stella fucking Reese - that's why. I narrow my eyes before scanning across the office from behind the glass walls of the conference room in search of the man-draining woman.

When my eyes finally land on her, they soak in the sight of her, famished beyond reason. Goddamn she is beautiful. Radiant. The essence of beauty. Pain slices through my chest as I watch her. The suffering is so excruciating that it causes my eyes to water.

"I can't take this shit any longer. She broke. Oh well. So did I, dammit." I dart from my chair and stalk from the conference room headed on a one way track to 'fuck it all' and 'damn the consequences' when that son of a bitch, Jude goddamn Preston, steps from my periphery and stands directly between me and my angel. And it pisses me off.

I can't do this anymore. I'm done. Finished. She's mine. Period.

It feels like I run smack into a glass wall that someone Windexed the hell out of when he leans down and she greedily accepts his kiss.

NO. NO. NO. NO. NO. NO. NO. NO. NO. What the hell is going on?

My feet are cemented to the floor.

I shake my head trying to clear these... these delusions. Please God, let them be caused by my mind playing tricks on me. Please.

A red mist floods my vision as I watch my woman in the arms of another man. She is MINE.

Stell's smiling up at him like... Shit, like she smiles up at me— or used to smile up at me!

Hell no! No. I'm Wesley fucking Jacobs. If I say it's mine, then it's mine! And that damn smile, that damn woman *–is mine!*

I storm toward them my fury like a tornado and ram my shoulder against into Jude's hard enough to cause him to back-peddle several steps to keep from busting his ass. Immediately my hand circles Stella's arm yanking her toward my office. I growl over my shoulder at Barby, "No one. And I mean *NO ONE* is to disturb us, is that understood?"

Her eyes are as wide as saucers as she nods her head.

I slam the door to my office locking it before spinning around and glaring at her. I watch her ease slowly further and further away.

"I do not know what in the *HELL* you think you're doing, but *IT STOPS NOW!*" I roar advancing towards her with my pointer finger stabbing the air with each word. "Are you fucking him? Is that what's going on? That weaseling author that has been chasing after you since day one." I'm towering over her tiny frame as I stare into her terrified face. I grab her chin harshly, my fingertips biting into her pale flesh. "*YOU'RE SUPPOSED TO BE FIXING YOURSELF! HELPING YOURSELF! YOU'RE SUPPOSED TO BE REALIZING THAT SUBMISSION IS THE KEY TO STOPPING YOUR NIGHTMARES! NOT OFF FUCKING VANILLAS!*"

I release her face and step away from her to keep myself from

174

bending her over my desk and tearing the skin off her ass. I shove my hands through my hair as I begin to pace the length of my office.

"How am I supposed to come to the conclusion or understand that my submitting to you will stop these nightmares that plague me *EVERY* damn night since *YOU* shut me out, *WHEN I DON'T HAVE MY DOM TO SUBMIT TOO?* Huh? *HOW, WESLEY?!?!*"

"How? What?!" I stop pacing and stare at her in confusion.

No - wait. Why does her argument stack against mine with the same amount of weight? Is it my need to have her tipping the scales? Am I allowing my mind to rationalize something irrational just to selfishly gain what I want - what I've been starving for?

She pulls her shoulders back, standing taller before speaking, "If my submission is essential then how, Wesley, will I ever figure it out without my Dom? A submissive isn't a submissive without her Dom there to demand she submit."

What the hell am I fighting for? I can't even remember the rationalization behind my argument. All I can manage to do is stare blankly at her and blink, trying to remember why the fuck I thought leaving my sub was the correct thing to do as a Dom.

SAFE WORD.

"You safe worded out, Stella! You might as well have cut me off at the knees, not because you used your safe word, but because you used it when you were panicked. You took your trust from me when you read too much into my question. Instead of relying on me, trusting me enough to realize I would not ask a question with intentions of trapping you. What you did, Stella, was total bullshit! You used your safe word to dominate *me!* Do you not understand that?"

Yeah! There it is! I knew I had a point, dammit!

I watch her face as my words settle between us. Confusion, denial, anger, defeat, resignation, shame, all flash across her features. When her eyes slowly rise and meet mine, all I see in them is cold determination.

In a tone as icy as her mask, she replies, "I understand now. But before you explained it to me?" She shakes her head, "No, I didn't. I'm entirely too new to this lifestyle to even grasp concepts at that level. You are the only man I've been with consensually. You are also the only man I have ever handed my total and complete trust over to. The only man I've willingly submitted to. The only man I've freely allowed to Dominate me. As my first teacher, Wesley... *you* let me down. How can the student let you down? *HOW!?* The *TEACHER*, the *DOM*, left *HIS* student, *HIS* sub behind to flounder without explanation? Explain *THAT* fucking riddle and we can try this conversation again!"

She shoves past me and slams out of my office.

"Because! You..." I close my mouth. Whatever I say, she'll just find a way to twist it up and use it against me.

Well, that and she's already gone, so she can't hear me.

Jesus. Christ. What the hell have I done?

Her words batter around in my chest and my mind.

There is no way I can effectively refute her argument.

I left my angel, and I let her down.

Chapter 30

No Choice

I don't even know where to begin with that five billion piece jigsaw puzzle of loop holes-finger pointing-rigmarole he just tossed in my lap! The hell? I cut him off at the knees? No motherfucker, you cut yourself off at the knees by cutting me out!

He has to be high. That is the only damn explanation I can honestly swallow. Anything less is an excuse he made up in his mind because he got scared and didn't have the balls to tap out while looking me in my face.

"Holy mother of God! The father of my child does drugs. Either that, or he's lost his damn mind." I declare out loud staring at a wall in my living room.

"Oh! Stell, come on! He is not a druggie and he hasn't lost his sanity either. He did what he, stupidly, thought was the right thing to do. Should he have talked to you first? Hell, yes! You want to know why he didn't? Because. He's never been in a relationship that lasted longer than twelve damn hours." Trina flops down beside me on the couch.

"Are you taking his side? Seriously, T?" I narrow my eyes on hers.

"I'm just being the voice of reason, bitch. Take it or leave it."

"Whatever. I hate you. I mean I love you, but I really hate you for drinking in front of me. A sip would not hurt the baby. I'm just saying." I reach for her glass but she's much faster than me. Doesn't even spill a drop that I could suck up.

"No, probably not. But a sip... Will only piss you off, sister. You forget. You can't bullshit me. I know you better than you know yourself, girl."

"Pssh... Whatever. I'm going to take a damn shower."

After I walk into the bathroom and start stripping, I glance in the mirror before stepping into the shower; but I'm frozen still when I see my reflection.

"Oh my GOD!!!!" In my boy shorts and sports bra alone I haul ass into the living room, screaming, "Trina! You said I had months before I started to show! I look six months pregnant, not three!"

I round the corner and yelp, "Oh shit!" When I find Bo, Eve, *and* Jude all standing by the front door. I quickly make eye contact with Trina and beg her wide, blinking eyes with mine in vain.

Please tell me they didn't hear that, sissy. Please! She knows me too fucking well, she nods.

SHIT!

Clears throat You see, the thing is, after my friendly 'Hey! You're pregnant!' doctor visit with Dr. Thomas, I immediately informed Trina, Bo, and Eve of my, ahem, 'diagnosis'. It was over my homemade chicken parmesan, and it was... Yeah, my chicken parm did nothing to soften the blow. They were just as shocked and horrified as me.

Now... I also sort of kept seeing Jude. Not anything serious, just... you know, we went on a few dates. *Shrugs* He may have taken it a little more seriously than I did. So, sue me.

Smiling as brightly and insanely as the woman on the 'Black Hole Sun' music video, I say, "Hey! Everyone! Wow. This is... Wow. Exciting, huh?" I look back over at Trina and her and Eve are just shaking their heads. "Okay. So, I don't feel so swell. Just... I need to hide - I mean shower! I need to shower." I spin on my heel and carry my ass back to the bathroom as quickly as I can.

Of course - Of course! - Jude reaches me before I can get the bathroom door shut and locked.

He shoves his way into the bathroom effortlessly despite my attempts at shoving the door closed on his face. It was his black boot shoved between the door and the door jam. Damn boot; can't move those damn things...works every time.

The torment on his face affects me like a slap across my face, I stumble back, gasping under the hand I have covering my mouth. I've never seen him look anything but cocky, flirty, and confident. Stark anguish stares back at me.

"Why? Why him? Why not me, babe?" His desperate whisper tears at my heart.

"Jude, it's always been him. I never promised you anything other than a Saturday night here or a lunch date there. Please... Don't make this harder than it already is. You're a great guy. I'm nothing. I promise. Nothing. If you knew even a fraction of how fucked up I am, you would run so damn fast away from me." I laugh at myself but it sounds as empty as it feels.

He shakes his head, his steel blue eyes never leaving mine. "I do know you. So much—" He cuts himself off and looks down. "You had a choice, babe; and I really wish you would've chosen different. Why do you always make things harder for yourself?"

His question confuses me until I remember the topic. The baby. He wants me to get rid of the baby. My hands slide protectively over my small baby bump.

"No." I shake my head. "That's where you're wrong, Jude. I've never had a choice. Not once in my whole life have I ever had a choice. You don't know a damn thing about me. If you did, then you'd know that with Wesley, I never stood a chance in hell against him." I open the bathroom door. "And I for damn sure never had a choice. Goodbye, Jude."

He nods and turns... And then he leaves.

179

Chapter 31

Red & White

Monster

Looking back on the decisions I made throughout the course of my life; all were what I - even now - consider accurate decisions reflecting that period of my life. I can easily look at each individual decision and justify every one.

Except for the one most important decision I ever had to make: When I set my Beauty up to fall, I did so based wholly on my need for revenge. She deceived me, made me fall in love with her, I placed her on a pedestal so high, she mattered more to me than even I mattered to myself. And, in the end, I allowed my hate and my love for her to decide her fate. Not rational thought.

So when I found her in the girls bathroom surrounded and covered in the very substance I craved in return for the redemption she owed me - the sharp contrast of her translucent pale skin against her dark congealed red blood caused euphoria to hum through me. Pure elation, so unlike anything I'd ever felt before, made me feel as though I was soaring. I leapt to my feet shouting out joyfully only to realize seconds later how fleeting that happiness turned out to be.

I shoved her back with my boot. When it didn't revive my joy, I spat on her before jumping and landing on her back with both feet. I jumped on her like a trampoline for several seconds before hopping off, shouting, "It's all your fault. You asked for this! You deserved this! Fucking wake up and look at me! Where are those eyes of every color at now, huh?! You tainted your pureness by allowing *that man* to fuck you. I'm only doing you justice, Beauty, I'm only staining your skin the color of pure driven snow with the blood of your trespasses! Do you see me now?!"

Her labored wheezing gasps of breath coming only once every thirty seconds registered with my anatomy and physiology knowledge, instantly spurring me into action.

I grabbed the first girl I saw standing outside the bathroom, "My sister! She went in there, I think she was bleeding. Please! Go help her." She nodded before scurrying inside. As soon as the door closed behind her, I ran as fast as I could, slamming into the school office out of breath. It took me a moment to stutter the words out. "A-A girl, she came from the bathroom s-s-screaming someone was dead. I-I came as fast as I could! She said..." I pretended to shiver, "...S-She said there was blood everywhere. I-I think she tripped on her."

Moments later, I sat perched atop the school watching as paramedics attempted to resuscitate my Beauty in vain. It was only when I witnessed the man covered in a sheen of sweat who was in charge of chest compressions step back and shake his head as they loaded her on a gurney into the ambulance, that I realized how wrong of me it was to make a decision based on my emotions.

Tears streamed down my face as I sat watching my Beauty be carried away, ironically in a vessel flashing lights of red and white.

Chapter 32

Investigation

WESLEY

I'm glad this shit fuck week is finally over. On the other hand, I'm pissed as hell another week has come and gone and I'm still left with no answers and no Stella.

Finally! Derrick has new information!

I grab at the pages, yanking them from the damn fax machine before they can print the page number at the bottom.

Who the fuck needs page numbers?! WHO?

After I lay all eight pages out on my desk and assemble them in what I'm pretty sure is the correct order, I sink into my chair. A Fresh bottle of scotch as my only companion—I pour my first tumbler full, swallow a huge gulp and let my eyes fall to the collection of pages in front of me... And I know without a shadow of doubt they are about to fuck me up.

Stella Jolie Reese

DOB June 10 1988

Female

Caucasian

Height: 5'7

Last documented weight: 134 lbs

Hair color: Brown

Eye Color: Hazel

Marital Status: Single

Mother: Unknown

Father: Fredrick Reese- found murdered 1/4/96 at 31 yo age. Police files indicate seven yo daughter (Stella Reese) was the only witness. All evidence concludes to the child committing the homicide in an effort to evade her father's sexual abuse—Child has no recollection of the events which occurred and refuses to answer questions related to possible shock. Charges were never filed and child was placed in therapy. CPS placed child in the foster care system where she was placed in a foster home.

Fred Reese- Sole guardian and named on birth certificate as biological father.

Wes, I looked over the notes from the first investigation. I'll try to keep these notes as a side by side

After the occurrence resulting in the patient, Stella J. Reese, being admitted to ER via EMS in 1997, Pine Bluff DA was interrogated by State of LA resulting in the reinstatement of case number 102.561, The State of Louisiana vs. Reese—Manslaughter 1st degree (Minor stipulations prevented charges being filed.)

The collaborative investigation between PBPD and the State of LA remained an ongoing investigation until autopsy reports of the exhumed body returned with nothing but circumstantial evidence.

However, during a meeting between State of LA and neighbors,

—After doing some digging and calling in some favors I was able to pull some strings and rec'd the following

four of the initial nine now recalled seeing a navy Ford Bronco in the Reese's driveway. No one recalls seeing the vehicle there before or after the date 1/4/96. No one recalls seeing the person driving the vehicle.

The case is re filed Unsolved/Cold Case due to lack of evidence.

FOSTER HOMES w/ Listing of ALL members living at residence the same time as Stella Reese:

Pine Bluff, LA

(1996-97)

Mr. & Mrs. Sims

Blake and Jenny Sims, married in 1988, no children of their own, began foster care program in 1994.

The Sims residence was a four bedroom three bath ranch style home in the Prairies Estates neighborhood.

At the time Stella Reese was placed in this foster home, there were two other children living there since 1994.

     1) Jeffery Pierce
Male; Caucasian
DOB: 9/10/86
Hair/Eye Color: Blond/Blue
Parents died 12/24/93 in Motor Vehicle Accident or MVA caused by a drunk driver swerving into opposite lane and hitting the Pierce vehicle at an estimated speed of 55 mph head on. When officers arrived at the scene there were no survivors.
Jeffery Pierce was taken by the state and placed in the LA foster care program in 1994. He was the first child fostered by Mr. & Mrs. Sims.
Initial Psych evaluation by the state of LA found the patient's mental evaluation WNL (Within Normal Limits) related to his developmental stage.
    Annual follow up evaluations:
1995: Patient diagnosed with depression and speech impediment. Therapy with a parish counselor and speech therapist was initiated for weekly sessions. State of LA will continue to monitor patient's progress and work closely with counselor and speech therapist. Follow up in one year.
1996: After six months of weekly therapy sessions, the counselor's six month evaluation showed dramatic progress and little to no depression symptoms noted. Therapy continued for six months. Patient's Psych evaluations by the state of LA were found Within Normal Limits related to his developmental stage. Speech therapy continues.
From 1997-2002 Psych evaluations by the state of LA were WNL (Within Normal Limits) r/t his developmental stage.

Child was removed from Mr. & Mrs. Sims foster care after an incident with another child, Stella Reese, which resulted in the foster parents being removed from the program. When the child was questioned about the incident he stated, "I never knew nothing like that. I never seen it. Hey, can I have a coke?"

    2) Preston Stone

Male; Caucasian

DOB: 6/29/86

Hair/Eye Color: Brown/Blue

Preston's file goes back to '88 when authorities were called to an armed home invasion. Four adult residents were found shot point blank to the chest. The fifth adult resident was found in the hallway grasping a telephone with four gunshot wounds to the back. 911 dispatcher was still on the line found in victim's hand. The only survivor was eighteen month old Preston Stone found in a back room.

Child was placed in the foster care system. In 1995, he was moved to the Sims foster care home related to his previous foster care provider being deceased. Cause of death was ruled positional asphyxiation during sleep.

Initial Psych evaluation by the state of LA in 1988 states mental and emotional state were WNL (Within Normal Limits) r/t his developmental stage.

Psych evaluation by the state of LA from 1989-1997: Other than continuing speech therapy for ongoing Selective Mutisim being displayed by patient, all evals were found WNL (Within Normal Limits) r/t his developmental stage.

Child was removed from Mr. & Mrs. Sims foster care after an incident with another child, Stella Reese, resulted in the foster parents being removed from the program. When child was questioned after incident he was unable to verbally answer related to his diagnosis by state psychiatrist and speech therapist of selective mutisim. When child was questioned using written questions, all answers were consistent with Jeffery Pierce's leading investigators to the belief neither male children were targeted by Blake Sims sexual assault.

Psych evaluation by the state of LA 1998: ***Patient's mood, thoughts, and behavior are highly unusual and disorganized compared to previous psych evals. Patient Therapy with a parish counselor initiated for weekly sessions. State of LA will continue to monitor patient's progress and work closely with counselor. Follow up in one year.

Psych evaluation by the state of LA 1999-2003: All Psych evaluations by the state of LA were WNL (Within Normal Limits) ***Except in 2000: There has been a change in mood or behavior noted during Psych evaluation by the state of the patients selective mutisim was finally resolved with speech therapy.

Alexandria, LA

(1997-1999)
Mr. & Mrs. Temple

Jonathan and Ella Temple, married in 1980, no children of their own, began with foster care program in 1985.

There were no other children in this foster home while Stella J. Reese was under their care.

Ruston, LA
(1999)
Mr. & Mrs. George Long

George and Marcia Long, married in 1993, one biological child (daughter *See note), began with foster program in 1998.

The Long residence was a three bedroom two bath home in the King's Terrace neighborhood.

Chelsea Long

Female; Caucasian

DOB: 11/19/95

Chelsea was evaluated prior to parents acceptance in LA Foster Care Program;

Psych evaluation by the state of LA in 1998; Mental and emotional state were WNL (Within Normal Limits) r/t her developmental stage.
After the removal of Stella J. Reese from Long residence, Chelsea Long had a Psych evaluation by the state of LA in 1999: Mental and emotional state were WNL (Within Normal Limits) r/t her developmental stage. When child was questioned with parents consent by Social Services Counselor she stated, "Nope, love mommy and daddy."

**After Stella Reese received extensive psych evaluations performed by the state it was ruled the mental breakdown caused by PTSD displayed during the therapy session in 1999 was related to the child's previous documented molestation, sexual abuse and/or rape.

Shreveport, LA
(2000-2001)

Mr. & Mrs. Smith
Joseph and Elizabeth Smith, married in 1988, one biological child (daughter *See note), began with foster program in 1988.

186

The Smith residence was a five bedroom three bath home in the Broadmoor neighborhood.

Jessica Smith

Female; Caucasian

DOB: 1/9/87

Jessica was evaluated after parents were accepted in LA Foster Care Program;

Psych evaluation by the state of LA in 1990; Mental and emotional state were WNL (Within Normal Limits) r/t her developmental stage.
At the time Stella Reese was placed in this foster home, there were two other foster children living there.

1) Michael Jones
Male; African American
DOB: 2/6/86
Hair/Eye Color: Black/Brown
Child's only living relative, his maternal grandmother died in 1998 r/t Cardiac arrest.
Michael Jones was taken by the state and placed in the foster care program with Mr. and Mrs. Smith in 1998.

Initial Psych evaluation in 1998 by the state of LA were found WNL (Within Normal Limits) r/t his developmental stage.
Annual follow up evaluations:
From 1999-2004 Psych evaluations by the state of LA were WNL (Within Normal Limits) r/t his developmental stage.
2) Sam Smith
Male; Caucasian
DOB: 2/6/83
Hair/Eye Color: Blond/Brown
His family members were fatalities in a house fire in July 1983, which occurred while the infant was hospitalized for pneumonia. The child had no living relatives. At the time of discharge, infant was placed in LA Foster Care Program. In 1988, he was placed in the foster care of Mr. and Mrs. Smith. The Smith's filed for adoption in 1989 and was granted custody by the state of LA.

Initial Psych evaluation in 1988 by the state of LA were found WNL r/t his developmental stage.
Annual follow up evaluations:
From 1988-2001 Psych evaluations by the state of LA were WNL (Within Normal Limits) r/t his developmental stage.

187

I'll continue investigating her whereabouts between 2001-2004, however from everything I found during the first investigation I don't think I'm going to find any other legal or medical documents. I'll keep digging. Just don't get your hopes up.

After rereading the files over and over and looking back at the initial files that I've read so many times I have it memorized, I begin feeling as though I'm getting closer to an answer. An answer to what? Hell if I know. I also don't really know where to start. So with nothing else to go on, I start with the first foster home and scour the internet searching for *ANYTHING* on the people that lived in those foster homes with Stella.

It's almost four am when I literally cannot keep my eyes open anymore. I make my way into my bedroom and crash face first into bed where I promptly pass the hell out.

Chapter 33

Beauty & I

Monster

I spent the rest of my childhood, teenage years, and young adulthood attempting to conform to society's expectations of me. With my vast knowledge, and my already stellar achievements in all of my classes, moving through high school successfully in less than two years was an effortless feat. I paid no attention to the other students, and my grades alone kept whomever I lived with - I didn't even pay attention to names any longer - happy and content enough for me to be left alone with my thoughts and study's.

When I graduated college at the young age of twenty with honors, no one was in the audience applauding as I accepted my Master's degree in Physics. And I was extremely relieved that I'd finally cut out every person to ever try to pretend they cared for me.

When I looked around at my life and had no idea what or where to go next, I went back to school; ready to master another subject.

It gave me direction. Without it, I was adrift. And being adrift, for me, is unacceptable.

Over the next ten years of my life I traveled following whichever collage offered my next conquest and mastered most degree programs offered by the numerous colleges I'd attended.

One day, out of the blue, I was no longer adrift. The urge to write consumed me. I locked myself inside my New Jersey studio apartment, and began to write. Finally, after almost twenty years, every single word, every phrase and assemblage of words I'd yearned to express and illustrate the depth of emotions my Beauty evoked - poured out, story after story.

I found after I had written several books, it did not suffice. I needed more. I needed affirmation from the masses that my reactions to Beauty's betrayal was errorless, despite what the demons within insistently sneered.

I was without insight on how to get my stories to the masses, so I revisited my old stomping grounds, city parks—with nothing more than a handful of my story's I'd printed, bound, and covered at the Kinko's across the street from my apartment.

I found it took more effort than anything else I'd ever attempted, however after studying the people in the city's parks and the interactions between them, I was able to adapt... I found myself for the time ever socializing; knowing this was a necessary evil to reach the goal that was my new main focus.

I interacted with people of every race, gender, and walk of life. All the while, selling my books. Sometimes as little as five a day, some days as many as fifty. I sold my books during the day, and wrote the story, our story... The story of Beauty and I.

It took me over a year and a half to finish our story. I had accumulated a few people I trusted enough, who loved almost to the point of worshipping my stories so much, that while I manically wrote mine and Beauty's story, they would sell my books on the corners and at the parks when I was unable to extricate myself from writing.

And one night that had turned to early morning, I finished. I closed the manuscript and wrote in my calligraphy trained hand across the cover the only title this story could ever truly be entitled:

Twisted Obsession

By

Jude Preston

Chapter 34

A Soul Becomes Sand

Stella

After I found Jude's note he left on my dresser while I showered, I settled into a night of restless sleep, tossing and turning as thought after thought assailed my conscious mind. "Such an asshole!" Every time my eyes closed last night, I saw his note.

If you don't tell him soon,

I will.

-Jude

Now I lie in bed staring at the ceiling fan as the blades endlessly circle, chasing the blade ahead. And I conclude that on this day - Sunday, April 20th - I will inform Wesley Jacobs of his upcoming fatherhood.

And then, I will assure him that this too will not destroy me - that I am more than willing to fight this battle alone, just as I have fought every battle before.

I shower, shave, and dress to the motherfucking nines. In my black strapless linen dress with an empire waist which hangs almost to the floor, I step into my six inch nude with black pin stripe heels before grabbing and shoving the sticks (there were twelve) that I pissed on after my visit to Dr. Thomas, inside my purse.

I walk into the living room and see Trina and Eve sipping coffee on the couch. Trina's eyes almost bulge from their sockets. Eve's? Eve's fill with tears. "Good morning!" I smile brightly. "I can tell from your expressions and tears of joy that what I have on my agenda for this morning, is obvious. Oh! For Christ's sake! You both knew this shit, I mean this day was coming. I look six months fucking pregnant, the cat's already out of the bag with Jude, and Wes... Well," I sigh, "I guess we'll see about Wes." Smiling through a shrug, I finish, "If I come home, I will be a crying hot mess in dire need of copious amounts of alcohol. With no possibility of supplying said dire need. If I don't, then *YAY!!!!*"

I clap my hands together with an excited look on my face trying to get my sisters to be a little more enthusiastic. My attempt is, as always... an epic fail.

Trina sets her coffee cup on the table before walking over to me and wrapping her arms around my neck. Hugging me tightly, she whispers in my ear, "I love you, Stella. I know this is going to feel like you're walking into the dredges of hell, sister. And I promise, if it were possible I would give anything to do it for you."

I steel my spine and pat her back, still hugging her and say, "T, it's what I do, it's what I've always done. And just like every walk through hell I've endured alone before this one, I'll come out in the end. That which doesn't kill me, only makes me stronger, sis." I kiss her cheek and step back.

When Eve comes running at me, all of her fine blond hair flying behind her, she wraps her thin arms around my neck and just falls to pieces, crying. "Shh...Evey, I'll be fine, honey. Come on. Look at me." I pull back, smiling at her while looking into her light blue eyes, "Don't cry for me, babe. Please?"

Through her sniffles, she sputters out, "If I-I don't, then w-who will?"

"Huh, never thought of it that way. Okay, I concede, cry your eyes out, sis." I smile mischievously at her, "However, if I'm not home by four pm, you and T better be having a cocktail, because I will be getting righteously fucked by, quite possibly, the most beautiful cock in the whole state of New York."

She smiles, blushing and shaking her head, "Of course you do." She looks at Trina, "Of course she does."

I slip my purse strap over my shoulder and turn to leave. When I get to the door and open it, I turn around and say before leaving, "Of course I do, if I don't keep shit light and let it roll off my back, this fucking world would've taken me down years ago." I hold up my middle finger and kiss it, flipping them off and blowing them a kiss. "Love you two bitches. Here's to hoping I don't see y'alls' asses later!" I laugh closing the door before making my way from my building... Making my way to my baby daddy's house, to tell him he's my baby daddy.

I wave and smile at the door man on my way into Wesley's building. After I step from the elevator and stare at the door to his penthouse, my nerves assault me, crippling me from moving forward and knocking on his door.

I stand, frozen in place, staring at the dark lines veining their way across the even darker wood. What if we can't figure this out? He said no forevers. My hands slide over my baby bump as tears fill my eyes. Everything about my new little peanut spells out forever. Baby and forever is universally known as... Forever. What if he doesn't want our baby?

I can literally feel my resolve steel. Determination courses its way through me. Conviction solidifies around my soul. My shoulders pull back, my head held high, I step forward and knock seven bold times.

After a minute of no answer, I scoop the keys from my purse and unlock his front door before walking inside. Each click of my heels sounding across the hardwood floor as I make my way through the living room ricochets with the same determination that continues pushing me forward.

The entire penthouse is cloaked in darkness, there are scotch bottles lined up on his glass coffee table. When I walk into the

194

kitchen, I see more evidence of a Wesley Jacobs bender.

Well, this should be fun.

I grab a garbage bag from the pantry and make my way through the kitchen tossing bottles into the trash bag. Once I'm in the living room I collect those bottles as well then straighten the cushions on the couch and chairs. On my way to the storage room on the opposite side of the penthouse, I round the corner and come face to face with his office.

Seriously? "Jesus, Wesley. How much fucking scotch can one man consume?" I sigh making my way into his office and head towards his desk. When I reach over to grab the two bottles my eyes snag on my name, my name written and typed over and over, paragraph after paragraph on what looks like records, or something. I toss the bottles of scotch into the garbage bag before picking up the piece of paper and scanning over it.

Over six broken bones noted via X-ray which appeared to go untreated. (See below):

Both clavicles, mandible, maxilla, left femur, right humerus.

The nurses notes also state there were multiple abrasions, lacerations and contusions. Some of which appeared to be recent as well as healing injuries.

Also documented and photographed: Numerous bite marks covering the patient from neck to knees, most of which where located on the patients anterior thighs, genitalia and rectum.

The bottles crash, shattering as the plastic ties slip from my fingers. I snatch the file from his desk, my eyes skimming the words as the memories strike, stripping the old scarred flesh from my soul.

Patient was brought into ER via EMS on a stretcher after students found patient (9 yo Stella Reese) in the bathroom of the school unconscious with copious amounts of blood around the patient. Upon assessment, after removing tampon and several pads, 4th degree vaginal and rectal lacerations were noted consistent with extremely severe sexual abuse.

"Why?" I choke out frantically flipping through the pages. "Why?" My whimpered question cuts through his silent office.

Stella Reese's whereabouts remained unknown from July 4th 2001 until January 3rd 2004.
In 2004, 16 yo Stella Reese was found living in an abandoned home on Texas Street.
Documentation states 16 yo Stella Reese admitted to living in both the abandoned home as well as sleeping some nights in her high school library she'd been attending without knowledge of the State of Louisiana.
CPS filed for a warrant to retrieve the following medical files:
July 5, 2001- Time: 0018:
911 phone call:
"Hey there's some chick passed out by Cross Lake." —
background unknown female voice—"Steve she isn't breathing! Tell them she's not fuckin' breathing!"
Male caller: "Umm... my girl says she isn't breathing. I would stay, but I can't be late for my curfew."
911 dispatcher: "Sir, I need you to remain where you are. Do you or your friend know CPR?"
—Phone call ends. July 5, 2001- Time: 0020.
Medical Records/ Doctors dictation notes/ Nurses notes:
Dr. Cole- Dictation notes of patient currently known as Jane Doe (age unknown):
Received patient via EMS to ER 1. Upon admission patient status is unstable with a weak and thready pulse noted. EMS documentation states that patient was resuscitated via CPR and defibrillation. After patient stabilized doctor assessment yields asphyxiation as well as first and second degree lacerations noted in and around vagina and rectum consistent with rape and/or sexual abuse. Lacerations were sutured using a 2.0 chromic suture times 2. Patient remains stable. Will continue to monitor. (Patient signed out Against Medical Advice less than nineteen hours after admission.) Prior to patient signing out AMA patient refused rape kit.
Patient's printed name and signature: <u>Stella Reese</u>

<u>*Stella Reese*</u>

My hands fist around the pages as tears stream down my face. I spin to leave his office, headed straight for his room knowing there is only one place a man that consumes that much scotch could be. I trip, staggering through the hallways, as savage pain brutally shreds its way through my heart; twisting and tightening, slicing it in two. Uncontainable sobs hiccup from my throat as I reach the double mahogany doors leading to the master suite.

With both fists clenched around the papers in my hands I shove both doors open before crashing into his room as insanity blankets my rational thought screaming, *"OF EVERY FUCKING MAN TO EVER FUCKING DESTROY ME, YOU'RE THE ONE I WON'T LIVE THROUGH! YOU FUCKING KNEW ALL ALONG YOU MOTHERFUCKER!"*

When my teary eyes adjust to the darkness in the room and my blurry vision clears, what I witness shoves my fractured sanity and scatters the sand that remains of my soul leaving absolutely nothing of me in its wake.

Chapter 35

Stella

WESLEY

I roll over looking at the clock on my nightstand. Holy shit! It's past noon! After I jump from bed and land beneath the hot pelting water spraying from seventy five showerheads, it dawns on me that it's Saturday. And I have nothing planned today, only my continuing efforts to pin the ghost of Stell's past down. Which is good, because I don't have the energy to shave.

After my shower I dress in khakis shorts and a V-neck black t-shirt, make a cup of coffee, and head to my office.

I sit behind my desk and with fresh eyes begin reading over the files and my scribbling notes down on Blake and Jenny Sims, i.e. Foster fucks number one.

More than two hours go by and I have yet to find anything on Blake and Jenny Sims online that I don't already have in my file. I glance up at the clock and see it's almost three thirty. Ehh... Scotch right now would be considered day drinking.

As I jot down Jeffery Pierce's name when the hair on the back of my neck stands on end I quickly type the kid's name, pulling up his information online and sink back into my chair reading the articles one by one.

Foreboding crawls up my spine, causing me to sit up straighter with every article I read. This motherfucker was seriously a fucked up kid. . The information I am reading online, in no way reflects the same kid in Derrick's files.

Every muscle in my body is strung tight. My alarms are so high it causes me to jump when the phone on my desk rings.

"Shit!" I shake the tension off before answering the phone, "Wesley speaking."

"Hey, what's up man, it's Jude." I glance at the clock. Fuck it. It's past five o'clock, I abstained as much as I care to.

"What's up, Jude?" My voice is as bland as the empty tumbler in my hand, at least until I fill it to the rim with Johnny Walker.

"Look, I don't really know how to say this other than just coming out and saying it. I like Stella, a lot, more than I should. Until yesterday I honestly thought you were just her boss. A boss she had a crush on, but still just her boss. I don't know what yesterday was all about, but honestly, I don't feel comfortable with an intern being behind my writing career. Yesterday cleared my cock from the equation when I saw your reaction to us being together, now, I have absolutely no problem conceding, you're obviously the better man suited for Stella. However, I can't— I refuse to settle for Stella parading around acting as my publisher Wes, I want you, man. You're the reason I came to Jacobs, I'm sorry my cock lead me astray momentarily, but fortunately," He chuckles, "My rational thought has returned."

I sit silently as his words roll around until they settle. "What exactly do you want from me, Jude? Stella may be 'parading' around as your publisher, but she's still getting her work done, the proof sits directly on top of your award for being a NY best seller. What is there left for me to do?"

"I know she did. She rocked 'Twisted'; but what I have in the works for my next project, man, it's going to kill, totally annihilate 'Twisted Obsession'. Hey! You got plans tonight?" I look at all my written notes scattered around my desk, drain my scotch and head to the corner bar to make another.

"Not really, just some personal shit I'm working on. Why?" I walk back to my desk eyeing one empty bottle while opening a new one and pouring my second drink.

"What time is it? Oh, almost six. Okay, meet me at Molly's, the pub on 3rd Ave near 22nd Street. I'll bring my manuscript's outline,

199

let's say...nine-ish? Is that cool?"

I sip my scotch while looking at the clock. That gives me at least two more hours to research this little fucker, Jeffery Pierce. Scrubbing my hand down my face sighing, I say, "Sure. Nine it is. But I'm not staying long, I'm stuck up to my asshole in personal shit that I need to get figured out. Understood?"

"Absolutely, man. Alright, I'll see ya then." The phone clicks dead.

I return to my research and my scotch.

I hate this encompassing premonition that something in Stella's past - in these files - is, has, or will damage what's left of my little angel that fights. But what I hate more is that I've allowed it to constantly come between us.

But fucking hell, if she ever knew, I'd lose her. For-fucking-ever. I would lose my angel. And I will never allow that.

So until I find whatever it is provoking me to search, or until I've exhausted every fucking lead, name and avenue, I will continue to keep myself from the only woman I have ever truly, fiercely, and unconditionally loved.

"This is good, man," I tell my driver as the car slows and I spot Molly's. "I shouldn't be more than an hour, two tops. Go grab a bite to eat." I step from the car and head into the pub.

Once I spot Jude, I nod and head in his direction at a small table all the way at the back of the bar and away from the crowd. "What the fuck you hiding by the backdoor for, Jude?" I ask sinking into the leather seat.

He looks at me like I've lost my mind before sliding a drink in front of me. "Johnny Walker, right?"

I nod accepting the drink. "Thanks, man."

"Yep, anytime." After taking a swig from his beer, he says,

"Why the fuck am I strategically sitting away from everyone? Really?" He slides a piece of paper across the gnarled tabletop, "Umm... Because I don't think the other patrons would understand or be able to stomach the shit we're about to discuss. Holding women captive as slaves, rape, sodomy and flaying their skin from their bones is generally frowned upon, buddy."

I glance down at his outline, scanning over it before nodding and look back up at him. Keeping my eyes locked on his, I chug my drink and set it back on the table. "This shit's good." I say looking back down to read it more carefully.

"Fuck. That shit's better than good, and you goddamn well know it. I need another beer, you alright?" He asks standing.

Without taking my eyes off the outline, I raise my glass. "Here, tell the bartender to start me a tab."

"It's alright, man. I got it."

Son. Of. A. Bitch! This is going to give CJ Roberts a fucking run for her money! The dual POV of the contrasting characters. Wow. What the fuck? This man is a goddamn genius! With the mind of a motherfucker straight from an asylum! SHIT! I want—no, I need to read 'Twisted Obsession'. I had no idea the kid had it in him.

"Here you go, man." He slides the drink to me. When I look up, the room tilts for a second before instantly righting itself.

Shit, I haven't eaten anything today. I grab my scotch and chug it back before telling Jude, "Honestly, when I handed your manuscript to Stell, I only fucking did it because yours was at the top of the stack, man. However, you and I both know that woman knows her goddamn shit. I haven't read 'Twisted', but I can say that her un-jaded enthusiasm over your work was - in the long run - a gift. To you and your first published work." He smiles setting another Johnny Walker in front of me like a damn magician. "Thanks. Now," I go to tap the paper with my pointer finger landing a solid foot away from it. "This shit? I'm all yours, kid." I smirk before sipping my drink.

Jesus. Fucking. Christ.

My fingers sink into my angels hair, fist and haul her up onto her knees as I continue to pummel her tight little asshole with my cock. "Whose ass is this, Ms. Reese?" I growl around my fat tongue.

"Yours, it's yours, daddy." I shove her face back into the mattress, trying to fucking shut Rachel's grating voice out of my mind before pulling out and ramming my cock into her pussy.

"I'm not your fucking daddy. Utterstood?" Fuck! What's wrong with me? And what the fuck?! Stell's pussy feels like it's been hammered by a tree stump.

My vision blurs before everything goes black. But not before I fall on top of my angel and pull her body over mine, whispering, "I fucking love you, Stella Jolie Reese. Goddamn it I love you so much."

Then I pass the fuck out.

The sound of Stella screaming, *"OF EVERY FUCKING MAN TO EVER FUCKING DESTROY ME, YOU'RE THE ONE I WON'T LIVE THROUGH! YOU FUCKING KNEW ALL ALONG YOU MOTHERFUCKER!"* Has me instantly bolting up in bed.

When I see my angel that fights face looking back at me in utter devastation, I lose any and all control I've ever held. As Stella runs from my room, the reins of rule slip from my fingertips, running away with her.

"Seriously, Wesley? You gave her a fucking key to your apartment?" Rachel's voice snakes into my ears before her arms slither around my neck.

Chapter 36

Why?

Monster

Oh! Well, Hello.

I'm so delighted to finally be significant enough to attract your attention. I know, the mind does boggle a bit sometimes, does it not? Especially when you're being mercilessly dragged through Beauty's sad and pitiful excuse of a life.

Now, where shall I begin? Oh, yes! Imagine my surprise when my little Sarah - sweet girl, who, however, possessed not a morsel of common sense - called to inform me that a Mr. Wesley Jacobs was willing to set up a meeting...with his intern.

This turn of events lead me and my demons on a sick mind-fuck consisting of hills of vengeance and valleys of retribution, until I learned with whom the meeting with Jacobs Publishing would include.

I had full intentions of walking into that building and telling Stella Reese, while my fingers curled and tightened around her throat, that *she* was my twisted obsession, that *she*, Stella Reese, was Renee, and that *I*, Jude, was John.

Instead, while standing in the elevator waiting for the doors to close a slip of a woman hurried inside. My hand shot out and hit the button for level three - even though I'd already hit the button for the top floor - when my Beauty turned, smiling up at me, with her eyes of every color before saying in awe, "If they ask, we'll say, 'Destino'." Beauty's laugh reverberated through the closed space.

When the doors to the third floor opened, I flew from the compacted confines. I ran, as fast as I could, I ran from the woman that was both my Lord and savior, as well as Satan herself.

Once I collected my wits, I called Sarah. "Look, I know babe, I haven't talked to them. But it's my family, my fucked up family. Just fill in for me at the meeting, if they have any questions, give them my number. I can do a quick conference call."

That night, having pushed myself to the brink, with orchestrated lie after orchestrated lie, I wrapped my knuckles, one in Rachel's hair, and the other shoving, fisting into her cunt. After I'd used and stretched every hole she possessed, I stalked from her apartment, praying she'd freak the fuck out when she awoke and tip the chair I'd barely left under her right foot, causing her to land on nothing but the strings around her neck... Before snapping it in two.

To say I've been waiting for this night is an incredible understatement.

Just like the first time I masterminded Beauty's downfall, I placed a note I knew would spur her into immediate action.

What can I say? I know my Beauty.

The next morning, merely a handful of hours after struggling to toss Wesley's drunken and drugged ass into bed, I sit outside Stella's apartment... Watching.

When I see her step out of her building, she steals my breath away for a moment. I would've let our decades of struggles fly out the window. Except she made the wrong decision. Over and over, she constantly made the wrong decision. And now, she will regretfully, pay...Again.

I follow her to Wes' in a cab behind hers. After I pay my fare, I walk around the corner and unlock the black van I parked here the night before. I double check all my items for the hundredth time. Chloroform snap capsule. Rope. Duct tape. Cable Ties. Thin dish rag. Annie Lennox 'Why'. Knife. Smith & Wesson M&P 9 mm. Let's hope she behaves so I won't have to use the last two too soon.

Thirty minutes later I'm standing in front of Wesley's building with a cup of coffee in each hand.

Thirty seconds after that my Beauty comes descending down the stairs with tears streaming down her face.

She is the goddamn epitome of perfection.

Before her foot steps from the last stair, I toss the coffee into the trash bin I was standing near and my arms are wrapped around her, "Hey, hey... Shh, its okay, its going to be okay."

"Jude! Oh my God, Jude, what..." Her arms slip around my neck and immediately the demons slamming against my rib cage begin screaming at me to hold and protect her. To love her.

Her head is shaking back and forth, her frame convulsing violently. My fingers run down her hair, my lungs inhale her for as long as I can. As long as she doesn't speak, I'll allow myself - my demons - to gently love her. "Shh...it's okay, babe, I'm here."

She tightens her arms around my neck before stepping back. "What are you doing here? I-I—" Her head starts shaking again trying to clear her thoughts, possibly. I really wish she would have kept her mouth shut just a little while longer.

My feet begin moving backward, toward the corner of the building, and with one arm around her waist, I reach the other behind my back, pull the thin dish rag from my pocket. Before turning to walk beside her, I replace the arm circling her waist with the one holding the dish rag - and lead my Beauty to her demise.

"I'm here for an assortment of reasons, an assortment of conflicting reasons." As we round the corner, I slide my arm from her waist to the top of her shoulder, hugging her to me while snapping the capsule and soaking the rag, all while unlocking the van with the key fob in the other hand. "The main reason however..." I move the arm hugging her to me slightly up before clamping my hand over her mouth, effectively covering her face from nose to chin with the chloroform soaked rag. "...Is your unique ability to consistently make the wrong choices. *WHY DO YOU ALWAYS HAVE*

TO MAKE IT SO MUCH HARDER?!" I slam her fighting body against the brick building.

"Do you have any inkling how extraordinary it was to lay beneath your bed listening to your screams and watching the mattress bow while old man Sims ravaged your little nine year old body? Knowing I was the one behind your desecration? Mmmmm...there has never been such sweeter bliss, my Beauty veiled in grotesqueness." Her struggles seem to have weakened during my declaration, but when I loosen my arms to open the backdoor of the van, they recover ten-fold. Her head connects, cracking against my chin.

My hand clamps down harder shoving the soaked rag against her mouth. In less than three seconds, her last surge of adrenaline submits to defeat and, at last, unconsciousness succeeds. After I lay her in the van, I grab the knife and gun and tuck them into my coat pocket. I zip three cable ties each around her wrists and ankles, then zip three more around those, binding her feet and hands behind her back. I wrap duct tape, circling her entire head, covering her mouth before anchoring her to the van with the rope.

I push the cd into the cd player and as 'Why' spills into the van, I pull the gearshift to drive, saying, "This is vengeance, Beauty, in its purest, simplest form. Only this time... You won't make it out alive."

How many times do I have to try to tell you

That I'm sorry for the things I've done...

But when I start to try to tell you

That's when you have to tell me

Hey... this kind of trouble's only just begun...

Chapter 37

That Which Destroys Me

Blood. Blood is everywhere. Soaking my hands, knees. It's everywhere. I'm scared. I'm cold. There are no lights on. It's dark, but I can still see his form silhouetted by the sliver of moon just outside the dirty trailer's window. It's cold. The blood is seeping into my sweatpants. It's everywhere. So are the screams. They are everywhere too. I cover my ears to stop them. But the blood on my hands smears on the sides of my head. When I feel the blood run down my face and neck, my vision blurs from my tears. Why am I crying? I don't like this man. I hate him. I can't remember a time where I didn't hate him. All he does is hurt me. It's all he has ever done, for as long as I can remember.

"Shhh… Angel, I'm here. I'm always here. I'll always be here." I hear Wesley right before I see him. He walks deftly around the cluttered trailer and bloodied floor. When he reaches me, he scoops me up and cradles me in his big warm embrace. "Every time you fall, I'll be there waiting to catch you. And no matter how hopeless things may seem, don't ever give up on me—I am what nourishes. Don't ever let them destroy you, angel. Never. Understood?"

Screams don't wake me, the silence of them do.

My naked body shivers against the cold, wet, gritty floor. I clench my teeth when they begin to chatter. I have to keep quiet. Silent.

When I first woke up in this cold dank cell I screamed. I screamed and clawed at the dirty walls until my nails bent, broke and bloodied; even then, I continued screaming, begging for help, for anyone to help. I curbed my screams when I realized they are what feeds him. Then I silenced my whimpers after I became aware they feed him too.

It's my silence that enrages him. My blank stare.

It's the rust stain that causes my silence, the long rust stain running from the ceiling to the floor I blankly stare at, watching the water slowly trickle down, drip after drop.

When he slashes my skin, splitting the tissue covering my chest, stomach, legs and back, the sounds he makes are tortuous, one would think it was his skin being split. He rages and spits, whales on me with strips of barbed wire and chains furiously…while I silently stare at rust.

He unleashes his frenzied, desperate rage, battering my numb body, spatting my past at me, castigating my actions of the past and present and sneering on and on about my defilement. However, all of it is in vain. My mind fractured when I saw Wesley in bed with Rachel and my body numbed the first moment my skin was flayed.

I'm uncertain what his plans are. If they end in my final death, then I only want to continue assisting in ending his plans as quickly as possible.

Whatever was left of my soul was destroyed when I fell silent. When my screams turned to whimpers, and at last my whimpers turned to silence, that was the sound of my extinction. The sound of Stella Reese ceasing to exist. All that remains now is a void. A vessel. A shell.

Every time I awake from my dreams of screams going silent, I pray that before I fall asleep again, I won't make it. I pray for the end.

Only to wake again and stare silently at the rust stain while he strips my flesh from bone.

Chapter 38

Lost & Owned

WESLEY

"What he fuck are you doing here!?!" I'm flying out the bed buck ass naked and storming around that motherfucker snatching clothes off the floor on my way to the other side. With a handful of clothes in one hand, I drive the other into Rachel's hair, yanking her naked ass off the bed before dragging her through my apartment by nothing but the wad of hair in my fist. Her feet struggle trying to stand, but my pace and the fact that she can't walk backwards fast enough has her falling back onto her ass with every attempt.

Once I get to the front door, I swing it open before throwing her ass out by her hair with every ounce of strength I possess. After her naked body slams into the elevator doors, I toss the handful of clothes at her.

"If I ever see your ugly goddamn face again, bitch, it'll be the last time anyone else ever does!" I slam the door shut, lock it and head into the library where I pour a scotch, slam it back, then repeat.

I sigh grabbing the bottle before sinking into my couch and muttering, "Fuck the glass."

And yes, I'm still stark naked.

Leaning my head back, my eyes trace the intricate detail carved into the molding of the ceiling when suddenly, my mouth starts voicing the thoughts plaguing my mind, "What the fuck have I done? What in the FUCK have I done?"

Okay, I gotta calm the hell down.

Think. Last night -I force my mind to return to the unwanted snippets of last night and flip through trying to piece together what I can.

I was at Molly's with Jude. I read his outline. But, other than remembering it was good, I can't fucking remember anything else!

No! Shit, I was... I WAS with Stella last night. Wait. Wasn't I?

I remember my eyes tracing her spine, the slope of her back. I remember sliding my hand from her ass to her hair. But when my fingers sank into it, it didn't feel fine and silky like Stell's hair, no, it felt dry and course like...Rachel's.

"Oh my fucking God! I did! Shit!" I kept telling myself there had to be an explanation, that somehow, no matter what it looked like, there was a rational reason for why I was in bed with Rachel and neither one of us had on a stitch of clothing! "Oh my FUCK! What have I done?!?!"

You've royally fucked yourself. That's what you've done, you stupid motherfucker!

I sit there trying to understand how I got from Molly's to my place with Rachel for I don't know how long. Long enough for me to polish off the fifth of scotch and talk my drunk ass into getting up and heading towards my office...for more scotch.

Hell yes, I'm sorry, but I fully intend on drinking until I can't feel the agony and torment caused by the look on Stell's face before she rushed out of my life, taking every good thing left of me with her.

Stumbling-slash-staggering my way from the library towards my office, my foot slips on something in the hall. Immediately I throw both arms out gripping the walls on either side to catch myself. Using both hands to brace me, I shake my head trying to clear my thoughts. When I open my eyes, I see trash - wadded up paper on the floor. I snatch them up from the floor and after scanning the first few words, I realize they're from Stell's file. Confusion sinks, weighing even heavier on my drunken mind.

Why would I wad that shit up? And why in the hell would I bring it from my office? It doesn't make any sense. None.

210

The first thing my eyes see are both of Stell's files wide open on my desk with more of the pages wadded up and scattered across the floor.

"The fuck?" I glance at a trash bag lying on the floor in front of my desk with broken scotch bottles spilling out. Then my confusion shifts from bearing weight to a noose tightening around my neck.

I would give almost anything to remember, or understand, what happened last night.

I flatten out the pages using the edge of my desk and start sorting them out. Half of the first file is missing and I honestly don't know how much of the second file is because—Fucking page numbers!

After I piece the second file back together, somewhat like the game Memory, I conclude that I've lost a little less than half of both files combined.

"This is such bullshit! And none of this makes ANY fucking sense!" Fury, confusion, and anguish are tearing through me like a goddamn hurricane. "GAHHHH!!" I leap from my chair causing it to smash into the book shelf behind my desk, sending books, decorative globes and bookends crashing to the floor. I begin assaulting the sheet rock of my office wall, pummeling it with my fists, while splitting the skin covering my knuckles; but I still keep hammering the goddamn wall as rage swells and swells inside, spilling over from my mind and onto my heart. I smash the wall until my fist goes all the way through it.

When I try to yank it back through, I realize my fucking fist is stuck and I yank; once, twice—thankfully on the third yank it, and chunks of sheet rock, come out flying out.

I grab my chair up, setting it right and slump into it. I pull open my desk drawer and grab the half empty fifth, chugging it back until I need a breath. Then I set it on my desk and allow my eyes to scan what's left of Stella's files.

Concentrating on what I'm doing becomes utterly impossible the more I drink; but I can't stop drinking until I forget Stella's face frozen in horror.

So I continue to hit the bottle... Until, finally, I face-plant onto my desk and pass the fuck out.

I'm not sure what time it is when I wake up. I do know it's dark outside. After I've cleaned my office of the trash, sheet rock and shredded, sopping wet files, (I may have knocked a bottle of scotch over) I place a call to the building maintenance manager and explain that my penthouse needs a little tape and float, and possibly some paint.

When I get to my bedroom door, I find more wadded paper littered on the floor from outside my bedroom to just over the threshold... Exactly where Stella stood looking at me like I'd just rammed a blade into her stomach. The memory of the blood draining from her face flips the switch and suddenly the puzzle pieces click into place.

OhmyfuckingGod! *She* found the files. She found the files, then busted into my room to confront me. SHIT! What the fuck did she say? Something about men... Of all the men? Goddammit! What was it?

Her words rush me, each syllable of each word a dagger to my heart. *"Of every fucking man to ever fucking destroy me, you're the one I won't live through! You fucking knew all along you motherfucker!"*

Like a loop, or a scratched vinyl record, playing over and over in my mind, *"You fucking knew all along you motherfucker!"*

That's... I couldn't be more fucked. I lost her. I knew I'd lost her when I saw Rachel in my goddamn bed. Even when I thought there was no way in hell I'd cheat on my angel, there was an explanation. I knew then, I'd lost her. And now, when I can't even lie to myself, now knowing I fucked Rachel, and Stell charged my room knowing I knew about her past all along, only to find me in bed with Rachel?

This is it. This is the end of everything. I've lost my angel.

I've lost everything which ever mattered.

But what I can't stand to bear, what cripples me the most, is as soon as I realize I've lost her forever, I realize that I have always

212

loved her, from the moment she walked into my office for the first time with her head high, her shoulders back, like she owned everything and everyone around her.

And she did. She owned me in that moment, and every moment after.

Chapter 39

Breaking Beauty

Monster

I will kill her.

It's obvious that my Beauty died days ago.

It's obvious that I'm ramming my cock into a woman who has checked out - mentally, physically, and emotionally.

And it infuriates me. Ever since I sat atop our school and watched as the ambulance carried her away, I have dreamed of being not only the reason for her screams but the hand that delivers the agony behind them. The thought alone swelled my cock until it ached. Only now...She won't even scream! Cry! Nothing! "*Fuck!*"

My flaccid cock slips from her.

Tracing the curve of her neck from her chin to the tops of her breasts with my eyes, I wonder, "Do you remember the cover photos you chose for 'Twisted Obsession'? How does it make you feel knowing I've raped you as both now? Knowing I've defiled you as both the epitome of his 'Obsession' as well as the fractured silent woman portraying his 'Twisted Obsession'?"

My fingers slowly wrap around the taped end of barbwire dried in her blood and old pieces of flesh before lashing it across the front of her body causing a new split in her skin from her lips to her cunt. "Knowing I'm the one responsible for carving you into... How did you word it? Oh yes, 'someone in the midst of a silent scream to stop their fracturing sanity. ' I know, it probably would have been more fitting had I used broken stained glass to flay your skin from your bones." I sigh briefly wondering where I might obtain stained glass and glance back down at my hideous Beauty. Disappointment and repulsion flood through me.

"You broke much sooner than I ever gave you credit for, Beauty. I find it difficult to wrap my mind around how quickly you shattered." I walk around the table she's lying on to stand over her head and put myself in her line of vision, gripping her face with my fingertips I whisper into her ear, "Easy or difficult, nothing will ever be as precious and sacred as destroying you, Stella."

When her eyes of every color clear and flutter then lock on mine, delight and excitement surge through my veins.

My usually worthless cock stiffens as I watch her slowly trying to sit up and other than wincing, her eyes never leave mine. My adoration of her swells as she sits up and turns her broken and bloodied body towards me, hanging her battered legs over the edge of the table. I moan when her bloody delicate hands cup my face. Our eyes remain locked. I know I'm bewitched, entranced.

I lean into her like a moth to a flame and as our lips brush, she whispers in a dry tone with her cracked voice, "Preston Stone, you could never be man enough to cause my destruction. Your worthlessness and pitifulness alone steal your ability to ever break me. I hate, no, no, no, no, no, I love to be the one to tell you this, Preston - Wesley Jacobs destroyed me, shattered me, cracked my sanity and left me ruined long before you ever laid a finger on me. You've been raping and paring the skin from nothing more than a void where Stella Reese used to exist."

She blinks as her hands slip from my face then turns, pulling her legs up onto the table before lying back down. Her head lolls to the side and she resumes blankly staring at the wall behind me.

Rage, as red as her blood, floods my vision.

CRACK. CRACK. CRACK. CRACK. CRACK.

Did you know when your sanity completely separates from your consciousness, it creates a sound?

Beauty's words unleash the rutting demons who've been

crawling and scratching just beneath my surface. Their fingertips brush the chain links before grabbing the electrical tape and taping the sharp new strips of barbwire and chain together.

After they've constructed a new apparatus for torture they continue where I left off; raining down strike after strike, slash after slash.

Standing on the outside looking in, I witness my brittle sanity separating from my consciousness - listening to the unmistakable sound it creates with every break. And it amuses me at how much it echoes the sound of the chain and barbwire splitting the surface of my already broken Beauty's skin.

Hell bent little demons seeking the pleasure of her warm wet blood splattering across their face.

Hell bent little demons seeking the thrill of breaking.

Unlike me, the hell bent little demons are unable to distinguish between the breaking of Beauty's bones and skin, and the breaking of Beauty alone.

When the obtuse hell bent little demons discern her skin has been as broken as it can be, they thrill at the sight of the sledgehammer.

Before grasping it, swinging it, and bringing it down to thud, cracking my Beauty's knees.

And I succumb to my new role as nothing more than a semi amused spectator by virtue of being robbed of my life long retribution of breaking my Beauty.

Chapter 40

The Quiet Little Boy in the Shadows

The motivation behind my actions and words to Preston came from where? I'll never know. And the flicker of desire to consider the conundrum burns out as quickly as it sparked.

I numbly – silently - lay there as Preston, the quiet little boy who always hid in the shadows, tirelessly continues shredding my skin into ribbons.

I'm sure you expect me to be grateful for the numbness, and I would be…but I'm numb. Every lash goes utterly unfelt. Unfelt physically and unfelt emotionally.

When Preston grasped my face with his bruising fingertips and cheerfully exclaimed, "Easy or difficult, nothing will ever be as precious and sacred as destroying you, Stella," it ripped me from my numb trance, blazing agony across every nerve ending, and pain unlike anything ever conceived by rational thought completely consumed me.

How I was able to squelch the screams tearing their way through my throat, sit up, deliver my reply and lay back down? I'll never know.

I can, however, easily recite the definition that every shrink, counselor, and therapist repeated during every session, over and over, throughout my life: Compartmentalization is an unconscious psychological defense mechanism used to avoid cognitive dissonance, or the mental discomfort and anxiety caused by a person's having conflicting values, cognitions, emotions, beliefs, OR

HAVING TO ENDURE TORTURE, within themselves. Yeah, I may have added to it a bit.

Now, I'm no doctor, but I'm willing to place a bet on either compartmentalization being somewhat held responsible, or I'm finally actually at the brink of death. The latter being preferred, if I were able to crave or yearn…if I were able to hope.

Instead, I numbly and silently lay here as Preston, the quiet little boy with blue eyes so dull they looked silver, whales across my knees and thighs with a sledgehammer, splintering bone after bone with every swing. And I continue to stare at the rust stain running from the ceiling to the floor, watching the water slowly trickle down, drip after drop, remembering the quiet little boy from my past.

"Hey, Jeff, has he always been like that?" I ask jumping from the tire swing when I spot Preston.

"Huh? W-W-Who b-b-been l-l-like what?" He stutters.

"Jeff, calm down, breathe buddy, it's okay. It's just me and you." Smiling at Jeff, I turn away with Preston at my back and my body obscuring his view I motion with my thumb for Jeff to look behind me. "Preston, see him up on the roof? Why is he always trying to hide, I wonder?"

"Oh, I-I d-don't know. H-he's always been that way." Jeff takes the stick from my hand and starts poking at an anthill.

I sit beside him and grab another stick, poking the anthill with him. "I feel sorry for him. I wonder what his parents did to make him so sad." I rest my chin on top of my knees, still poking the anthill.

"S-Stella I don't think he's s-sad. H-he's really really really m-mad. Don't t-tell n-nobody, b-but I-I'm s-s-scared of h-him."

I look up at Jeff, "Scared of him? Why? That's dumb."

"I-It's j-just that one t-time, on m-my way h-home, I t-took a s-short c-c-cut through the woods, a-and I-I s-s-saw…" He shudders and clenches his eyes shut before finishing, "…H-H-He h-h-had a knife, a-a-a-nd w-w-was c-c-cutting up a-a, s-s-some kind o-of a-aanimal." He shudders again before gagging.

"Really? Nuh uh! You're so full of it, Jeff." I playfully shove his shoulder.

"S-Stells, I'm n-n-not l-lying! I s-s-saw him!"

"Okay! Okay! Sheesh, Jeff chill out."

I never did believe Jeff, though.

Every time I saw Preston, he either looked like the saddest boy I ever saw or like he was in terrible pain. And I always felt so bad for him - when I remembered him - and I only remembered him when I saw him. Which was pretty rare.

Now, as the quiet little boy from my past raises the bloody sledgehammer over his head while standing over mine - his deranged silver eyes jump from my left eye to my right eye - I feel absolutely nothing for him at all; even as I watch him swing it back over his head, bringing it down, down, down, I feel nothing for anything except numbness.

And when the head of the bloody sledgehammer smashes into my face, finally, blessedly ending my life, I feel peace.

Chapter 41

Missing Angel

WESLEY

It's been a week since Stella left me alone in the depths of Hell. A week. Seven days. A hundred and sixty eight hours - of pure torturous hell. I've lost motivation to do anything. I've lost desire for everything—other than scotch. Mostly, I've lost hope of ever having contentment or happiness again in my life.

The only explanation for my actions last Saturday night that I can conceive is someone drugged me. At first, I blamed Rachel; but I had to discredit that line of assumptions because I don't remember seeing Rachel until Sunday morning.

I looked at Jude, stacking blame on him was incredibly tempting, because I hate the motherfucker. But hating him doesn't fall in line with explaining why the hell the cocky bastard would drug me. I didn't wake up in bed with *him*, a date rape victim. I am left with nothing. My current state of misery is the product of some ass hat drugging the wrong persons fucking drink.

Goddamn drink drugger. I hate my life has been severely altered and I have no idea who the culprit is. I am left looking at every single person who walks by, wondering if they are responsible.

I tried to go to work on Monday and Tuesday, but ended up unable to function and going back home. I worked the rest of the week from home, conferring with Barby over the phone and telling her to tell everyone else I'm ill and I said to go fuck themselves. Barby being the good, proper girl she is, only relayed the first half of my message.

Monday morning has arrived and I'm pulling into the parking garage of the JPH building, I pull into my reserved spot parking my R8, grabbing my espresso, and step from the car.

A solid nine walks by eye-fucking me and I glare at her, "You gotta problem? Didn't your daddy teach you staring was rude?"

"Never had a daddy, but I sure could use one." She saunters towards me while she croons her response. I throw my hand up.

"I'm sure you may find this shocking, Candy, but believe it or not, I find absolutely nothing about you attractive. Your voice alone makes me want to stab my eardrums out. Turn around, walk away, and never fucking speak to me again. Understood?"

"Candy? Who the fuck is Candy?" she shouts as I head in the direction of the building's elevator.

When the doors open, I stalk inside, hit the button to my floor and turn around to glare at her and reply, "The name of every whore I've ever had the displeasure of meeting."

I'm behind my desk going through the hundreds of messages Barby stacked on it last week when she comes into my office.

"Hey, you doing any better?"

Without looking up, I shake my head.

"Oh, sorry. I wish there was something I could do to help." She says sadly.

"Its fine, Barby. Thanks for feeling sorry for me. Even though it does nothing to help, it's the thought that counts. Got the schedule?"

She nods smiling, "Yes, sir." After handing it to me, she and I go over the day's meetings. When we finish and she's walking towards the exit, I ask, "Has Stella called, have you talked to her at all?"

Her head shakes no. "I'm sorry, Wes. I haven't."

"Okay, I…I just wanted to know. Thanks." I nod before looking down, pretending to know what I'm looking at until she closes the door behind her, leaving me in solitude.

Cupping the back of my head with my linked fingers I look up at the ceiling and wonder what the fuck to do next.

I had Derrick resend the files he has on Stell last Wednesday; but as I stared at the information on the pages, the ghost I'd been chasing disappeared. Nothing. No inkling, no niching at the corners of my mind, no sick feeling of dread in my stomach. I felt nothing staring at the information as minutes turned to hours and hours turned to days - all the way up to staring at it last night until the words blurred and I lost consciousness, passing out on top of Stella's past.

Whatever it was gnawing at me - whatever I chased for months - simply vanished, leaving not even a hint of its presence behind.

The phone ringing jars me from my bleak thoughts. "Wesley speaking."

"Wes, what's up ya kinky BDSM energizer bunny?!"

"Trina?"

"Ahh...Yeah. Wow, way to make a girl feel special. The least you could do is pretend remembering your baby's auntie. Has Stell taught you nothing? Oh wait..." She bursts out laughing before continuing around her giggles. "...You two have been too busy fucking each others' brains out for the last week. But don't worry, you'll get your education in Stell and Trina 101 soon enough, daddy. Congrats, by the way."

Three words. Nothing but three words are left in the carnage of what hers do after slamming into me like a fucking freight train.

Whatthefuck   whatthefuck   whatthefuck   whatthefuck whatthefuck!?

"What the fuck?"

"Huh?"

My voice roars, "WHAT THE FUCK?!"

"What the fuck?"

"WHAT THE FUCK ARE YOU TALKING ABOUT, TRINA?!?!"

"Huh? What the fuck am I talking about? No! What the fuck are you talking about, motherfucker. And stop yelling at me!"

The phone clatters to the desk as my fingers grasp my hair, holding my head up. My eyes fall to the papers on my desk, but I see nothing except my angel's back as she runs away.

Where the fuck did she go? Where the fuck has she been? And what the fuck is Trina talking about? A baby? Whose baby?

"Congrats, by the way."

My fumbling hands grab for the phone. When I finally grasp it, I yank it to my ear. "Wesley! Wesley, what in God's name is going on!?"

"Trina, where the fuck is Stella? And what the FUCK are you talking about a baby?!"

"Oh my God! She never…You never. SHIT! She went to your house last Sunday! A week ago! She went…She left our apartment a week ago, headed to your place to tell you about the baby! Did you see her? Did she show up?"

"What fucking baby!?!" I shout.

"Your fucking baby!!!"

My baby? My baby? What fucking baby?

"Wesley, we both need to calm down. I'll say what I know, and if you can add to it, then do so. Okay?"

"Understood."

"Stella, she woke up not yesterday, but the Sunday before. She got dressed, then told me and Eve she was going to your place to tell you she was pregnant. She said if she came back…well, it didn't go well. And if she didn't, then it did go well. And in a roundabout way, to let you two have your time, your happily ever after go undisturbed by me bugging her for deets. Then she left. And, Wesley…I haven't seen her since."

"She's pregnant? With a baby? She's pregnant with my baby? And she came to tell me? Oh my God, Trina, oh my fucking God, what have I done? Trina. Holy mother of God."

I hear her calm voice slowly but sternly say, "Wesley. Did you see her on that day?"

"Yes."

"Okay, did you speak to her?"

"I don't—No. I didn't. Oh my fucking God. I didn't even speak to her when she came to tell me she was pregnant, that I was going to be a daddy, and found me in bed with Rachel. Oh my fu—"

"Okay! Whoa! Focus. We're moving on, but don't you DARE think that Rachel shit has gone unnoticed. I'm guessing, like the Stella I know, instead of having tea and discussing what she caught your piece of shit ass doing, she ran. Am I right?"

"Yes. Correct."

"And what? You ran after her? Please Lord tell me you ran after her."

"No. I didn't"

"Right, because your dick was shoved in someone else's pussy! Have you seen her since, Wesley?"

"No. Have you?"

Click. The phone line goes dead.

And with eighteen thousand questions, scenarios, and 'What the fucks?' screaming through my mind, I try calling Trina back, over and over. After the, hell I don't even know how many calls, I dial Derrick's number.

"Speak."

"D, as of this morning's email from my personal accountant, I have a little more than five hundred mil, it's yours, ALL of it, the minute you bring my angel home. To me. Is that understood?"

"Hang—" There's a shitload of noise in the background, clattering, some scattering, then silence. I'm certain he just leapt from his seat and knocked over a bunch of shit. "Sorry, I had to find a pen. Okay, angel? I'm guessing we're talking about Stella?"

"Correct." See? I told you he knocked a bunch of shit over.

"Last time you saw her?"

"Sunday, April 20th, around ten in the morning."

"Friends? When did they see her last?"

"D, I was the last person to see her alive."

"Fuck. Again, friends, when did they see her last?"

"When she told them she was headed to my place. To tell me she was pregnant with my child."

"Fuck! Okay...and how did that convo go?"

"It didn't. She found me in bed with another woman, after she found all your files."

"FUCK! Motherfucking bitch ass FUCKING shit goddamn hell FUCK!"

"My thoughts exactly. Look, I just hung up with her roommate, Trina. She's the one that called trying to find Stell. I can almost guarantee that when she hung up with me, she called the cops. So...yeah, man, five hundred mil, all yours. Just get me my goddamn angel back, and do it quickly."

Chapter 42

Monster in the Shadow

MONSTER

Do you have any conceivable concept of the difficulty, messiness, and wretched taste involved in resuscitating someone who's facial bones mimic mush? In case you were wondering, it's almost impossible, it's a bloody mess, and quite possibly, the vilest thing to ever coat my tongue.

I told you I would kill her. I warned you that I would.

My question is, where have you fucking been? You could've stopped this. You saw the trajectory of my madness. So why? What caused you to idly sit aside? What caused you to do nothing to save my Beauty?

I hope you're happy.

I hope you sleep well knowing that you fucking killed her.

For the last hour, I've been following every CPR algorithm by the American Heart Association I've learned, studied and memorized. Alternating from breather to chest compressions back and forth, over and over.

I stop to assess my gallant interventions, and instead of finding a weak thready pulse and hear her labored breath twice a minute, I feel no pulse at all - radial or carotid - while watching for two whole minutes, and not once observing her lifeless body attempt to breath.

Without even fully understanding, my role as spectator is stripped. And without any self preservation or rational thought, I dial 911.

As the dispatcher's tone remains somewhere between assertive, calm, and disciplined, telling me to continue CPR, I hear the ETA (Estimated Time of Arrival) of the paramedics is less than three minutes.

I disconnect the phone line by ripping its cord from the wall as my eyes search and locate the shadows to hide amongst before continuing CPR in vain.

There isn't anything anyone can do. I've killed my Beauty, then resurrected her to only kill her again.

Breathe. Breathe. Link fingers, one hand on top of the other, palm to back, at nipple line, then shove the heel of your hand between. Thirty compressions, then two breaths. Breathe. Breathe. Link fingers. One hand on top the other, and at middle of her sternum, I resume chest compressions.

When someone hurries me, by…let's say, dying, it causes my temper to shorten and my reaction to sharpen.

This is why Beauty's sternum cracks under the heel of my hand. I lie. I tell myself that isn't what I heard or felt. However when my second and third compression create the same crack along her sternum, I concede.

I concede that you've not only allowed this to occur, but facilitated it.

And now, thanks to you, I'm left leaving my Beauty alone with the paramedics as I slink to hide in the shadows.

Where I can comfortably do what I have always done best…Watch.

Chapter 43

Ghosts

WESLEY

I get the call that night. Derrick heard the first few pieces of information over the police scanner and called me. I'm at my house on speaker phone listening to Derrick go over what he calls 'ironic non conclusive evidence' while the police scanner repeats in the background. '911 dispatcher states caller was an adult male. Sounded panicked. 10-14C, Possible 187.'

"Okay, Wes, in the Sims foster home, there were two other kids living there with Stella." I hear shuffling paper in the background. "Jeffery Price. I looked this kid up and he checks out. Married, two kids, he's an accountant for some huge storage company in Baton Rouge. Now, the other kid, Preston Stone, this kids like a fucking ghost, man. An extremely well educated ghost. He has his master's in almost every damn degree imaginable. And his doctorate in Physiology, Anatomy, and Physics. But, the thing is, he just vanishes after that. Gone. No record of a Preston Stone that I could find."

You see, this is why Derrick is the best. Even with his head buried in information about Stella's past, he still hears and processes other shit going on around him. Things you and I would either not even pay attention to, or brush it off as nothing, he notes and investigates.

"What does that have to do with anything, D? Put a star on the kid's name and go to the next."

"I said that 'I *could*', as in past tense. You see, where Preston Stone falls off the face of the earth in Newark, New Jersey; your

228

boy, Jude Preston lands."

As his words register in my mind, then begin to process, I hear the police scanner in the background.

'Police arrived at the residence of Preston Stone after a call was placed to 911 from residence requesting help. After initial knocks, police officer Lieutenant Jones requested backup and entered residence. Finding no immediate cause for alarm during a brief walkthrough, Lt. Jones awaits for backup.'

"Wesley?" Derrick's voice sternly asks.

"Jude fucking Preston drugged me. I don't know what the hell for, but after that..."

"I'll call you back."

The line goes dead.

"*FUCK!*"

I've tried calling Derrick, the police, Jude, Trina and every fucking hospital in New York City over the last hour.

I still have no answers. No angel, and no answers.

I swear to Christ, I'm five seconds from losing my goddamn mind. I pour a glass of scotch and toss it back before pouring another when someone starts beating at my door.

I drop the bottle of scotch and haul ass to the door. When I open it and see Derrick, I start pelting him with questions. "The fuck, man? Shit! I've been losing my mind. What the hell did you find out? Is Stella with Preston, or Jude? What did the cops find? Did the scanner say?"

He won't look me in the eye. Hell, he won't look me in the face. "D?" I shout trying to get something out of him. Anything.

When his eyes look up at mine dread to swallows me whole and ice courses through my veins. "Wes, you're gonna want to sit

229

down for this. Where's your bottle of scotch at, man?"

"NO! Fuck that shit! Tell me where Stella is! Now goddammit!"

As he walks from my foyer into the living room, he begins speaking, "Preston Stone kept diaries. You remember that movie with Brad Pitt and Gwyneth Paltrow? Seven? Remember all those diaries they found in Kevin Spacey's apartment? Preston Stone kept diaries like that. NYPD found over eighteen hundred diaries. They have an entire group of officers dedicated to reading them. From what they've learned so far, Preston was morbidly obsessed with his foster sister. He calls her his Beauty. Used to sleep under her bed when they were kids, hide in the shadows and watch her all the fucking time. She knew nothing of it. In this Preston kid's eleven year old handwriting, you read as he gloats, calling himself the master of being unseen. Apparently while he was 'being unseen' one night under Stella's bed, he woke to the sounds of Mr. Sims raping young Stella."

After walking over to the bar and pouring us each a scotch, I hand one to Derrick and we both sit.

"Now, Preston, being the sick little fucker he was, blamed Stella for being raped. Then…he plotted for over a year. And the results of his plotting were the incident which had Stella removed from the Sims residence."

"Well, there's my motherfucking ghost." Those words are the only ones I can manage as I try to process what Derrick is telling me.

"Only, little boy Preston thought he'd accidently killed her. For damn near twenty years. Now they haven't gotten any further into the diaries, so I don't know when he came to the realization that she wasn't dead."

"His book, 'Twisted Obsession', the synopsis alone. Derrick, it parallels what's in his diary. I haven't read either, but I swear to Christ, it parallels."

"Mmmm…" I see him nod from the corner of my eye. "Probably does. They didn't find him though. They will, they have the whole goddamn state police task force looking for him now."

He sips his scotch before motioning to my glass. "I'll pour you another," After standing, he grabs my glass in his other hand and heads to the bar. "We're not quite through talking."

"They did find her though, right?" When I see him nod it feels like a million tons of weight have lifted from me. "Thank fuck."

He shakes his head before turning and walks back towards where we're sitting. "No, Wesley. Don't thank fuck." He slides a piece of paper across the mahogany table between us. "Stole a copy of her ER admit assessment."

My eyes don't move from his. "What does it say?"

"Drink your scotch and read it, man."

After draining my glass I slam it on the table, shattering it. *"WHAT THE FUCK DOES IT SAY?!"*

"It says that at 8:32 pm, Lt. Jones and his backup team entered Preston Stone's residence. They searched the first and second floors finding nothing out of place - no sign of occupancy, no sign of struggle - nothing. Several of the officers in the office area of his residence came across a bookshelf of diaries, while another officer stumbled upon a trick door slightly opened in a closet inside the office - that led to a concrete walled basement. Inside that basement, there was a cell made of two basement concrete walls, and two walls lined in steel bars, four inches between each bar." He clears his throat and drains his glass then sets it on the table next to my shattered one.

"They found a Caucasian female, dark brown hair, possibly mid to late twenties. Other than that, there were no other discernible features useful to identify her."

I shoot from my chair and I'm in the foyer grabbing my keys and shit off the table and shoving them in my pockets. "Come on! What hospital is she at?" When I look over my shoulder at him expecting an answer, my hands stop as my mind processes. Not only has he not moved, but he's shaking his head. His eyes alone tell me what I've known but denied since he walked through my door.

He goes to speak, but gets choked up and coughs before finally speaking, "Wesley, the reason there was no other identifying characteristics the officers were able to discern," Leaning forward and sighing, he says, "She barely had a thread of skin left on her entire body. The soles of her feet, her palms, those are the only way they were able to determine her race." His eyes narrow on mine. "There are nine bones from a human's waist to their ankles. Nine. The Jane Doe they found in Preston Stone's basement, directly beside the blood covered sledgehammer whose head mold castings match the impressions covering the victim, she had seven of her nine bones from waist to ankle shattered; consisting of a fractured pelvis, two shattered patellas, or knee caps, an open compounded fracture of the left femur, and an impacted fracture to the right. Both of the victim's tibias were hit repeatedly. From the medical documentation, it appears the initial impact to both tibias caused open compounded fractures. Meaning, when the bones split, they pierced her already shredded skin. In most cases, even though it looks horrid, those types of breaks are easier to set. However, not in this case. Stella was pummeled repeatedly from her knee caps to her ankles. When he finished on the lower half of her body, he sledgehammered both her clavicles, as well as the inside of her elbows, effectively breaking all six bones of her arms."

Derrick stands heading towards the bar, grasps the bottle and while walking back to his chair, he takes long pulls of scotch before sinking back into his seat. Lolling his head back and looking at the ceiling, he whispers tortured words that resonate through the room, "Wesley, what I'm trying to say is, Jude Preston, or Preston Stone shredded Stella's skin with chains and barbwire for six days straight; and on the seventh day, after there was no more skin to shred, he broke her bones, crushing them, one by one. And after Jude was done breaking her skin and bones, he bashed her face in."

His head comes up and our eyes lock before he delivers the final blow, "Stella Jolie Reese was pronounced D.O.A., by not only paramedics, but the ER admitting RN."

Chapter 44

Life

I've always considered my childhood, the reason for me being everything I was, both the good and the bad. Any strength I possess, I earned from my ability to withstand being drug through hell, time after time being broken, only to emerge from hell every brutal time stronger. Scarred, but stronger all the same. On the other side of that coin, it's the scars left behind, the shattered pieces I glued back together after every horrible perversion I experienced which caused my nightmares to slowly creep into my strength and invade any sacred peace I held closely to me in life.

Don't pity me. Don't feel sorry for me. Everyone's life is different. Everyone has their own issues and obstacles to overcome in life. Some worse than others; but it still doesn't take away from the lessons.

Everything I experienced in my life led me back to Wesley Jacobs. Led me to the first and only boy I've ever loved. Wesley healed me. When I was wrapped in his arms, I became whole again. Wesley's love is all consuming; it's beautiful, courageous, fierce, and it was utterly precious. I will cherish the tiny moment in time, when I was his and he was mine, now and into my next life.

I was broken and scarred by the sins of others before Wesley came into my life and broke the ugly sins that bound me and held me as a prisoner. After he broke every piece of ugly I had left in me, he wielded me - bending me until changing everything I ever believed of myself, and then he covered me in his praise and protected me in his love.

So no, don't pity me. Yes, I may have lived in hell, but in the end, it led me to being fiercely loved by a beautiful, strong man I fell in love with at twelve years old. How many women can claim they had a snippet of time in their life being loved by a man who is the epitome of their perfect, who is truly their soul mate?

Life is so poetic. The course and rhythm of it, the pulls and pushes, the give and takes, when what's been reaped from what we've sewn.

When what nourishes us, heals us, and strengthens us sadly becomes the very thing that which destroys us.

All my life, I considered myself broken. What's worse than being shattered? No one wants a broken thing. No one can love someone whose broken. I know now there is a difference in being broken and being destroyed. When you're broken, you're just broken; but when you've been destroyed...There's no coming back.

Broken people are still living, destroyed people are not.

Chapter 45

Destroyed Angels

WESLEY

Trina, Eve, and Bo just left. It's only Derrick and me in the waiting room. I keep telling him there is no need to stay, but he shakes his head mumbling, "I'm fine."

Stella has been in surgery for over six hours. The admitting ER physician came in to call the time of death. As he walked through the door, the flat line on the heart monitor spontaneously indicated an agonal rhythm, a blip of a random heartbeat, meaning her heart began beating again while the ER nurses continued their CPR efforts. When the physician saw this random heartbeat he immediately reacted. She was instantly prepped for emergency surgery.

And over the last six hours, she has died on that OR table eight times… But today, she's come back to life nine.

I don't care how many times she dies on that table, but she better come back every time. I can't live this life without her. I won't. So as long as she keeps coming back, I'll refrain from blowing my head off, right before I fall from the top of my building.

I will not live without her.

Derrick nudging me brings me from my thoughts. When I look over at him, he nods and I follow his line of vision. I see the doctor headed in our direction and I leap from my chair. "Doc, how is she? Can I see her? I need to see her. Now."

"She made it through the surgery. To be honest with you, I don't know how. Sometimes, especially with cases as critical as

Stella's, as a physician - a surgeon - there's only so much I can do. And frankly, it's just a last ditch effort, a last resort that has me doing any and everything I know to do JUST to get through the surgery alone and my patient still be alive. In Stella's case, I scrubbed in for her surgery wholly prepared to give everything I have to keep her alive and truly believing that it was an impossible feat. Everything I did, her body responded to almost miraculously. Now, Wesley - we wait and pray she lives through her hour of recovery. After that, we wait and pray she makes it through the night." He pats my shoulder and smiles. "I want you to stay steadfast; but Wesley, try not to let your hopes get too high."

"Thanks, doc. What room is she in?"

"Wesley you don't want to see her right now. Just head home, get some rest and come back later." He moves to walk around me and I stop him, grabbing him by his shoulders, shaking my head.

"Room. Tell me what room she is in. Do not tell me what I want, where to go, and that I need rest. You tell me what room she is in."

"Recovery room three." I spin and head towards the double doors.

When I see recovery room three, I take a deep breath to calm myself before walking in.

Nothing. Nothing could have ever prepared me for what I see.

Tears hit my eyes and I choke on a sob. "Angel?" I whisper across the dimly lit room.

I step closer towards the bed as my eyes scan her bandaged body, when I see her black and purple hand resting on top of the white sheet, I sit beside her, gently pick her hand up and cradle it in mine. Tears blur my vision before streaming down my face in rivulets as I sit there, staring at her tiny battered hand in mine. "I'm so sorry, I tried to protect you, but I've never protected anyone before and I failed you. I knew there was something. I just didn't know what it was. I'm so sorry." Laying my head on the bed next to her hand in mine, I gently kiss it and try in vain to hold back the sobs. "Please, I know I'm a selfish bastard, I know I let you down, and I know I'll never deserve you; but please, Stella, don't leave me...Angel, please don't die and leave me here alone."

The sound of the door opening and closing behind me causes me to sit up and rub my hand down my face wiping away the tears before looking to see who's walked in.

"Hi. I'm Dr. Hughes, Stella's obstetrician. The attending physician consulted me after the SAFE RN finished collecting any evidence they may have found during the rape assessment."

"Jesus fucking Christ." Agony slices through my already shredded chest. "Crucify me now. She was raped? A-fucking-gain?"

Why in God's name is this woman still alive? How? How can one person bear so much excruciating torment, time after time, and continue to live?

Stella may have made it through the surgery, and she may make it through the night. If she makes it out of all this alive, there's no way she'll ever be the same.

"You'll have to wait and see what comes back after they've run all their tests. But, usually if they do a rape kit, rape is suspected. I'm sorry. And I do need to do an assessment. If you'll step out, I'll have the nurses let you know when I finish." She smiles. She won't be smiling for long.

"No. There isn't any reason for you to be sorry. And no, I'll not step out. Anything you need to do to Stella, you can do with me sitting right here. I'm not leaving her side, and I'm for damn sure not leaving this room, is that understood?"

"I'm sorry, but I'm about to perform a trans-vaginal ultrasound to verify IF she's still pregnant. So no, sir. It is not understood. Do I need to have security called? Because I will in order to protect my patient's privacy."

This bitch doesn't seem to get it does she?

I keep Stell's hand in mine and lean my other elbow on my knee before narrowing my eyes on her, "Dr. Hughes, let me be more clear. Stella is mine. That includes her pussy and her baby. Now, if the hospital policy states that the father of a woman's baby cannot be present during the ultrasound of his own child, then I would probably call security if I were you, because you're going to need help removing my six foot four, two hundred pound ass from this chair."

I guess the hospital's policy was in my favor. After Dr. Hughes puts Stell's casted legs in some leg holders she turns on the ultrasound machine. "Mr. Jacobs,—"

"Dr. Hughes, please—That's my father's name. Wesley's mine."

Yes. I apologize. I know I'm being a total dick. But you have NO idea what the hell I'm going through! What if she lost the baby? I want that baby, that's my baby. I made it, it's mine. What if it's already gone? What if it isn't go—Oh my God...I'm about to see my baby. If it isn't already gone. Please don't be gone, little baby.

"Oookay. Wesley, I don't want your hopes to get up. Stella has, well we aren't certain she'll live through the night. If she's still pregnant after what she's gone through, it will be a miracle alone. And if she is able to carry this child to full term with the stress of recovery and rehab... I just don't want you to get your hopes up. Please keep those things in mind, okay?"

I can't stop the dread. It just keeps coming and coming, more and more, and my damn cup runneth over with dread eons ago! I can't handle anymore!

But I do. Even though I swear I can't take it, I do and I continue to. Because I refuse to accept defeat. I refuse the alternative option. I will sit in my Hell of dread and pain, knowing I could lose Stella any second, knowing I could have already lost my baby and I will remain here, because I can't live without Stella. *That* is what I cannot do.

The doctor's said to pray Stella made it through her hour of recovery; and after that, to pray she lived through the night. I did -

and those prayers were answered. However, no one told me I was supposed to continue praying for her to live through the morning, noon, and night that followed the first night she survived. Stella did live through that first night, however she coded the morning that followed. It was her last time to leave me - and the first time she did not came back.

Today is May 1, 2014. The day I bury not only the woman I love, but also our twins whom Dr. Hughes had found still very much alive and very active on the ultrasound.

As I watch my angel being lowered into the ground, it resonates through me that I will never know happiness or contentment in this life. I've never had to protect anyone before and because of that, I wasn't prepared to protect the only important thing to ever come into my life.

I said I wouldn't live without her, and I won't. However, because my angel spent all of her life being broken and, in the end, destroyed, I will remain amongst the living, unattached and unwilling to pretend I am not dead.

This devastation, this hell that my life now consists of, is my reparation for any and every wrongful penance bestowed upon Stella during her life.

I was unable to protect the woman that changed me, and for that I must endure this atonement, refraining from snipping any time off my life that the same God who allowed my angel that fought to cease fighting, may deem necessary for me to suffer. I shall carry that which destroyed her, knowing – hoping - it will someday soon also destroy me.

Chapter 46

MONSTER

Insanity: Doing the same thing over and over again and expecting different results.
—Albert Einstein

I don't know how much more I can take of being in the shadows, a nameless face always amongst the crowd.

How much more does she think she'll get away with? How much longer does she think I'll allow Wesley to continue living?

What? Because she so easily succumbed? Does she think by sacrificing herself and dying, I will allow him to live?

She is absolutely absurd if that was her rationale for breaking so easily.

My inability to physically endure - as well as witness him continuing to live as if I don't even exist- will lead to her soul mate's demise.

My inability to physically stay away from her, even in death, may lead to mine.

But not before I initiate my new plan of attack. Not before delivering the corpses of anyone and everyone she ever loved at her doorstep or the mantle of her tombstone.

You see, it dawned on me in a fit of rage while standing in the corner of the OR suite wearing my badge 'Preston Stone-Trauma

ER Resident'. As I watched her come back to life over and over again, I realized my plans for truly destroying Beauty were flawed: I was using physical pain and mental anguish to destroy Beauty.

No. No, no, no, no. It's so simple. I couldn't see past my loathing and contempt for her and her alone, to discover what the real clear answer was.

Destruction with physical brute strength isn't the key. Stripping her of the very things that nourished her would destroy Beauty...And yes, I could continue destroying her even after death. This is how immortal, how powerful, I am.

Even now, as I stand hidden near the forest - again, nothing more than another face in the crowd - watching as her body is lowered into the ground, I cannot help but be astounded at the simplicity of my plans. Excitement thrums through me, endorphins flood my system.

"So intricate, yet flawed, were my orchestrations. All along, I needed nothing more than to patiently wait for you to find your disgusting little happy ever after, kill you, and then kill everything you loved. All along it was only as simple as taking anything and everything that you loved and loved you in return and snuffing the life from it." Sighing, I push away from the tree before turning around to leave, only to have some brute run into me. "Excuse yourself, you imbecile."

"There's no fucking way that's gonna happen. Long time, little chase, motherfucker."

"Excuse me?"

"Now you expect a pardon?" He shakes his head, chuckling like I'm the one who's insane. "That's not going to happen either. I will tell you what is going to happen." He keeps crowding my personal space causing me to step back. "I'm going to introduce myself." The white of his teeth contrast starkly against his dark face as he smiles before stepping forward again; and again, I step back. "My name is Derrick 'The Click' Jackson. You fucked with some of my shit, important shit. And for that reason alone, you get to learn about my middle name. Preston, do you wanna learn why it's 'The Click'?"

"No, I want you and your black ass to get out of my—"

"Because motherfucker, I'm the one who makes goddamn sure that it's the last sound you'll ever hear."

CLICK.

Dear Reader,

I struggled with this ending more than I've struggled with any phrase or wording of a sentence, ever. Eighty percent of this story literally fell out as I stood aside and merely transcribed. The last twenty percent, not so much. I fought it with every single thing I am and I lost. There is an alternate ending out there, however right now I can't tell you whether or not it will ever published. I do want you to know that I loved Stella, and I swear I did fight for her, hard. Unfortunately, sometimes as a writer, all you can do is write the story. Especially when the story demands it's own…story.

Love Always, Kimber

Acknowledgements

Ahhh... Okay, first and foremost to my street team! You bitches have pimped your asses off!

Trina Taylor, I love you, sissy. Dammit, I love you!!! You are and will always be more than my best friend. You're my sister! XoXo

Donna Pemberton, thank you for pulling back my reins when I needed you too!

Francette Phal, thank you SO much for believing that I could write more than a book review! Thank you for always being there when I need your help, momma! To call you friend is one of the most kickass feelings in the world!

Jennifer Cothran, you are always there for me, no matter what, and I fucking love you for it, girl!

Yessi Smith, Hells yeah! So damn lucky to have met you! And dammit, honestly, I have NEVER clicked with anyone as quick as I clicked with you! NOLA has no idea what's gonna hit 'em ;)

Natalie, Amanda, Sandra, Heather, Isa and Debi... Holy shit! You damn ladies are freaking 'Pimpin', pimpin'! Y'all knock me on my ass with your pimping style! I'm so damn happy Lil and the voices in her head brought y'all into my life! Every damn one of you I consider a fucking awesome friend!

Dolores Montz, 3 words! New Orleans, BITCH! We're gonna light that bitch UP in August! CANNOT WAIT! Thank you SO much for talking all those baseball moms into reading my smut, lmao! I love your pimpin' style, momma!

Kimber's Bitches, THANK YOU! There is no damn way in hell I could have made it through Wesley's story without each and every one of you badass bitches! XOXO

MaryAnn Breedlove, YOU! Are more essential to me and my writing development, than you'll ever know. No rainbows, No bullshit… You are the whisper in the corner that turns me from an unpolished, four letter word littering writer into a mothafuckin' author! And I love you for it!

To my editor Melissa Willis! Wow! I don't even know where to begin! I'm utterly humbled to have you even read my book, but to edit it? WOW! You're my fucking Madonna, PERIOD!

Kari Ayasha from Cover to Cover Designs, girl! There will NEVER, EVER be another cover artist that fucking touches my books! You are one of the best things that has happened to me since coming into the author world. Every damn cover I have in my crazy head, you don't just make it happen, you make it perfect!!! Xoxo

Lauryn, Meg, and B, y'all are my reason for living, my reason for breathing, and if weren't for you three, I would have lived my life like a woman gone mad. You are each sweet blessings that I could never live without, and I love each of you so very much in your own specialness.

Momma and Daddy, I know I am the least conventional kid to have and also the hardest daughter to love, However, ONE DAY, I WILL make you both proud. Thank you so much for giving Bobby and me the wonderful and loving family we grew up in. Momma, thank you for raising me to be strong and to never back down. But most of all, thank you, Momma, for being my greatest friend. Daddy, thank you so much for being the best daddy in the whole wide world. I'll always be Daddy's girl first, even when I'm a hundred years old. I love you both so much and pray that I can make y'all proud. *Psst... Momma, don't let Daddy read any of my books—the acknowledgments ONLY!!!!*

Author Bio:

Who is Kimber? Shit, sometimes even I don't know, lmao. However if I had to type up an author bio (which, son of a bitch, I do) this is how it would read. BTW, caught a lot of shit for this author bio. Really don't give a fuck though, because I was asked to type up a bio. And if I can only say one thing for certain about myself, it's this: I'm real, I don't back down from what I believe, I say what I mean, and I mean what I say. I don't bite my tongue and I never try to hide the ugly parts of who I am... You either love me or hate me, but if you love me... I'll always be loyal, no fucking matter what ;)

I can be called a billon different things—daughter, wife, mother, labor unit nurse. I sell pussy on the side. *Coughs* That would be Persian kittens, thank you...you dirty-minded scoundrel. I'm a book blogger, book pimp, and a book whore. My two indulgences are my Jack's in life...Jack Daniel's and Blackjack. My biggest dream, the day I'll acknowledge that I've succeeded in life and can I die a happy woman, is the day I get to go two stark-naked hour-round sexual bouts with Jason Statham. *Sighs*

I was born and raised in Louisiana... and No, I do NOT live in a bayou, I actually see the beaches on the gulf coast more than I see a bayou, lol. I started writing poems and short stories very early in my life. You know, for the Michael's and Leo's and Nick's in my life. I've been a book hoarder since I was eleven years old, but then a couple years ago something wonderful happened! The 50 Shades of Grey craze brought to life my inner smut whore and I commenced to read anything and everything smut affiliated. When reading wasn't enough anymore and I noticed that so many of the authors of my favorite indie authors and their books weren't getting the exposure their work deserved, I turned it into a mission, starting my own blog, buying their books and reading them one by one. I then wrote my reviews for my blog and didn't hold back in writing them (Hell yeah those motherfuckers are profanity laden). I've never done a single thing in my life halfway. I always go all in. After the success of my Blog, and the insistence of one of my bestest friends, my sister from another mister, Trina Taylor of Bad & Dirty

Books, I was ready to finally take the plunge and see if I could write a book that was worth a damn. I'm a Southern girl to my core, a self-proclaimed smut whore, and I keep hearing that I'm an author, but honestly... I don't believe the rumors, lol. I don't feel like a kickass bitch spittin' out lyrics, or stories, like a motherfuckin' rockstar.

Tattooed across my ribs are the words I have always lived by: 'Aut viam inveniam aut faciam tibi.' Latin for: If I cannot find a way, I will make my own.

Made in the USA
Las Vegas, NV
06 May 2022